THE ISLE OF GOLD

SEVEN JANE

BLACK SPOT BOOKS

This Book is sold subject to the condition that it shall not, by way of trade or otherwise, be lent, re-sold, duplicated, hired out, or otherwise circulated without the publisher's prior written consent in any form of binding or cover other than that in which it is published and without similar condition including this condition being imposed on the subsequent purchaser.

ISBN Print: 978-0-9997423-8-9

ISBN Ebook: 978-0-9997423-9-6

Cover design by Najla Qamber

Edited by Melissa Ringsted

Interior design layout by Rebecca Poole

Black Spot Books

All rights reserved.

This is a work of fiction. All characters and events portrayed in this novel are fictitious and are products of the author's imagination and any resemblance to actual events, or locales or persons, living or dead are entirely coincidental.

To MR, my captain and my sea.

ACKNOWLEDGEMENTS

I am indebted to the following people for their contributions to this book:

To the fabulous team at Black Spot Books, including Lindy Ryan, Melissa Ringsted, Rebecca Poole, and Najla Qamber. I am eternally grateful to work with such a fabulous group of creative and passionate women.

To my first readers, Toni Border, Cat Skinner, and Jennifer Flath for their support, insight, enthusiasm for this story—and their valuable criticisms as the story and characters found their way.

To Katlin Blake, Evan Cloyd, Andrew Kruczynski, and Angel La-Coursiere for bringing Merrin, Winters, Tom, and Claudette to life.

To Sarah Miniaci and the team at Smith Publicity, for helping to make an author's dream a reality, for talking me off the ledge at regular intervals, and for being the greatest champions.

"*Take courage, my heart: you have been through worse than this. Be strong, saith my heart; I am a soldier; I have seen worse sights than this.*"

— **Homer, The Odyssey**

1716

For as long as men have set sail, they have told stories about the sea—of its women, of its treasures, of its beasts, and of her.

She's been given many names by the sailors who have traveled her waters. Calypso. Amphitrite. Ursula. Mélusine. A goddess, a queen, a witch, a daughter. In all of these, she is the sea, and the sea is a cruel mistress.

PART I

I

T HE FIRST TIME I MET THE CAPTAIN, I WAS DRUNK, FILTHY, and damn near destitute, clinging to the arms of a troubled woman like a piece of wreckage caught in a storm. Not unaccustomed to ferrying the sloppy weight of inebriated men, Claudette held me upright, with one arm low around my back and the other stretched firmly across my waist. She was a friend, not a lover, but her strong arms were tender around me as the two of us stumbled toward The Goodnight Mermaid, a tavern known as much for its ale as for its hospitality to women of the night—like Claudette—and the disreputable men who fancied them. The crew of the *Riptide* was foremost among the latter, though its captain—a man named Winters—did not waste his time on such frivolities.

"This is a fool's errand, Merrin Smith," Claudette hissed in my ear. The pretty lilt of her Caribbean accent was flat with frustration. "You've had too much wine. I think you should sleep off this compulsion before it becomes the end of you. I do not wish to see you dead." She had pleaded with me alongside every step of our slow, shuffling walk, imploring me mercilessly with her words and eyes to abandon my reckless impulse to pretend myself a man and join the *Riptide*'s infamous crew. I trudged onward, doing my best to ignore her save for a grunt of rebuttal now and again when she became particularly insistent, or when her nails bit painfully into my skin. Luckily for me, women in Claudette's profession were more concerned with parting sailors from their coin than they were with worrying over their impulses, and thus she was as unfamiliar with begging as with suffering nonsense—men's, mine, or otherwise. And so it was not long before her pleas became bitter with irritation and then narrowed steeply into fury before ceasing entirely. By the time the tavern loomed into view, my lifelong friend had become so silent that the only noise left to accompany our walk was the labored sounds of our own breathing—mine heavy and uneven from drink, hers labored from shouldering the burden of my added weight—and the scratching of her linen skirts on the gravel beneath our feet. In truth, I would have preferred her nagging to the ghastly combination of these sounds. With every footfall, they raked like cold, deathlike fingers against my ears, growing louder and more incessant as it joined with the bothersome drumming of my own heartbeat. Together the noises swelled to form an ominous cacophony, drowning out every other sound that hung in the salty, humid air until it even filled the space between my heartbeats with dread.

I refused to acknowledge the truth of Claudette's warning, even as it echoed horribly in my chest. This compulsion would very likely be the end of me. The thought should have sobered me—it *should* have stopped me in my tracks—but still my feet compelled me ever forward. I had been waiting for this moment for as long as I could remember, so much so that even the threat of imminent death would not stop me. And so I marched ever forward, stopping occasionally to slow the spinning of the world around me before moving on.

The clamor pounding within my head grew as we neared The Goodnight Mermaid, bloating itself as it fed off the racket that poured forth from within the tavern walls and wafted out to us on the street. The whole of it washed over me in a drowning tide so dense and overwhelming that I nearly passed out from the sheer strain of it, and I struggled not to let my mounting terror show. If I gave Claudette even the smallest hint of hesitation, such a master negotiator was she that she might be able to dissuade me from my goal and lure me home. I'd hate her for it when I awoke tomorrow, warm and safely on land in the hammock I kept in the brothel's kitchen, but she and I both knew that she'd gladly accept my hate if it changed the course of what I intended to do.

Alive and hateful was still better than dead, I supposed. If I was sober, I would very likely agree.

When we reached the door of the tavern, I shrugged myself out of Claudette's steadying grasp and fell softly onto my arm against the frame, waiting for strength to replace the tingling sensation in my legs. I caught an expression of piteous contempt as it washed over my friend's face in the lamplight. She had little patience for drunken stupor. "It sours even the best men into scoundrels," she was fond of saying; never mind that there were piteously few decent men to begin with, particularly in a place like Isla Perla. It was also costly and muddied the mind, she'd reminded me when I'd emptied a cask of wine early that evening. The wine had given me the courage to make the trek to The Goodnight Mermaid, but had indeed taken its price in strength. After several minutes of walking, feeling was only just beginning to return to my wobbling limbs, and as my strength grew my bravery waned. I hoped, now that we'd arrived, that it had been a worthwhile trade, but I knew what Claudette would say if I shared my thoughts so I did not.

"I have to do this, Claudette," I told her finally as the feel of my boots, still awkwardly large though we'd stuffed the toe with cotton, became firm on the gravel. I drew in a deep swallow of air, wishing one could drink bravery from the wind. "It's now or never. Go."

She sucked her teeth at me. "I have never left you before," she spat. "I will not begin now."

"If someone sees you, they might recognize me, and then it would be bad for the both of us. Please, ma chère amie, you must," I pleaded, using the French words of Claudette's native tongue. With a deep sigh, I allowed my gaze to roam over the woman's beautifully tanned face, her delicate neck, and the ripeness of her figure, wishing that I were capable of loving her as I knew she did me. Like her sisters at the brothel, Claudette had no interest in romance. Nor did she keep the company of rough men or women, or abide by the compulsions that so often earned one an early grave at the bottom of an unforgiving sea. That Claudette had become my friend was a small miracle; that she had grown to love me was a mystery. She and I were brothers in arms, sisters in secret. She was the closest thing to family I had ever known, and very likely the only person alive who cared anything for my fate. It was this loyalty more than anything else that kept her by my side this evening. She had not frequented The Goodnight Mermaid much at all in the past few years, preferring to meet her clients in the parlors at The House of Swallows.

"Please, go," I repeated, pulling the brim of my hat low in an attempt to shield myself from her eyes. I tested my footing again on the loose boards of the tavern's porch, satisfied by the creaking noise of the rotted wood. I pushed myself off the doorframe and stood solidly on my own in the door.

Claudette stood still for a second longer, the tips of her

fingers gently tucking away a stray lock of hair that had escaped my hat as she committed to memory her final view of me. She'd stolen the hat for my purposes from a client who had left it behind in her room when he'd sailed the week before. It was slightly too large for my head, but we'd wound a bandana around my disheveled brown hair to anchor it in place and it had done a fair enough job. The rest of my ensemble we pieced together from items harvested from other men who'd frequented the House of Sparrows over the last several weeks, as well as what we could purchase surreptitiously in the market. A pair of odd-fitting cotton breeches, a shirt with a torn sleeve, and a wide cow skin belt that carried an assortment of knives, a pistol with two bullets, and a small pouch of odds and ends, including a rusted compass and a small flask of rum. To these we'd added a cutlass Claudette had stolen from her procurer, a sweaty, beetle-eyed man called Maurice who made a habit of liberating weapons from his clientele whilst they were otherwise engaged in the arms of women and drink. Also, a brass-buttoned linen waistcoat the color of wet sand that Claudette had won in a bet and tied with a sash fashioned from one of her dresses (this had not gone over well with Mrs. Emery, the madam of the brothel who oversaw the women's wardrobes). The boots I'd pulled from a corpse with a bloody leg. The little bits of silver and gold that we'd decorated my slops with had been donated from the collections of the other women in Maurice's employ—and which could escape the notice of Mrs. Emery, who was as keen of shiny things as was an octopus. All told, it was a convincing outfit and I looked the part of a proper pirate, although I'd never been farther out to sea than to visit the merchants along the beach. Even so, the water had always called to me, beckoning me so insistently that finding my path to it was inevitable.

Claudette softened. "Adieu, ma chérie," she whispered, her voice now returned to the gentle whisper she reserved just for me. "I hope to see you again." Then her lips brushed against my cheek and she was gone.

I watched her shadow disappear into an alley between buildings and wondered if I would ever see her again. I had never been much of an optimist, but the parting was as somber in my mind as it had been on Claudette's lips. I would never see my beloved friend again, of that I could almost be certain. But it was as much for her as for me that I had made my way to the tavern, and for all of us on Isla Perla, and so I steeled myself for the task ahead, adjusted the belt's rest atop my hips, and took my first step inside The Goodnight Mermaid with the hopes of becoming a pirate.

II

THE TAVERN WAS—AS IT ALWAYS WAS—TEEMING WITH RAU-cous sailors and their purchased women. The men drank and laughed and, on occasion, beat at each other for the sport of it while the rest of the throng gambled their fortunes on the winner, and the women clung tightly to their arms, awaiting their share. The tables and floor were littered with half-emptied bottles of liquor and scraps of forgotten food; a thin layer of sand covered every surface. The flames of uneven candles flickered above their thick pots of wax to reflect in the glass of mirrors whose gilded frames were tarnished from the salty air.

Yet even unkempt and in disarray, the tavern was a wonderful sight, warm and inviting and slightly otherworldly, a fitting starting point as it was this tavern's mistress for whom I sailed. It had once belonged to an enchanting creature by the name of Evangeline Dahl, a woman who had seemed to be sculpted from the finest treasures of the sea, with milk-white skin, tumbles of curls the color of spun gold, and eyes of chrysoprase that sparkled like waves under a brilliant sun. She had held no equal in her loveliness, or in her nature, which had been likewise as wild and unpredictable as the sea—a disposition that was requisite for survival in a place as feral as the tropical, Caribbean paradise of Isla Perla. Even in its golden age the land of pirates kept an uneasy peace, held in place largely by an abundance of riches, rum, and loose women who knew how to manage the men the rest of the world had cast away. No one quite knew when Mistress

Dahl had been delivered on the beach, only that she had arrived one evening by way of a red-sailed merchant ship and had proven to be as smart as she was beautiful, possessing an uncanny intelligence that made her particularly adept at navigating the tides of trade between the pirates and merchants who visited the island. She'd been clever and fierce, and as sharp as the knives she wielded like they were simply another appendage, wearing them tucked in her bodice and lashed to her ankle, even concealed deep within the looping curls of her hair. Within a fortnight of her arrival Evangeline Dahl had established herself both as proprietress of the tavern and as a new force on Isla Perla. Within a month she had charmed the island into submission, providing new avenues to keep it bathed in wealth and seduced by its own debauchery so perfectly that almost none had been the wiser to her intent.

Those who benefited from her loved her, and those that did not watched her with envy and respect. Those who neither traded with her nor envied her still feared her, for in addition to her tribe of loyal men that kept watch over her tavern, she also held the favor of Captain Erik Winters—a man known either for his quick temper or savage nature, but very rarely had anyone lived long enough in his presence to witness both.

Though the two had kept their romance in confidence, it had nonetheless been a well-known secret on the island that Mistress Dahl and the *Riptide's* tenacious captain held a contentious and fervent affair. It had evolved into a sort of local legend, and over the years it had become difficult to distinguish where the truth ended and the fantasy began, which only made the tale more captivating. Rumor had it that though the two often found themselves at opposite ends of their own interests—hers the manipulation of trade and the seagoing men whose prizes sustained the island, and his the oft contrary struggle to maintain his seat of power under both her conspiring gaze and his crew's—yet they were drawn to each other as unavoidably as the sea is to the shore. Their love, it was said, was ardent and dangerous, the sort that would compel one to hold a knife to their lover's neck while kissing with such passion that the edges of their blades cut at their own throats.

This romance between Mistress Dahl and Captain Winters was the essence of Isla Perla itself. It was wild, and untamed, and unyieldingly beautiful, and I had loved them both for as long as I could remember—she the governess of the sea and him the man who sailed it. Their story was as entrenched in my spirit as was the island that had been my home, for though I could not remember when I had first arrived at Isla Perla many years before, I could, in the murky haze of my earliest memories, just recall the delicate shimmer of Mistress Dahl's golden hair as she waved at me from the stoop of her tavern. That singular memory, although treasured, was also unreliable. For one, it seemed both recent and ages ago and I could never be sure exactly when, nor if, it had really happened. And, for another, it stubbornly insisted that Winters was sitting at Evangeline's side, but so bright was the halo of her hair that it outshone everything else and so I could never quite be certain it was he.

When the news of Mistress Dahl's sudden disappearance had swept the shores of Isla Perla two summers before, none had returned to harbor more racked than Captain Winters, whose already capricious temperament had become terrifying to even the most surly of rogues. His fury was afforded a wide berth by all, even his own men, and none were immune to his ire. When he had first arrived, Winters ransacked Isla Perla searching for Evangeline. Without hesitation, he and his crew cut down everyone who had ever so much as raised their voice at the island's most beloved proprietress as they moved from the pink-sanded beach through the quayside and into the lush green wildness at the interior of the island. No evidence of her had been found on the island or in the blue waters of the neighboring seas, which in the months since Evangeline's disappearance the *Riptide*'s murderous crew had run red with the blood of any that sailed across its path. They overtook ship after ship, merchants and Navy and pirate alike, leaving few alive in their wake. The captain's reputation, savage at the onset, had risen to the level of madman, and he'd taken to wanton marauding and plundering with a fury only a man who wished for death could have as he boiled the waters in search of his ladylove. His hunt had thus far been unsuccessful, but this was of little concern to his crew, whose interest in recovering Mistress Dahl was tempered by an appetite as sufficiently whetted by the riches of the prizes they took as by the blood they spilled to obtain them. When at long last the *Riptide*'s hull was stuffed full and Winters and his men had finally had their fill of gold and vengeance, the ship retired once more to Isla Perla, and so it remained until now.

For the past several weeks the crew had helped themselves to the luxuries of the island while Winters, already a taciturn man, remained disturbingly silent and out of sight. He spoke only to his quartermaster, a loyal and sturdy man by the name of Mister Brandon Dunn, and remained locked away in the former bedchambers of The Goodnight Mermaid's mistress. The women who attended him, friends of Claudette, gossiped that so taken was the captain with studying the mythical texts of the waters he'd stolen in his raids that he barely seemed to notice them any more now than he had before. He had instead become convinced that no mere mortal was left alive that could be responsible for the vanishing of Mistress Evangeline Dahl. Now, he nursed a determination to take her back from the sea itself. It was, they said, more than an obsession—it was a *consumption*. Rarely had they waited on Winters and not heard him locked in manic debate with Dunn while names like Poseidon, and Amphitrite, and Calypso passed between them in harsh whispers. The very gods of the seas, Winters insisted, had stolen Evangeline away, and he would sail to the heart of the ocean to bring her back.

And so with baited breath, the people of Isla Perla—I first among them—waited for Winters to reemerge with his plans to make way. When he finally did, announcing that the *Riptide* would sail for the fabled Ogygia, the surreptitious Isle of Gold where Calypso had held Odysseus prisoner, to rescue Evangeline, none dared to challenge his sanity or his resolve. Above all else the seafaring lot are a superstitious bunch, yet they are also men of greed, and so the prospect of such fortune—even if it tempted the fury of the gods of the ocean deep—aroused their appetites into frenzy. If Winters were able to lead them to Ogygia, the entirety of the spoils each of them had taken in their short, violent lives could be multiplied by infinity and would still pale in comparison to the mystical island's incalculable bounty. Were Winters unable to find the island, the crew was satisfied in the knowledge that their gold thirst would be satiated on the high seas, their targets growing ever-larger and more profitable as Winters' frustration mounted. Their heading set, his men made ready to pour back into the seas, while I had taken immediately to the task of outfitting myself as worthy to join with them.

And so it was that tonight the crew was making ready to set sail and I found myself at the captain's table, scratching some shaky bit of penmanship that could have been my name onto a piece of parchment under the studious gaze of Mister Brandon Dunn, the *Riptide*'s redoubtable quartermaster.

"Are ye certain you know what you're doin', lad?" Dunn asked in a manner that said plainly that I did not, and that I should leave the tavern immediately lest I become next in line for a beating in the skirmish that had broken out behind us. The sound of his voice queued a wave of nausea to roll up from within my stomach, and I wished for Claudette's steady arms at my back. I tried not to vomit as I felt the man's eyes wander over me—hard and black and soulless as they were—and by the time he finished his examination I was certain they were able to see all the way to the very core of my soul.

When he didn't signal to the pair of men hovering with arms crossed sternly across their chests behind him, I shifted, uncomfortable under the unfamiliar bulk of my new wardrobe. I pulled loose the lock of hair that Claudette had carefully hidden beneath my hat and twisted it around my finger. "A-Aye," I stammered, unable to return Mister Dunn's skeptical glare. I swallowed back the bile that had collected in my throat. I had hoped, foolishly, that I could sign the contract and move inconspicuously aboard, existing below deck in the secretive company of the bilge rats until we reached Ogygia. Now I said a silent prayer that he wouldn't see through my flimsy disguise and reveal my deceit to the throng of rowdy men surrounding us. I was unfit to sail with the *Riptide*'s crew in more ways than I could count on one hand, and none of them had to do with the fact that I had never set foot aboard a ship, pirate or otherwise. A woman seeking to stowaway on a pirate ship was a punishable offense by the order of the brethren code.

Mister Dunn adjusted his considerable size on the other end of the table and kept his eyes locked stiffly on me. Up close, he was a larger man than I had expected—thick in the chest and reedy in the limbs in the way that men accustomed to a hard life are. Weathered skin crackled around his eyes and nose. He had a thick shock of greyish-white hair that was clipped wildly and un-evenly, as if some drunkard had taken to it with a pair of shears. It flickered about wildly in the air above his head like blowing blades of silver grass, and seemed to move independently of the rest of him. Matching ragged fur the same shade of silver worked its way down his jaw to ring a thin, unfriendly mouth. He wore a necklace around his neck that ended worryingly in what resem-bled a piece of human bone. Still, there was a sort of smoothness about him that marked him as different than the rest of a gener-ally rough and unpleasant lot. Possibly this was a consequence of his role as diplomat between captain and crew, or perhaps a necessary adaption to survive so intimately in the company of a man like Winters. Or perhaps I imagined it all together. It was so dark in the tavern, and my vision so blurry as much with anxiety as it was still with wine, that it was hard to be sure.

"What's yer name, boy?" Dunn bowed his head to the con-tract before him where I had scratched my name, squinting to make out the sloppy signature.

"W-Westley," I stuttered, forcing out the name I had carefully prac-ticed. "Westley Rivers, sir." It rolled off the tongue believably enough, even if I did swallow heavily afterward. Having only read the name in a book I'd found in Mrs. Emery's office, I had never heard it spoken out loud, and so I said it as I'd imagined it, breaking syllables at the *t*.

in a loop on his belt. An odd-shaped sliver of a glistening white stone stone dangled from a thin black cord on his neck, and on the forefinger of his right hand he wore an iron ring with a compass stamped on its face.

Winters did not need his reputation to immediately incite fear into those who found themselves caught in his company—the presence of him was quite enough. Still, it was easy to tell that behind his unwavering glower was an undeniably handsome man, though it could only have been a woman as brave and beautiful as Evangeline Dahl to tame him, assuming such a thing were even possible.

When he finally spoke his voice was deep and gruff from disuse; it rumbled with a thunderous quality like the roar of a storm at sea. He held the nub of a cigarette pinned between his lips, and a thin tendril of smoke curled into the air in front of his face. "You want to sail to the Isle of Gold."

I was unsure whether it was a statement or a question, and I did not trust my voice to speak on either account, so I nodded and hoped it was sufficient. My pulse beat so strongly against my throat that it felt like there was a bird trapped in my neck, threatening to break free.

Winters stared at me, saying nothing and everything at the same time, and I very nearly lost my nerve under the suffocating weight of his eyes. Luckily, Dunn broke the silence before I could take my last breath. He introduced me by way of another one of his disapproving gazes. "Lad's name be Rivers," he grumbled to the captain's back. "Barely wet behin' the ears and thinks himself ready to join the *Riptide*'s men." He raised an eyebrow in my direction. "Best be sendin' him on his way. We have preparations to ma—"

I rediscovered my voice just in time to interrupt the quarter-master—an action that earned me another stern look of reprimand from the older man. "I d-do," I spluttered, starting forward awkwardly. My damned hat slipped down too far over my eyes as I shuffled gracelessly to a sudden halt, and I tried not to look embarrassed as I pushed it back into place. I attempted to cover my discomfiture with additional tugging on the waistband of my pants, but my efforts were foiled by a startling, clinking sound of metal on my belt, and I couldn't help but feel like a child dressed up in a pirate's costume. "I do mean to join your crew."

Winters loosed a puff of smoke from his cigarette, and continued to hold me in his silent, icy stare. I could feel the coldness of it hardening around me, the razor sharp teeth of frostbite creeping up my toes despite the musky warmth of the crowded tavern. Frozen in place, I couldn't help but wonder if the captain had been born with his name or if he'd earned it from some former enemy. Both would have been just as likely.

"The crew won't like it," Dunn added. A faint note of caution had crept into his words though I wasn't sure who it was aimed at. The men behind him, I noticed for the first time, had disappeared since their captain's arrival, their previous shark-like intensity diminished to lesser fish in the company of this new danger.

Winters remained unmoved as he passed his eyes over me in a final, lingering appraisal. His tongue flicked out in a swift movement—a quick flash of a red tip against the dark auburn of the stubble around his mouth—and the small nub of cigarette disappeared between his lips. "He'll sail," he decided, and then rose up from the table so swiftly that the smell of wood fire and gun smoke rushed into my nostrils. A last wisp of cigarette smoke escaped the corner of his lips. He paused momentarily, his taller height swathing me in shadow, and as I bravely raised my eyes to meet his, I was of the distinct impression that any choice I had had in sailing with the *Riptide* had now been replaced with an order. Whether I wished it or not, it was to be a pirate's life for me.

Without another word or a backward glance Winters moved briskly away, sliding through the throng of his drunken men to retreat behind a door at the other side of the tavern. Dunn and I watched in silence as the … *our* captain disappeared, and with a heavy sigh the quartermaster stood and extended his hand over the table to me. Without hesitation I took it, neither of us missing that my hand slid too smoothly into his, like silk into sandpaper. His mouth bunched into a disapproving look and his black eyes glittered with suspicion, but much to my relief he did not remark on it.

"Well, Mister Rivers," my new quartermaster grumbled in a tight voice, "welcome to the crew."

III

I SPENT A DIFFICULT NIGHT STRIVING TO CONCEAL MYSELF AMID the rough stonewalls and dim corners of the tavern, and doing my best to avoid the skeptical eyes of the *Riptide*'s men. Over the past several hours the announcement of my addition to the crew had spread throughout the tavern, prompting more sour looks and obscene hand gestures in my direction than I was entirely comfortable with. In my eagerness to join them, I had naively assumed that these hardened men would have little interest in me, and that I would slip unremarkably into their ranks without a second thought, and minimal, if any, disturbance in the usual course of such things. I had not, however, considered the possibility that they would be so opposed to my coming onboard, nor so openly hostile.

Shrunken down as small as I could make myself in my ill-fitting pirate's costume, I felt like a sheep running blindly into a pack of wild dogs, led by a wolf, and cursed myself for thinking that I was bold enough for such a mission. It had been easy enough to daydream about setting out to sea to find treasure, and answers, and the secret to Mistress Dahl's disappearance when I had been safe in the brothel's kitchens, surrounded by familiar faces and familiar frustrations. Now, I could only hear Claudette's words echoing in my mind. *"This compulsion will be the end of you."* I'd scoffed at how wrong she was. Never mind living long enough to return back to Isla Perla at the end of this journey, I'd be lucky enough to survive my first week at sea. If as the small boat bumped against her glorious sides. I stared up at her full height with awe as I waited my turn to scale the ladder embedded into her side and set my feet upon the deck, watching carefully as the men in front of me scrambled up so that I could mimic their motions as smoothly as if I'd done them myself a million times before.

The *Riptide* was a large English galleon, and even by a pirate's standards she was an exquisite ship, possessing two gun decks and three fully rigged masts that billowed fresh canvas sails of foggy grey, a mark of Winters' command. She was an older ship, although expertly maintained, and rumored to have been seized originally in the Mediterranean before finding herself somewhat recently in the hands of Captain Winters on the other side of the world. Unlike many similarly decorated ships, the *Riptide* boasted the image of a goddess—fierce and ethereal and with a countenance eerily similar to that of Evangeline herself—as its figurehead rather than the large-breasted merfolk or busty angels which were more usual. The sides of the ship's hull were lined with well-worn gun ports of carefully arranged canons, and its stern galley was wrapped in windowpanes with the name *Riptide* lettered in gold filigree underneath. Waving languidly in the air above its topmast was Winters' flag—a skull atop a pair of golden bones, flanked by red claw marks and resting on a black cloth.

I climbed the ladder and boarded the ship, then stood uneasily on the deck as I took in the flurry of movement around me. The men, an assortment of characters of every age and nation, worked with the speed and agility of an army of ants loading and storing barrels of food and supplies as they filled the ship's stores for a long journey at sea. I tried not to catch the attention of any pirate swirling around me, still weary from last night's murderous glares as I watched crate after crate come aboard—flour, rum, gunpowder, and other assorted items concealed in barrels and sacks. A portly man, who I guessed was the ship's cook, supervised a pair of men as they lifted a spit carrying a giant roasted pig onto the deck, then stepped it below deck.

The men did not seem to tolerate my presence on the edge of the main deck any more than they had the tavern, and not wanting to appear useless I quickly fetched a mop from the bannister and begin to busy my hands with polishing the planks around me. The men barked their sentiments as they shoved past me:

"Out of the way, power monkey."

"Shove off, swab."

I pretended not to hear these.

Then, "Oi," an unfamiliar, affable sounding voice called in my direction. I kept my eyes locked on my mop and counted my breaths. The voice came closer. "Oi," it said again, this time obviously to me. "What's that you think you're doing?"

I looked up to find none other than Tom Birch standing with his hands crossed across his chest, his torso tanned and laced with thick, sinewy veins and flecked with small hairs that reflected the yellow mid-morning sunlight. I tried not to gape at him as I moved my eyes up his bare chest to his face, a long sweep that eventually reached deep, saltwater green eyes that glinted curiously at me. He was so tall that from my position below him his head almost entirely eclipsed the harsh, mid-morning sun, leaving the blotted light to cast a halo behind a crown of dishwater blond hair that had been clipped shorter than was common so that it stuck up in little tufts around his head. Thin sideburns ran the length of his face and curved around the ridges of his jaw and surrounded a pair of plump, soft-looking lips that were, at the moment, slightly parted as he waited expectantly for an answer. He wore a pair of plain woolen breeches topped by a wide leather belt, and a thick strap of frayed rigging rope hung around his neck. A small pail of oakum and pitch dangled loosely in his left hand; a brush thick with the black paste was stuck handle-deep within. From afar the boatswain had appeared lanky and unassuming, but up close he was much more arresting though he still had smooth skin that had not yet been hardened from salt spray. He was distractingly handsome, and by the looks of it, only a few years my senior, but now was not the time to enjoy such a view— the puzzled expression stamped on his face said clearly that I had committed a greenhorn's error.

"Well?" he inquired again, harder this time as he gestured agitatedly at the mop in my hands. The rope swung heavily from his neck, ticking like an impatient pendulum. I had nearly forgotten is question.

"I-I was swabbing the deck, sir," I answered, my voice squeaking a bit with surprise. I cleared my throat and lifted the mop as if it were explanation enough. I hadn't the slightest clue what I was doing, but I was familiar with mopping—it had been a common chore in the brothel to mop up blood and other vile fluids from the floors several times every day. "Readying for the waves, sir."

The tall man cocked an eyebrow at me, and his upper lip stretch backward in annoyed bewilderment. For a moment, he just looked at me, stunned into silence by what I could only assume was my own stupidity. Then, he slumped forward, as if he thought he might have misheard whatever I'd said and a closer proximity would clear the confusion. I tried not to notice how inviting his lips looked, still parted, or that his teeth were brilliantly

THE ISLE OF GOLD

white. "Readying for the waves?" he echoed incredulously. His eyes dropped to the deck and he waved his open palm around in a sweeping gesture, the can of tar swinging in his hand. "What are you playing at? Can't you see that it's just been caulked?"

Being unfamiliar with the nuances of nautical maintenance, I was foreign to the term *caulking*, but as I looked to where Tom Birch motioned at my feet I could plainly see that old rope had been pressed between the boards and sealed over with tar. I assumed this was what he referred to as having been caulked, though I didn't dare confirm it with him and incriminate myself further. The sudsy saltwater from the mop bubbled around it pitifully in the light. I would have been less speechless had a mermaid suddenly appeared and flopped about on the boards, and I struggled to find a suitable response. No words filled my throat, and I braced for punishment. I had often heard that sailors did not take kindly to mishandling of their ships, particularly by young, already unwanted new recruits.

After a painful moment during which he just stared blankly at me, a thought bloomed inside Birch's eyes, making them somehow even greener and more lovely. A look of clarity smoothed his furrowed brow though his face retained some of its previous irritation, and he looked at me with new recognition. "You must be Rivers, then?" he guessed, visibly relieved that he was dealing with a novice and not a moron. Without waiting for verification, he thrust the pitch pail in my free hand and snatched the mop from the other. This last he tossed uselessly on the deck. A man with an impressively long beard made to yell at him, but upon seeing it was the boatswain who'd thrown the mop he let it go and kept waking, mumbling something under his breath. Mister Birch pulled a cloth from the band of his belt and wiped the sweat from his brow, then flipped the rag over his shoulder. "I'm Tom Birch, the boatswain." He nodded at me in introduction but did not offer his hand, which was just as well as I was using both of mine to hold the pail, which was heavier than I had expected it to be. "Ol' Bullet said to look after you."

I glanced from the tar in my hands to Tom, wondering what sort of manual misery "looking after" might mean, and then, noticing the much taller man eyeing me, I nervously managed one hand away from the pail to reposition the brim of my hat as low over my eyes as I could without blinding myself. It had only been one day and I was becoming rather practiced at seeing from underneath the brim of that bothersome hat. I tested the give of the brush in the pitch paste and found it to be sticky and stiff. If my lot on this ship was to be tarring planks, then so be it. Then again, had Tom Birch said to lick the deck I very well might have done that for him just as willingly.

The boatswain was still watching me fiddle with the tar pail. "Bullet?" I asked, certain I'd never met anyone called Bullet.

"Aye," Tom said slowly, and I saw irritation overtake his eyes once more, this time tinged with a hint of pity. The expression on his face showed that the man now evidently thought me daft—not exactly an improvement from stupid, but still it was better than suspicion. He pointed off the starboard side of the ship, and I followed his eyes down the length of his arm until my sight landed on Dunn, who was still several yards away on shore. "Bullet. Mister Brandon Dunn, obviously."

The moniker brought to mind a certain speed and gracefulness that didn't seem to fit the man I'd met in the tavern last night. However, even across the water, he was easy enough to distinguish by his standing grey crest and tall, rail-like stature that did have a sleek, bullet-like quality about it. Standing half silhouetted beneath the groaning awning of a rickety shanty, I could see the tense set of his white-ringed jowls in his profile. He seemed to be arguing with someone who stood just out of sight; he was moving his hands in slow, deliberate gestures that suggested he was trying to explain—or perhaps convince—his listener of something. I watched curiously as he gradually appeared to relax, until he finally shrugged and rubbed his lips with the back of his hand in a manner I suspected was acquiescence. Either he'd won the argument, or he'd given up.

Finally, he reached in front of him and laid his hand on an unseen shoulder. He bowed his head, and bobbed it lightly a few times in a listening manner. After a pause he withdrew his arm and turned away, his quick steps bringing him marching into the full sunlight as he made his way toward the small boat waiting on the water. As he neared the edge of the sand, I watched as he waded into the shallow depths and climbed into the vessel, and then returned my eyes to the awning as the person he'd been in intense conversation with stepped out of the shadow. I was stunned to see that the person with whom he'd been so engrossed was not one person but two, and a most unlikely pair at that— my sweet Claudette and Mrs. Emery.

IV

I WAS STILL STUFFING BITS OF FRAYED ROPE AND PITCH BE-tween planks midship when the sun began its downward descent to the west. My back was aching and my fingers had been worked to the edge of bleeding, but after a bustling afternoon in the blazing Caribbean summer sun, the ruckus on deck was finally growing still and the sky was fading to lighter shades of indigo blue. As a lazy quiet fell, the sounds of the waves could be heard again as they lapped gently against the sides of the ship, and the evening wind blew a cool breeze against the sweat-drenched fabric of my clothing. I arched my back like a midnight cat, satisfied by the popping sounds and yielding twinges of my spine as I stretched upward. When that was done I inhaled deeply, simultaneously clearing my nose of the bitter scent of the pitch and oakum tar and refilling it with the delicious salty scent of the sea at dusk.

As was custom, the captain had been the last to board the ship, and had come aboard only moments before. When he'd arrived he had walked the length of the deck, stern to forecastle, several times over, surveying the crew's work and occasionally barking an order or adjusting a bit of rope or canvas himself while the men assisted. The rank of captain aboard a pirate vessel was a democratic one, earned and kept by bloodshed and wit, and pirates were not widely known for their appreciation of hierarchy. However, Winters' men seemed to regard him with a deference that I had not expected—and with a sort of unspoken agreement that suggested to vote him out of command would be no easy matter, nor ultimately to their benefit. To my great relief, as the captain roamed the ship he only casually glanced at my caulking work and had not shown any special interest in me since. Neither, for that matter, had anyone else—save for Tom Birch, who'd appeared briefly only once to refill my supply of tar and then rejoined the rest of the more able-bodied crew on other ship ready tasks.

Once satisfied with the condition of the *Riptide* and the preparations necessary to make way, Winters had disappeared below deck and then reappeared briefly for a final inspection, speaking shortly with Tom Birch and Brandon Dunn, and then retired to his cabin with a flagon of rum in each hand and a heavy slam of the door. Another twenty minutes had passed and now at long last the small boats had been secured and the remaining crates and barrels stowed below deck or lashed to the walls of the interior of the ship. Most of the crew, their work finished for the time being, had receded to the galley to eat and rest before the heavy work of manning the capstan to lift anchor was given. A few men still hung about the deck, working with the rigging or dozing to the surprisingly relaxing sound of blades being sharpened on hard stones. Even though we had not yet formally returned to the water, the *Riptide*'s crew seemed now to be a more subdued lot than they had been the night before. These were men born and bred of the sea; it was as if just moving about on the swaying decks of the anchored ship had returned a piece of their souls that had been held in escrow during the time they'd spent on land.

We'd set sail at sunset. It was the captain's habit to weigh anchor as the sun slipped beneath the horizon and the strong gusts of the evening wind gave life to the sails—or so I had noticed from my many watches of his ship as it came in and out of Isla Perla's harbor. Our heading was set out of the islands of the Caribbean and into the open waters of the Atlantic Ocean, and the ship was to lie with her head northeast. This last I'd heard in the chatter around me while I remained more or less unmolested in my work, finishing the tedious task of caulking the last planks of the edge of the quarterdeck. I'd covered nearly the whole of the length of the ship, about forty-seven meters in total.

I slathered on a final stroke of pitch and was just sitting back to rest on my haunches when two shadows descended upon me, blocking out the last rays of setting light. I looked up to find Misters Tom Birch and Brandon Dunn towering over me, boatswain and quartermaster both observing me with the same bothered looks on their faces as though they had just stumbled across a suspect rodent and were unsure whether to kill or capture it. Dunn had added a worn leather vest and a dirty neck scarf to his attire along with a long, basket-hilted sword; Tom was now wearing a linen shirt overhung with a baldric that boasted a pair of polished flintlocks that lay heavily against the muscular swell of his chest. I'd come aboard with only the clothes I'd been wearing the night before, not that I'd owned much else or would have brought it if I had. It had been a job enough for Claudette and I to scavenge the items we did. The only extra articles I had were not visible on my body: a ring with an odd cow's milk white stone—the same strange hue as the one the captain wore around his neck, and a small leather journal tucked deep in one of the low pockets of my coat. The shape of a sand dollar was etched on the cover of the book. These had been the only clues to my identity when I'd arrived at Isla Perla. The ring had never left my body,

THE ISLE OF GOLD

although fearing theft I had always kept it hidden within my inner garments and never worn it on my hand. I had debated on bringing the book with me, but in the end decided that my notes were too important to leave behind. They were the accumulation of my life's work as I'd cobbled together hints to my past and myths of the ocean, and I expected the notes within those pages might be of critical importance on this journey. If anyone were to stumble across my diary, I would try to convince them that it was nothing more than a stolen keepsake. If it came to the worst, I could simply toss it overboard and return its secrets to the sea.

I set my hand against my side, comforted by the thick feel of the leather book against my hip as I looked upward at the two men. Working my fingers in the cloth, I could feel the outline of the ring, tied with a length of string and wound around the book.

"He'd make a decent deckhand," Tom observed with a tone of approval, his eyes contemplating the swatch of deck beside me while I tried not to get sucked into their path. It would not do well for the man to notice the way I couldn't help but look at him. No man had ever caught my attention the way he did, and the magnetic pull of it made me uncomfortable. He stooped down to look closely at the job I'd done caulking and gave a sharp nod of confirmation while I fumbled about, wiping bits of crusted blood from my fingernails onto the fabric of my pants. "Aye, we won't sink from leaks anytime soon if we set him to the shoring up what's needed in the hull. Plenty to keep him busy down there."

The praise was gratifying, although after having spent a day on deck in the sunshine the idea of being sequestered in the ship's dank underbelly was less than appealing. The sounds and smells of the water were addicting, even after only a mere few hours, and I couldn't bear the thought of being locked away from them in the stale darkness of the ship's womb. I opened my mouth to say this, but the two men continued to talk about my fate as if I weren't present, so I resigned to listen and hope for the best and stood, dusting granules of sand from my pants. When I reached full height, I was pleased to see that Mister Dunn was only barely taller than I, although nearly thrice as wide and densely stacked like a Bahamian pine. Birch loomed over both of us still, his lean, limber frame swaying in the evening breeze.

"Aye," Dunn was saying now, although he sounded uncertain as he observed me in kind, taking into account my slim stature. A disdainful grimace contorted one side of his face so that the ring of white around his mouth nearly met that which marched down the side of his ear. "He's done a good job of it, he has, but ain't no one below deck to keep an eye on him other than Jomo," the two men exchanged a knowing look, "so it might be best not to send him down that way."

"Right," Tom agreed, shortly. He lifted one eyebrow and crossed sinewy arms across his chest, then adjusted his footing on the deck.

The men, for the moment, fell silent, each considering what was to be done with me—Tom Birch with his studious gaze and Brandon Dunn with his more suspicious smirk. Finally, desperate to fill the silence I asked, "Who's Jomo?" So far, his was the only name I'd heard that was sufficient enough on its own to not be preceded by the weight of an honorific.

"The cook," they answered, nearly in unison, as if that explained it all. I made a mental note to decide once I met the man for myself. I wouldn't have guessed that the portly man I had seen directing the haul of meat earlier today would have been so formidable a companion below deck, although now I was not so sure that I was eager to make his acquaintance if Dunn and Tom Birch thought I was better off outside of his path.

"What else 'an you do, lad?" asked Dunn.

I almost said cook, but then I remembered Jomo. Serving pints would not do, nor would washing clothes. These were womanly tasks, and I feared they would give me away if I took to them too comfortably. "I can help with the equipment," I suggested, eager to learn my way around handling the weapons on the ship. "Sharpen blades and stack cannon balls and the like."

This did not interest either of the men; there were over two dozen others onboard who could have carried five times my weight without breaking a sweat, as well as a gunner and carpenter on the crew who already managed these jobs. "I can handle tasks as needed on the ship," I tried again, racking my brain for skills that might be useful at sea. "I can sew fair enough, so I can mend the sails if need be. Learn the rigging and try my hand at knots." I hid my bloody hands behind my back. Many of these tasks were under Tom's domain, as the ships boatswain.

Dunn grunted at Tom and he shook his head. "Sails are fresh and we've spares in the hold," the latter noted. "Won't be much to do there until we've been at sea for at least a month."

I thought back to my duties at the brothel. Tidying the rooms and keeping up with the kitchens had accounted for the bulk of my work, but as the only female who did not take clients I was expected to earn my keep by completing any other tasks that needed done. One of these, an unfortunately regular duty, had included seeing to the women's minor medical needs—bandaging, ointments, and even on the rare occasion, stitches or bone resetting—and so next I offered, "I know my way around treating an injury. I can aid your ship's doctor with mending bandages and the lot. I've not had any formal training, mind you, but I don't mind the messy bits."

"Mister Clarke is our medic onboard," Tom informed me with a tightening of his arms. He crooked one arm upward to scratch idly at his perfectly squared jaw and I resisted the urge to watch the veins dancing in his arm. "But he'll not have much use for you until the time comes ... and when it does, you'll probably need attending to yourself." Then he added, somewhat doubtfully, "If you survive, that is. You've not seen a rough night at sea yet, not that a strong gust of sea wind wouldn't be enough to carry you off."

I shrugged. The only other tasks I'd performed in the brothel had been a bit of record keeping when I'd, on occasion, help Mrs. Emery's failing eyes catalog receipts from the women's business and check expenses in the brothel's log. This duty, I knew, was largely the responsibility of Mister Dunn onboard, and if there were one man who I expected wouldn't be interested in my company, it would be him. Nevertheless, I noted the skill, lest I be resigned to shoring in the hull next to Jomo's kitchen after all—or worse, with Jomo himself. "I can read some and perform a little math, so I could help with the books, if you so wish it. I don't know the details of the ship's—"

Dunn and Tom exchanged startled glances before curiosity slipped out of Tom's mouth and tumbled downward in my direction. "Oi, you can read?"

I squinted up at him beneath the brim of my hat. "Aye, I can."

"Any good, or do you just be knowin' yer letters?" I didn't have to look at Dunn to hear the skepticism in his voice, though I looked anyway. When I did I noticed a shimmer had appeared in his beady eyes. Most men on the island were not learned men, but then again, I was no man—not that the matter would be of help to me here.

"Nay," I replied firmly, and then restated with all the confidence I could muster, "I can read." I'd learned to read the same place I'd learned to handle a sword, not that it was any of his business.

For the first time since I'd met him, Mister Dunn's faced contorted into what I suspected might have been a smile. He nudged the much taller man beside him with a hooked elbow. "I think we 'an find a place for you aboard the *Riptide* yet, Mister Rivers."

ONCE THE ORDER TO WEIGH ANCHOR HAD BEEN GIVEN, THE MEN had slid the long planks into the hungry mouths of the capstan and pushed it until the anchor had been totally lifted, a job which took the better part of two hours, and the *Riptide* had slowly begun to make her way out into the twilight waters of the open sea. Mister Dunn found me watching as the last vestiges of Isla Perla faded into the distance. Even shrouded in the darkness, the crystal blues of her bays and the lush, swaying palms at her shore were majestic, and my heart tinged with unexpected sadness to see her go. Nevertheless, in the space of a few seconds, the sea had risen above her on the horizon, leaving nothing but a stretch of white-crested blue. For the first time I understood what it meant to be surrounded by water. The ship rocked gently on the calm waters, and I gripped the railing as we sailed through the bioluminescent bays of the Caribbean, a trail of glowing blue light left in the ship's wake. It was a beautiful sight, and more lovely than I could have imagined in my nights longing to be free of the island. My nascent sea legs were as wobbly now as my man's legs had been last night on the walk to the tavern, but they would steady in time. Luckily, the motion hadn't stirred any sickness in my stomach, as I had expected it would. Rather, the sensation filled me with a thrill unlike I'd ever known, rushing through me like water pouring into an empty vessel. As I stared at the expanse of never-ending blue waves, a surreal sort of feeling that I had always been meant to be on the water struck me—or, more accurately, I felt as if I had finally returned to a home I had never known. On a whim, I pulled the hat away from my head and allowed the salty gales to whip through my dark tresses while I sucked it in through greedy deep breaths that filled my lungs until I feared they might burst. I closed my eyes, letting myself become lost in the sensation.

"Firs' time out to sea, I expect?" the rasping voice of the quartermaster interrupted my thoughts. He appeared beside me suddenly, chewing on the unlit nub of a thick cigar as he cast his eyes out over of the water with mine.

I shook my head, waking myself from my watery reverie. Quickly I slipped my hat back into place and pushed the lengths of my hair into the neck of my shirt. "It is, aye."

"It's a whole big world beyon' that lit'le island, lad. Not so big as one might expect, but a mite different from a life safe on land."

I didn't know what to say to that, so I simply nodded.

"Ye not be leaving much behind then, I expect?"

Claudette's lovely face blinked into my mind's eye, and quickly vanished. "Not compared to what I hope to find."

"Aye," he sighed, as if I'd said something familiar, and then gave me a sharp, considering look as he clipped the head of his

THE ISLE OF GOLD

cigar and let the cap roll between his feet. He struck a match on the handrail, brought it to the tuck end of the cigar, and took a slow puff, letting the taste of the smoke sit in his mouth. A few seconds later he blew it out again, setting silver rings to sail over the water. Returning his eyes to the water he said, "Although be warned that sometimes the things you be settin' out lookin' for don't be what you end up findin'. Or might be the things you're hopin' to find be better off left unfound, if ye catch my meaning."

I didn't, but I didn't want him to know that. Unsure of what to say to Dunn's cryptic comments, I nodded again, trying to appear agreeable. An odd feeling rose up within me—an impression that Dunn knew more than he was willing to say. The thought was unnerving, but as there wasn't much I could do to test my theory, I left it alone.

For a moment we stood side by side in silence as Dunn drew deeply from his cigar in long pulls, sucking in smoke and loosing it back out. I counted the smoke rings as they floated upward and then dissipated into the mist above the waves—one, three, seven, nine.

"The sea be a different place than land, youn' Mister Rivers," he repeated at last, a thoughtful expression pulling at his features. He stared at the water in the direction the smoke rings had gone. "Have ye ever heard the stories of the beings that inhabit these waters?"

I studied the man's profile. Each pull on the cigar cast him in a brief orange glow, making him look less than entirely human. It was a fitting caricature for a conversation that had wandered into the fantastic.

"Aye," I answered. Indeed I had.

"Ever be thinkin' they might be more than jus' old sailor's

stories?" he asked without looking at me.

I scoffed but didn't mean it. "Do you mean like beautiful mermaids and sea sirens that lure sailors to their deaths with their songs and magical islands that appear and disappear, never in the same place?" I thought seriously on the question as I stared at the bottomless blue water. "I suppose I do," I said. Given my circumstance and that I had signed to sail under the command of a man who sought to win his love back from the gods of the sea, it would have been foolish to say otherwise.

"Aye," he said. "Mermaids and magical islands be one thing, but there be other things that lurk in these waters, too." He snubbed out the end of his cigar and tucked what was left of it inside his vest. "Not everythin' be pretty fish and songs, lad. There be evil things that live in the deep." He sighed solemnly, talking around the smoke in his mouth, and even in the dim light I could see a shadow move through his eyes. "Dark things that don't much be carin' for the likes of men in their territory, they are."

A final smoke ring wafted like a lonely spirit atop the waves and disappeared. "Ashrays and devils," Dunn muttered gravely.

"Ashrays?" I questioned, assuming I had misheard. "Pardon?"

"Sea ghosts," he explained in a wistful voice. "Nocturnal beasties that play with men's eyes. Can take us with 'em to the bottom of the sea, they can, right down to the heart of the ocean if they be so wantin'. Them and the other things that live in these waters, they don't always be friendly to the men of land. The sea takes what it wants, lad, and she don't be givin' back other than what we take. Pray you don't learn that the hard way."

I wasn't sure what to say to this, so I said nothing, nor did I dare another nod. I looked for ashrays, but saw only the mist on the water, and once more was glad that Dunn did not know the

THE ISLE OF GOLD

truth of my sex. Perhaps women's eyes were not as easily fooled as men's, or perhaps I was simply too much a land dweller to know anything about what happened when among the world of water.

He gave me a crook-eyed look, as if there was more he'd intended to say, but he decided against it and shook his head. "Well, come on, Mister Rivers, it's best we be puttin' you to work."

I HALF EXPECTED HIM TO LEAD ME BELOW DECK AND DELIVER ME into the hands of the faceless man called Jomo, but Mister Dunn escorted me, much to my surprise, to the captain's cabin at the far end of the ship instead. He didn't speak again as he rapped on the thick wooden door once, pulled it open without waiting for a response, and ushered me inside.

Captain Winters' cabin was surprisingly warm and richly appointed. The flames of a dozen or more lanterns and candelabras cast flickering light around a large, spacious room that was wrapped in windows that were, in turn, hung with red drapes sporting thick golden tassels. A lovely woven rug covered the floor, which was scratched but had been recently shined, and littered about the room were spoils of previous battles—a few gilded artifacts, barrels and chests that brimmed with sparkling trinkets, and more swords and other pieces of discarded weaponry than I could count. More prominent than these, though, were an abundance of books and maps. Rolled and unfurled alike, they covered almost every surface of the room, many covered in markings and languages unlike any I had ever seen before and all well-worn, as if they had been studied and read a hundred times over.

Among his research sat Captain Winters, reclined in an ornate wooden chair at the head of a heavy oak desk. His legs were lifted on its surface and his leather boots were crossed carelessly beside a thick, open book that was held open under the weight of a large brass sextant. He looked the same as I had last seen him, although like the other men he had added to his seafaring attire. His simple garments now included a thick leather belt, a wide-breasted brown leather coat, and even more weapons than he had worn the night before, along with a well-stocked baldric of his own. An empty rum bottle rested in his lap and he was twisting a compass in his hands, appearing to be lost deep in thought.

The captain did not look up as Dunn and I approached his desk, me following a pace behind the other man. "The fuck you want?" Winters demanded when we reached the end of his table.

Dunn cleared his throat and waved me forward, giving me sideways look as I inched toward the desk. "I've found you an apprentice, Captain. Seems to be our new mate, Mister Rivers here, knows how to *read*." He said this with particular emphasis on the last.

Winters lifted his eyes from his compass and fixed me a steely glower, but said nothing. He took one last, lingering look and then snapped it shut. As the case closed I noticed that a portrait of Evangeline was tucked within its hood, her smile striking even in sepia, and I wondered which he had been studying more intently—his charts or her face. Then, he set his boots upon the floor and shifted in his chair, trading the compass for a cigarette that he slipped from a breast pocket of his coat and lifted to pinch between his lips. He leaned forward across the desk and lit its tip with the flame of a dripping candle, and then rested on his

THE ISLE OF GOLD

elbows as he let smoke unfurl between the crack of his lips. The whole gesture was painfully slow, and deliberate, and disturbingly dispassionate, and I tried not to show my discomfort while I waited for him to ready his response.

"That so?" he said flatly at last, as if this didn't interest him in the least.

I glanced nervously from Dunn to the captain, and cursed how the man seemed to ask questions that sounded like challenges. "A-Aye, Captain," I stuttered. "I can that."

Still glowering, he lifted the sexton and pushed the open text in my direction. "Read, then," he commanded with another puff of smoky breath.

It was too dim in the cabin to easily make out the fine, swirling script on the faded parchment pages. Without daring a look at the captain, I picked up a candle on the edge of the table and held it in the space between the book and my face, careful not to let any wax spill onto the pages. The book appeared to be old, and although it was thick and heavy it was delicate, and I dared not spoil it as much for its sake as mine. Such ancient texts were lovely things.

I studied the words, clearly an English translation by way of their uneven cadence and grammar although I could not be sure of the original language. The clumsy passage spoke of the journey of a Venetian navigator named Cabot who had, in the year of 1480, led an expedition to find the mystical island of Bracile, an island believed to be the same as Odysseus' Ogygia. The island itself was described as one that was cloaked but for one day every two years, when it would became visible, as if it had been birthed magically from the depths of the sea. During this brief time the island could be seen but not reached, as it existed only in a mist between the sky and the sea, somewhere the passage described awkwardly as "inside the ocean's heart." Further, it was rumored to be under the guard of a terrible creature of unknown design. Beneath the slanted text the page included a rough illustration of a small, circular-shaped island—labeled "Illa de bracile"—just southwest of Ireland, far out on the western edge of Europe. It featured a thin river that ran east to west across its middle, ending at a small cove in the center of the island.

"It's the story of an island," I said, trying to force my voice to sound steady and assertive in my translation as I passed an unsure finger beneath each word, confirming again the tale I had read. "An enchanted island, called Bracile née Ogygia, that appears only once every two years and can only be reach—"

Before I could finish, Winters abruptly slammed the volume shut and pulled it back across the table, his palm heavy against its cover. He righted himself, and then stood, the swift motions causing the empty bottle to drop from his lap and roll violently across the floor. With one palm still flat on the book and the other on the tabletop, he spat the cigarette away and stared at me for the space of two terrified heartbeats, his nostrils flaring with angry breath. He breathed fumes and then, with a grunt that must have meant something to Dunn, set his eyes on the man beside me and jerked his head backward toward the corner of the cabin. A canvas hammock was hung there, currently occupied by another stack of dusty texts. Then, Winters snatched an empty flagon from the table and, with it clenched tightly in his fist, swung around the desk and stomped out of the room without a backward glance, which apparently was his usual method of exit.

"That's settled then," said Dunn with a breath of relief. His pinched features relaxed as he raked long, knobby fingers through the white tufts of his hair.

I looked at him incredulously. "What's that, then? I don't know what to make of what's just happened." I gestured at the path of fury left by the captain. "He asked me to read it, didn't he? But then is angry that I did?" My own questions startled me in their candidness, but so much was my confusion that it was impossible to hold them at bay.

Dunn looked like he might say something useful, and then instead he said, sharply, "The captain be a complicated man, Mister Rivers, and you'll do well not to be forgettin' it. Now, that hammock will be your bed, and you'll keep wit' the captain and help him with deciphering these texts and whatever else he asks of you." He paused for a moment, and then lowered his voice and took a step closer toward me. "Listen, lad, I've been knowin' Erik Winters for a long time and there's a good man in him, but ain't one of us seen the likes of him these past few years. I'm not even sure he's still in there, though for the sake of us all I hope he be. Be that as it may, he'll treat ye fairly so long as ye don't be givin' him any trouble. Read, write, make your mark on his charts, and do your best to keep to yourself. You wanted to join his crew—this be your lot."

My confusion mingled with fear and excitement to form an incomprehensible cocktail of emotion. I had, of course, wanted to get closer to the captain, but had not expected to be in such tight company, and had never anticipated that it would happen so immediately—or that he would live up so readily to his reputation. Now that I'd found myself there I was terrified and thrilled, and more than a little sick from the conflicted blend of both.

"All right then," was all I could finally manage, along with a small nod. I couldn't help but feel a measure of certain doom, and wished I were back caulking the deck, fingers and back be damned. I might even prefer for company of the formidable Jomo if it was safer than being locked away with Winters. Still, if there was a man who could lead us to Evangeline Dahl and the mysteries that kept her company—and what might contain the answers to my questions—it was Erik Winters.

"Mind ye keep your wits about, Mister Rivers," the older man counseled in a softer voice. He rested one hand upon my shoulder in a fatherly manner and pushed a thin woolen blanket inside my arm with the other. "In here ye be safe from the likes of them outside, but don't let that fool you. The one you should really be afraid of is the one you're locked in here with."

V

WHEN I AWOKE THE NEXT MORNING, IT WAS IN MY NEW hammock in the captain's cabin of the *Riptide*. My former hammock in the kitchen's brothel had been scratchy and uncomfortable—and often so chilled by the incoming breeze from the open windows that my sleep was fitful and uneven—but the canvas of my new bed was soft from wear and it rocked gently with the motion of the ship in a room warmed by a candlelight. I had fallen asleep quickly and rather recklessly, too exhausted from the day's excitement and labor to conceal myself as I had intended with nothing but the thin blanket to cover me, and slept more soundly than I would have expected. Luckily, my new residence in the captain's quarters afforded me more privacy than I would have had otherwise, and so any clue to my secret womanhood had mercifully gone unnoticed while I slept. I lay still for a few more moments, enjoying the easy rocking and the dull hum of movement on the deck outside of the cabin. Then the realization of my surroundings slammed into me and my eyes snapped open eyes with a start. I jerked so suddenly that the steady rolling of the hammock swung off kilter and I nearly tipped out of it. I gripped my hands against the edges and willed the swing to still.

I might have had more privacy in this room than I would have had elsewhere on the ship, but that certainly did not mean that I was secluded—and, alone or not, the captain's cabin of a pirate ship was not the place to indulge myself. Dunn's words of caution the night before echoed in my mind. None of these men onboard were my confidant, not even the quartermaster or the handsome ship's boatswain that had distracted my thoughts and been so amiable toward me. I might have been sailing alongside the dozens of men who crewed the *Riptide,* but this was a journey that I took on my own.

I held my breath as I blinked the sleep out of my vision, ignoring my eyes' burning protests as I forced them open despite the glow of filtered light that flooded the sweeping windows of the cabin. Some had opened their curtains wide to the morning sun. Every fiber of my body was red hot with alert, but I strained to remain as still as a corpse so that I might get my bearings without being discovered. The room was still and quiet and my eyes immediately found the captain's chair. I had not expected him to be there, and yet there he sat, at work at his desk and hunched over a pile of documents. I wasn't sure when he had returned, or if he had slept at all, nor where, so deep had my own slumber been. I silently cursed myself for being so careless. Were my true identity to be discovered I could not think of a worse place for it to happen than alone with the captain within his quarters. For that, both he and I might suffer the crew's response. Since Bartholomew Roberts, the pirate captain known as Black Bart, had penned the articles of the Pirate Code, women had been forbidden from sailing aboard pirate's ships under the penalty of death. Of course, there were some notorious seafaring women who ignored this entirely, and others braver than I that challenged the rule openly. Still, I was unsure how such a thing might be handled onboard the *Riptide,* and while Mistress Dahl would likely warrant an exception, even if simply because none would dare challenge Winters, there was little hope that I would as well. I was no one.

While I waited for my heartbeat to return to its normal speed, I used my vantage point from behind to examine the man without the weight of his gaze on me. He looked much the same as he had when I'd see him the night before, layers of linen and leather, sinewy flesh bulging from underneath tight-fitting cloth that tapered downward from his thick, broad shoulders. He'd removed the coat and baldric, and his wavy auburn hair spilled down his back in windblown tangles that were held together at the middle with a piece of twine. A pile of weapons sat beside him—a pistol inches from his fingers atop the desk, a cutlass leaned against his knee—and a half empty cask of red wine waited within his reach. I could hear the scratching sound of a quill on parchment.

"You're awake then," he said suddenly without turning around. His gravelly voice boomed in the small open room, and it was so startling that I nearly flipped myself from my hammock again. I hadn't thought I'd made a sound that would have given me away, but he must have sensed my waking like a wild animal could scent its prey, perhaps by a rise in heart rhythm or a change in breathing. My slowing heartbeat accelerated once more. When I didn't answer he cast an impatient look over his shoulder. One icy blue eye speared me across the few feet of cabin between us.

I realized with a start that his comment had not been an idle observation, but a call to duty. It was an order to get out of my bed and to work. I was obliged to obey though I was surprised he'd allowed me the luxury of waking naturally. It did not seem a fitting way for a captain's apprentice to behave, and a wave of anxiety washed over me. "Aye," I confirmed in a voice hoarse from sleep. The sound was barely more than a whisper. I cleared my throat. "Aye, I'm awake, Captain."

With this, Winters' eye returned to his papers and I righted myself in the hammock, swinging my legs over the edge of the canvas and adjusting the brim of my hat as low as I thought reasonable. I smoothed back loose hairs behind my ears and then pulled my boots back into their proper place on my feet before I stood, re-tucking loose bits of clothing. I double checked that the journal was still concealed safely in my jacket, and tested the reach of my blade, just in case I should need it—not that it would do me much good, but it was reassuring to feel its cold steel just the same. Rubbing my sore hands across my face, I plucked out bits of sleep that had dried in the corners of my eyes with scabby fingertips. I wished I had a basin to wash in, but thought better of inquiring about one.

The captain didn't bother to look at me as I rounded the desk and stood before him. Instead, of all the questions I had expected he might ask of me, he chose the one I'd least anticipated, asking it directly with no preamble whatsoever. "What do you know of Evangeline Dahl?" he demanded as he resettled his quill in its pot of ink and took up the wine, drinking deeply as I fumbled for a reply. When he returned the cask to the table, it was nearly empty and I was still searching for an answer.

"I know only that she was the proprietress of the tavern on Isla Perla, The Goodnight Mermaid," I began, speaking slowly and taking care to select the right words. I paused, but he added nothing, and so I kept talking, filling the silence with the minimal information I had and thought safe to say aloud. "I know she vanished from that island two summers ago, and that you've been searching for her ever since, but that is the extent of it."

The captain lifted his quill again from the ink pot and, eyes still on the paper in front of him, consulted the book he had shown me last night before drawing a new mark on a map. "She

THE ISLE OF GOLD

didn't *vanish*," he said, his voice reducing to a growl as it landed on the last word. He drew another line, measured it with the compass that held Mistress Dahl's portrait, and then sat back from his work. "She was taken."

"Taken, sir?"

He rolled his eyes upward, managing to make me feel small beneath his gaze though he was seated below me. "Yes," he said. His words were so sharp they might have been a blade.

"My apologies, Captain," I offered, my thoughts still clouded and slow from sleep. "But I'm afraid I don't understand."

"She was *taken*," he repeated, a rumble of new frustration clipping the end of each word as he paused pointedly between them. "Stolen by the gods of the sea. But I will find her," he slammed his fist on the table, setting the quill to roll off its edge unnoticed, and fixed me with eyes so frozen that they would never melt, "I will take her back. And when I have, even the gods will pay for what they have stolen from me. You, Mister Rivers, will assist me in all things that I require, or you will join the dead at the bottom of the world. Is that clear?" The last three words bit into the air in turn, each punctuated with a snap so there could be no mistaking the threat that loomed in them.

I swallowed down a lump that had risen in my throat and nodded in agreement, now fully awake. There was nothing else I could have said or done but agree. Besides, I, too, would have fought the gods of the sea to have Mistress Dahl returned, as well as to force from them the answers that I so desperately craved. At least in this Winters and I wore in accordance, and he needn't concern himself with that, but apparently he had no intention of doing so. Already he had produced a new quill and returned to his charts, seeming to forget about me altogether.

As the appetite for my own pursuits lingered in my mind, a sound gurgled forth from my stomach, signaling another kind of hunger. It was an embarrassing consequence of life—that one must continually worry over such simple things as food. I prayed silently that Winters hadn't heard it, though I suspected if he could hear me pretending to sleep he would hear that telltale rumble as well. He could probably hear my thoughts, too. Luckily they were fixated now on a longing for some biscuits and fruit.

Winters loosed a deep sigh and leaned back in his seat, studying me with something akin to pity on face—the same way one might look at a suffering dog. "When's the last time you ate, boy?" he asked. From anyone else such words of concern might have sounded warm and welcoming, but from him they were just as cold as his previous warning, although they'd lost some of their normal hostility.

"Night before last at the tavern," I responded sheepishly. "Mister Dunn provided me with bits of bread and a tank of ale." In truth, I had been so consumed yesterday in preparing to make way that I had forgotten to eat.

Winters rolled his eyes and pushed the nearly empty flagon of wine toward me, giving a permissive nod to drink. I watched as the thick red fluid sloshed against its own container in a way that was eerily similar to the feeling happening my stomach, and struggled not to gag. The thought of wine on an empty stomach was almost sickening enough to diminish my appetite all together.

An amusing face must have accompanied this thought because the captain's mouth unexpectedly propelled its left corner upward in a tight, uncharacteristic smirk that might have broken a lesser man's face. His hand reached for the wine and he swilled the remainder of it, and then laughed so good-naturedly that the sound was more frightening than any he'd made so far. He clapped one palm heavily against the tabletop and waved the empty bottle toward the door of the cabin with the other. In the blink of an eye his face had hardened once more to its normal impassive glower. The transition was so quick and imperceptible that I wondered if I had imagined the whole thing. "Go on then." He waved the bottle again, all hints of laughter passed. He pulled a small red bead, no larger than a bullet, from his pocket and tossed it to me across the table. I caught it easily. "For the cook," he explained, although I wasn't sure what it meant. "Be back within the hour."

I nodded gratefully and excused myself, stealing one last brief glance at the good man that Dunn had said had once been the captain as I stepped out of the cabin and into the milieu of the deck beyond.

THE FIRST PERSON I SAW WHEN I MOVED OUT INTO THE SUNLIGHT was Tom Birch, who was sitting at a makeshift table formed from two half-rotted wooden crates that had been stacked atop each other. His legs were so long that even bent at the knee they stood taller than the combined height of the crates, and he had to hunker down over the table as he sat, shirtless in the hot sun and peeling the skin from an apple with a small dagger. Boatswains, I knew, were largely responsible for overseeing the majority of activities to keep the ship afloat, but currently he was holding a wedge of the fruit in one hand and wearing eyes wide with surprise while a coil of rope sat forgotten at his feet. I stepped out of the cabin's door and closed it softly behind me.

"Oi, what's that then?" he asked by way of greeting, waving

the dagger in the direction of the captain's office. His curious eyes landed on me, and I stared at the apple to avoid melting into them. "Was that the captain I heard," his voice dropped conspiratorially and he whipped his head around to make sure no one was listening before whispering the last word, "*laughing?*"

"Aye," I confirmed, glad I'd finally been asked something I could answer. I bravely met his eyes. "And at my expense at that," I said, pressing my hand against my stomach as it rumbled again. Tom cocked an eyebrow at the noise though he was polite enough not to comment. "What does it matter to you?"

He slid the fruit into his mouth and chewed it thoughtfully, the dagger left to dangle loosely between his long fingers. "Doesn't much really, I guess," he replied after swallowing. "Just I can't remember the last time I heard that. Don't think he's so much as taken a breath without scowling in at least a year." He sliced another chunk of apple from the rind and stuffed it into his mouth, squinting up at me in the sunlight. "Maybe more."

"Glad to be of service," I quipped, feeling embarrassed. I hoped my reputation on the ship did not become that of the comic relief. That might be worse than being found a woman. At least then they'd kill me quickly and not make me yearn for it.

Tom nodded amiably, then stood, stretched, and tossed the apple core overboard where it landed with a dull thud on the top of the water and sank. He wiped both sides of the dagger against the thigh of his pants—a movement I watched with a completely different type of hunger than the one banging around noisily in my stomach—before tucking it into the wide waistband of his belt. "Come on then," he said, turning to walk away. "I'll show you down to the galley."

My thoughts immediately turned to Jomo and I almost

protested, but my stomach twisted painfully against my insides and so I followed safely in Tom's shadow as he led me down into the belly of the ship.

WHILE I AVOIDED STUDYING THE MAN'S MUSCULAR BACKSIDE, Tom led me down through the tween decks of the ship and into the cargo hold, and then navigated us smoothly through stairwells and short halls as we made our way through the ship's pantry. Soon we reached the galley nestled into the bow of the ship's hull. Descending into the interior of the ship had not been as dark as I had expected with sunlight pouring through the grating between decks. Flickering wax candles cased in lanterns were stationed on shelves and tables adding light into the corners. With most of the crew either busy above deck or sleeping in their quarters, the lower decks were surprisingly empty save for a few men here and there who were tending to tasks in the hold. It was a good thing, too, as the recently stocked belly of the *Riptide* was full with supplies. Stacks of wooden crates and barrels, some standing and some laid on their sides, lined the walls and cluttered the floors where sacks of flour and thick coils of rope hadn't already taken up residence. Baskets of fresh fruits and vegetables hung below hooks jammed full of fish and other slabs of meat; kegs of rum stood at the ready with taps already hammed in their husks. A goat, tied to a post, napped in a bed of straw. A short milking stool lay at her feet, and nearby a small wire cage was crammed full with nesting hens while others pecked around the floor, hunting for bits of loose grain. Fresh and plentiful now, I knew that these stores would soon be depleted and we would subsist on little more than hardtack and salted meats.

The ceilings of the decks were shorter than those in the captain's quarters, but still taller than I'd anticipated, though more than once the tall boatswain had to duck to avoid hitting his head while I followed quietly behind him. He was at least three hands higher than me, perhaps more. Likewise, these rooms below deck were not like what I'd seen above. They were cramped, dingy, and unkempt, and had largely gone to ruin—not like the tidy, spacious room at the back of the ship that belonged to the captain. Long wooden tables stretched between the pantry and the galley, flanked by wooden benches for seating.

When at last we reached the kitchen and my sights set on Jomo, I was glad that I had Tom Birch's company to soften the introduction. The portly, soft-bellied man I'd seen on the docks yesterday couldn't have been more of an opposite to the terrifying vision of a man before me now—nor would I have been able to conjure anything the likes of this man even if I had spent a hundred nights dreaming of monsters. He was garbed simply and in a similar fashion to the rest of the men onboard, in layers of linen and leather, and his neck was embellished with length upon length of necklaces strung with various bits of beads and bone and feather, but where the man I'd witnessed in the harbor had been thick and fair-skinned, Jomo was midnight made flesh. He was slim and muscular with broad shoulders and a narrow, tapering waist, and covered in skin so dark that it was of a black so dense it might have been sculpted from ink. It was not the color of his skin that startled me—no, nothing quite so superficial as that. I had seen many darker hues color the skin of the peoples on Isla Perla, from burnt olive complexions to dark, mud brown, and rich, gleaming ebony. They were a mixed and dynamic people of lovely colors and even lovelier heritages. My own dear Claudette wore skin the color of whipped, delicious caramel that was several shades darker than my own. Pirate vessels, too, were diverse lots, crewed with men of every color and nation, although many still held the same prejudices as other white men and were known to treat runaway slaves or peoples of coastal Africa no more kindly than just another commodity in their stolen prizes. This man, though, with his hands buried deep within the stomach cavity of a large fish, looked like no runaway slave or coastal native that I had ever set eyes on before.

The coarse black hair at the crown of his head was braided tightly against his scalp, the remainder shaved away completely to expose long, raised scars that ran the length of his face. There were seven in total, each beginning at the top of his head and raking in concentric lines that ended at the edge of his jaw. A smaller set, four atop four, formed a hash mark above the steep cliff of his brow, and another line—this one fresher and noticeably thinner, ran diagonally across the bridge of his nose. A small, hook-shaped scar, oddly similar to the one on the captain's eye, decorated the top of his unmarked eye. He wore no less than a dozen silver hoops in each of his ears, another in his nose, and a series of small, raised circles adorned his upper lip. More scars ran the length of his collar and disappeared beneath his clothing, which I noticed now was more colorful than was customary, dyed in shades of crimson and sunshine.

"Jomo, this is Mister Rivers," Tom introduced me with a wave of his hand to the exotic creature gutting the dead fish as he rummaged about for something else to eat. He spoke slowly, pronouncing each word clearly like the man were hard of hearing, or prone to startling. "He is the captain's new apprentice, just come onboard in Isla Perla."

The whites of the man's eyes flickered in my direction and then returned to his business with the fish. Mine, however, stayed glued to his curious scars as I traced them top to bottom several times over. I had heard of such intricate scarring rituals in the Congo, but had never seen them with my own eyes. They were as striking as they were beautiful, and I had a morbid urge to touch them, trace them with my fingertips. However, I also had an urge to live, so I did not dare.

"What have you got for grub?" Tom continued jovially, nosing about the room as if we weren't in the presence of some displaced tribal god. "Lad hasn't eaten since two nights past. We can't afford any man to get sick this early in, not when we've got plenty of food to go 'round. Right, mate?"

Jomo grunted, jerking his head toward a table where a pile of uneaten scraps sat awaiting disposal. Among these I saw bits of a crumbling ship biscuit, a chunk of yellow cheese, and a small pile of red grapes. My stomach lurched and I inched toward the table. The cook's eyes darted quickly back to me and he lurched forward, his fish momentarily forgotten while strands of innards dangled from his hand, which now gripped an unsheathed blade, the business end of which was pointed at me. I noticed a gap in his grip; he was missing a finger.

"Payment," he demanded, his throaty voice sawing out words in blunt grumbles that had a strange, songlike quality. He sneered at me and I noticed that the few teeth he had left in his skull had been filed to sharp, carnivorous points.

My hands flew instinctively to the air in front of my face, palms facing outward in supplication. If I fainted, then perhaps I could blame it on my hunger.

"Oi," came Tom's voice from somewhere behind the cook's hulking figure. A tanned hand landed lightly on the cook's shoulder as the boatswain moved between us, his movements echoing that slow and careful manner that he'd spoken with before. He spoke to the air between us, his eyes on the knife that hovered threateningly in the air. "Mister Rivers here ain't familiar with how we go about business on this ship, Jomo. Are you, Rivers?" This last was directed at me.

"N-No," I spluttered, palms still in the air as I swayed uncertainly on my feet.

"See, that's right," Tom went on, nodding as Jomo's blade stilled and dropped slightly. "No harm done, mate."

"Payment," the dark man repeated. He lifted the dagger again but with some indecision this time.

"See, Mister Rivers," Tom explained, still speaking into the air above the knife, "our esteemed cook here has a different sort of arrangement on our ship. He don't care much for gold, so he takes his wages in other forms. What have you that you can pay him for your meals?"

I opened my mouth to say that I had nothing and that I would be fine to starve to death, thank you very much, but then I remembered the red bead the captain had given me. I pulled it from my pocket—watching nervously as Jomo's blade quivered threateningly when my hand disappeared from view—and held it forward in my outstretched palm.

Immediately Jomo stabbed the blade into the body of the fish and snatched the bead from my hand, turning it over appreciatively in the glow of a nearby lantern. He grunted again—apparently this was the common language used by men like Winters and Jomo—and Tom smiled approvingly at me.

"Well, Mister Rivers," he winked, shoving past me as he made his way back to the upper deck, "breakfast is served, mate."

I cast one last nervous look at Jomo but found that he was still admiring the red bead. With both hands I stuffed all the food I could into my pockets and hurried in the direction the boatswain had gone.

VI

ILEARNED LATER THAT THE COOK, JOMO, HAD INDEED BEEN found aboard a ship that had sailed from the islands off the coast of Africa with over one hundred of his people destined for lives as slaves in the New World. That dreadful ship had been caught and boarded by the *Riptide*'s men, its crew thrown to the ocean, and its hold emptied of its cargo, which—by the accounts of the men who'd been willing to share the tale—had been a profitable one, something to the tune of fifty tons of iron, twenty pipes of brandy, several bales of linens, and, of course, the stolen children of Africa. Among the men, women, and children still alive in the squalor and stench of filth at the bottom of the ship—which had been pitifully fewer than had originally been brought aboard—had been Jomo, clad in irons and chains like a feral beast. He had been beaten to the edge of death, and driven half mad by the same. In the little communication the *Riptide*'s men had with the captive passengers the story was told that Jomo had been the leader of their people, and though he'd defended them bravely he'd been no match for the weapons and the sheer numbers of the slavers crew. He'd been kept barely alive for nothing other than as a means to ease the crew's boredom on the long journey west. His missing finger was a souvenir the slavers' captain, now buried in the dirt of Davy Jones' locker, had taken for himself.

Winters, as savage as he had often shown himself to be, was a man of honor. He did not traffic in the trade of people, and so he had ordered the execution of the slavers and the slaves themselves freed unharmed, even allotting a portion of the ship's stores to feed and mend them as they returned to Isla Perla. Many of these people had taken up residence with the tribes on the island, some in the employ of Mistress Dahl or the brothel owner, Maurice, while others had found passage on safer ships headed back to their homeland. The captain, however, had taken a special interest in Jomo, and between he, Evangeline, and Brandon Dunn the man had been nourished back to health. His mind had not enjoyed the same recovery as had his body, but nevertheless Winters and Jomo enjoyed a certain friendship. When Winters had invited him to join his crew, Jomo had agreed, sealing the contract in the customary ways of his culture. Now, the two men wore an identical symbol above their left eyes in a mark of brotherhood.

STORIES SUCH AS THESE I LEARNED AS THE DAYS CAME AND WENT, passing uneventfully in a quiet rush on calm seas. For my part, I kept to my work as assigned, reading and translating as best I could stacks of old books and papers that Captain Winters left in unorganized heaps about the cabin whilst he stirred about the ship with a restless anger that left permanent goose bumps in my flesh. Many of the documents were unintelligible and some were waterlogged and useless, but either way I worked through their pages and provided detailed notes to the captain. I also took care to document some of the more interesting passages for myself in my diary, scribbling them in the dark when I was supposed to be asleep. Many of the tales were similar, with small but clear distinctions. All, however, concerned the gods of the sea, and sea witches and fairies that both loved and hated men.

After our first few encounters my conversations with my captain had become increasingly scarce, sometimes nonexistent, though a kind of companionable silence now existed between us. He did not speak to me of Bracile again, nor did he impart any of his own interpretations of the texts we studied together. If anything, he was even more secretive with his intentions than he had been before—keeping them not only from me but from Mister Dunn as well, a new normal that the older man who had previously been privy to all of the captain's confidences had not taken to well. I had also noticed on one evening when Winters pulled out his compass that the portrait of Evangeline had been removed, though I later saw it tucked beneath the inkpot on his desk. At times he was ruthlessly enigmatic, prone to violent fits of fury where he would curse and sling pages or empty rum casks or even daggers across the cabin. Other times he was forlorn and melancholy, and would ask me to read aloud to him or regale him with memories of Isla Perla, which inevitably—as I'm sure he knew they would all along—wound their way back to Mistress Dahl. Nonetheless, over the passing weeks I grew to learn his mannerisms, and to anticipate his moods, and so I had come to understand when my attention was required, and when it was best I leave him alone. The latter were far more often.

On those lonely nights—as it was often at night that the captain was most want to sit alone and brood and smoke and drink in isolation—I had taken to visiting the decks, usually joining in with Tom Birch as he attended to various odd tasks about the ship. I did my best to ease the loneliness by making friendly company with some of the less fearsome men aboard, including Jomo who, as it turned out, was a rather pleasant fellow so long as he was kept in fresh supply of beads and other trinkets one could find lying about the ship. He was partial to the color red, I learned, and so as I went about my duties I had made it my habit to collect any bit of red I could find—beads, scraps of cloth, beautifully colored shells, even an occasional bit of glass or sealing wax. I'd bring these to him in exchange for my daily meals, which were now met with something as close to a smile as the man could manage beneath the weight of his stone-studded lip. In fact, it often found its way into my nightmares: Jomo with his filed teeth and claw-like scars. Still, he was a gentle giant, and though he spoke little he was an excellent cook and enjoyed playing cards to pass the time.

Aside from the unique history of the ship's cook, the rest of the men who manned the *Riptide* were united by nothing more than their love of the sea and her treasures. Chiefly among these were the common suspects of gold, jewels, and other prizes, although some named more unusual item—linens, spices, even women. Most of the crew had spent their lives on the water, with many having little knowledge of life on land other than that which was required to attend the ship itself, such as careening or the particulars of restocking supplies. Others, like myself, were more recent recruits to the *Riptide*'s crew, having elected to join rather than perish when their respective former ships had been plundered by the men that were now their brothers. Many of these were still becoming accustomed to the vessel, as such large and well-appointed galleons were rarely found under the command of pirates. In a much smaller assembly of men, others, like Mister Brandon Dunn, had sailed with Erik Winters longer than I had been alive, and longer, as was in the case of Tom Birch, than they seemed able to properly recall. None were able to remember exactly when they had met Captain Winters, or how old they had been when they did, nor did they seem to care. In any event, all were loyal men, and I found no quarrels among them other than the usual disagreements over food or gambling debts.

Much to my surprise, as I worked my way through the captain's books, I also managed to finesse my way into the good graces of the majority of the crew—both new and old—and so the murderous glances that had welcomed me on my first day aboard were gradually replaced. These new relationships came at best with budding friendship, at worse with indifference, and only very rarely with anything more troubling. Only one man onboard seemed to be especially disapproving of me—the ship's carpenter, an olive-skinned man who went by the name of Domingo "Left Eye" Díaz—called so by the fact that he had only one good eye, the other being shaped from an orb of ivory that he was prone to removing from its socket and rolling worryingly around in his mouth. I discovered he had been the man who wore the handkerchief over this face that night at The Goodnight Mermaid. Domino had, on more than one occasion, made it clear he was not interested in so much as learning my name, never mind considering me an equal on the crew. He mostly sat at his table, busy with ship repairs. Since he disliked me so much, I reserved my praise of his ability to fashion fixes for the ship or repair dulled weapons, both of which he was quite skilled at. Like gathering trinkets for Jomo, I made it my habit to keep as much distance as possible between myself and the single, scathing eye of Mister Díaz.

Among the men I came to know best was an eccentric Dutchman called Gregory Nip. He seemed to never bother to wear a full set of clothes, and was always eager for a game of liars dice, though he seldom could finish a round without losing his temper and accusing his partner of cheating. Such a thing normally evolved into a mild skirmish although none took to it too seriously. In fact, the whole exercise seemed more of a way to relieve the tedium of long days spent at sea than any serious grievance, and usually ended in laughter all around. The portly man that I'd seen that first day in the harbor turned out to be none other than the ship's doctor, Mister Horace Clarke, who seemed in equal parts fat and sloth to be by far the unhealthiest man aboard. He was seldom without a chunk of food in his hand, and it was common knowledge that the meat I'd seen him direct onboard had been held in his private collection.

Lastly, in the quietest parts of my nights loitering about the deck, I often found myself in the company of the ship's navigator, a blond-haired man that was known simply as Rabbie. I doubted this was his actual name but more likely a consequence of no one being able to understand his thick Scottish accent, which was rivaled only by Tom's muddled British one. Such excellent navigators were a rare find I had been told, though not by Rabbie himself, who seemed indifferent to the role. Instead, soft-spoken and generally aloof, he spent most of his time lost in his own thoughts, eyes turned up at the night sky in careful consternation and humming to himself under his breath. When I visited, he taught me the names of the constellations that guided the ship as she made her way across the wide, boundless waters of the Atlantic Ocean. Were it possible to be paid in stardust, like Jomo, Rabbie would have likely obliged. Rumor had it that this man had been scooped from the very sea itself, a victim of another battle although no one, including Rabbie, could recall which.

"'At thaur is th' constellation Cygnus," he instructed one evening, his eyes cast skyward while I delivered a new set of charts to his post on the ship's bridge. He glanced quickly at the orders and then returned his eyes to the heavens, and without looking he adjusted course by a few clicks, turning the wheel slightly with his enormous paw of a hand before he continued. "When he was a cheil he stole th' gods chariot an' dove repeatedly intae th' water tae search fur phaethon. It ay pity, th' gods turned th' puir dobber intae a swan an' sent heem up in th' heavens."

"Is that so," I inquired politely, not really wanting an answer. I took a meager step backward, signaling a retreat. Though the stories Rabbie told were interesting, the stars had never held much interest for me, and learning them was usually not worth the trouble it took to unravel his accent. My apologies, of course, to Cygnus. I pondered that such a large, lumbering man could be held enrapt but something as delicate as stars, and stifled a giggle when I pictured him housed among them—the great oaf a human embodiment of Ursa Major itself.

"Aye," he returned, eyes locked above, and the conversation was done.

Mister Dunn and Tom Birch were, as they had been from the beginning, my two most ready allies, though my attachment to these two men had diverged along an unexpected continuum.

Firstly, my initial attraction to the handsome boatswain had mounted into full-blown infatuation. Hard as a might, I could not keep my thoughts, or my eyes, from him. As the days passed I found myself being swept away in the presence of his gentle, carefree manner and his clear, striking green eyes—his boyish charm knit inside a tall man's body. More than food in my body or breath in my lungs I craved the sound of his voice; the image of his strong, lean muscles rippling as he pulled at the ship's rigging or practiced with his cutlass; the accidental brush of his fingertips when they touched my flesh, unaware of the aching strum they played upon my heartstrings. It was consuming and maddening, and distracting in the most thrilling of ways. I yearned for Tom Birch with the same feverish intensity for which I longed for the answers to my own mysteries, and yet I would have thrown the rest away if I could have had him. Worse, still, was the truth that my affections were not just unrequited, but completely unknown—the poor man had no inkling that I longed for him so desperately, nor that I was even capable of doing so. And so the only recourse I had was to be the instrument of my own misery, keeping as safe and far a distance from him as I could tolerate—toeing the line between addiction and withdrawal like a drunk who could see the wine but not wet his lips. Still, I could not resist the pull to him, and I found myself often in his presence, fearing that the sounds of my palpitating heart giving me away as I worked at his side while he oversaw his many consuming boatswain's tasks.

My aversion to the constant attention of the ship's quartermaster, on the other hand, was of a decidedly different flavor. Every inch I attempted to add to the distance between Tom and myself, Dunn seemed anxious to fill with himself, hovering incessantly about me in a suffocating way that I came to distrust. He was never far from wherever I was, even when I lay in my hammock in the captain's quarters where he had now taken up residence, too. I often caught him observing me out of the corner of his black, beady eyes. When we spoke it was usually about ship's business, though on the occasion he could find an opening he would launch into a discussion on the various myths and legends of the waters and the fantastical creatures that lived within them. He seemed to desire both my opinion on such things as much as how the captain was taking to them. This I found odd as I had so very little information to contribute in the shadow of his apparent mastery of the subject, but still his questions persisted.

It was during one of these conversations that he had affixed the vanishing of Mistress Dahl directly to the story which he seemed most obsessed, that of the feminine water spirit named Mélusine. Drunk on brandy one evening, the quartermaster had cornered both Tom Birch and I—a situation that I found most distressing as the three of us were sat so closely that one of my knees bumped rudely against the bony nub of Dunn's while the other caressed the length of Tom's—and regaled us with his story, whispering so that it would not reach the ears of the captain, who had been particularly malcontent that day. A flickering stump of a candle sat in the space between us, casting a pale light onto our storyteller.

"She be born of a water goddess an' a mortal man, she was. Not just any man, mind you, but a pirate at that," Dunn informed us, his breath sickly sweet from liquor. "But the gods frown on such things—man's world blendin' up with theirs—and so they were furious and demanded they return to the sea and be punished. They wanted to be settin' an example of what happens when the women of the sea mix up in the world of men. So's they took her to an island, tryin' to keep her safe by comin' on land, but bein' that her father didn't know the full story of what she was, he didn't know what such a thing would do—keepin' the water separated from itself like that. That poor bastard had no idea what he was gettin' himself into, and that water goddess, she was so in love with him that she didn't think to stop 'im. 'fact, she gave him a piece of herself so that she could stay there on land with him. Bound herself to him, she did."

He took a full drink and pressed on, leaning in closer so that our three foreheads nearly touched. "Then that man, damned pirate that he was, he left them poor creatures stuck on land, and took back to the sea, tryin' to find a way to buy their freedom, but he got taken by a lust for gold alon' the way and had a bit of a jumblin' of priorities, yeh might say. Not a very wise thing to do to the water, aye? It ain't something' that can be tamed, and it don' play seconds to no one." He jerked his head violently from side to side and kept talking before Tom or I could respond. "So's Mélusine grew up and became a great beauty, as lovely as e'r was the sea itself they say with golden hair and all the like, but her mother, the goddess that she was be growin' colder and meaner all the while, too. She decided she be takin' revenge on Jones for leavin' her, and she used her powers over the sea to send it after tha' wily pirate and swallow him down whole. Then she went back to the sea, she did, leavin' before Mélusine found out what ha' happened. But when Mélusine did she was terrible mad, and she went about controllin' the waters the best she knew how, tryin' to find a way to free him and avoidin' her mother, who would of destroyed her, too, for the sin of havin' been a child born of man."

Here he paused again, drinking deeply from the flask of brandy while he thought on Mélusine's story. "And so the curse was born, as just like her mother, Mélusine fell in love with a mortal and her mother punished her for it, takin' her back to the ocean so 'at she would lose her happiness, too, just for the spite of it."

"Oi, and then I bet that water fairy turned her daughter into a fish," Tom broke in before the older man could finish his tale.

He winked at me out of the corner of his eye and I was grateful that the darkness hid the heat that bloomed in my cheeks as a result. It was not easy to look at him straightly when the talk of forbidden love was hanging in the air. "I suspect this story won't be getting a happy ending then?" He shook his head disappointedly and then shoved backward off his chair, taking the quartermaster's flask along with him as he straightened up and looked out at the black night water, alight with the twinkling of a million stars. "That's why I don't listen to your old damn stories when you've been drinking, Bullet. They're bloody depressing."

"Aye, don't nobody know for sure," Dunn admitted, waving Tom and his criticism away. His sharp eyes, even swimming heavily in brandy, did not miss the way I watched Tom as he walked away, flask still in hand. He went on, his black eyes locked on me. "Some say 'at she was cursed, turned into a serpent from the waist down and banished to live in that form forever. Others say she simply went back to the sea and wasted away into it, melted apart like soap in water. I once heard a tale that she'd been banished to a forbidden place no man may visit, turned into some sort of golden statue as a warnin' to pirates' greed. Don't nobody know for sure, though." He paused, looking around for his flask. Finding it gone he made a growling noise, like he was clearing his throat, and went on. "All's tha's known is 'at she simply up and vanished one day, cursed by her mother. Worse, that her own lover be bound to the ocean where he be sailin' the world over searchin' for her still, never to be findin' her."

With this he reached out and clutched his hand firmly around my wrist in a move so quick and startling that I nearly toppled off my chair. He leaned into the light of the flame and I saw that his eyes were suddenly sober, clear, and bright. The expression on

THE ISLE OF GOLD

his face was no longer that of a drunken sailor, but of a haunted man. "Now you tell me, Mister Rivers," he insisted, his grip tightening meaningfully, painfully, into my skin; it hurt, but I was too shocked by his sudden change in countenance to struggle to break free, "who do yeh think this story be soundin' like it be about?"

"I h-hardly believe in such st-stories," I managed to stammer out. "Old legends are just that—myths and fantasies."

With a sneer the man released my wrist, then blew out the candle so that we were covered in shadow. "Perhaps ye best be rethinkin' your notions, *Mister Rivers*," he snarled in the dark as I watched the white tips of the water glisten as they crashed into one another. *Ashrays*, Dunn had mentioned before, and I saw now how the white streaks in the water looked less like waves and more like the shapes of ghosts swirling beneath them. "We've a long time to be at sea yet, and you know nothin' of what lies in these waters, boy."

VII

SINCE THE EVENING HE SHARED THE LEGEND OF MÉLUSINE, I had avoided Mister Dunn as best I could, although he scarcely seemed to notice. Perhaps he was avoiding me in turn, or maybe I imagined it all together. It mattered not. Either way, his attentions had been called elsewhere, as the demands on the quartermaster's time were nearly as heavy as the boatswain's. Having been at sea for months we had made our way far into the vast emptiness of the ocean, and without so much as another pair of sails to be seen on the horizon many of the crew had become restless and grumbling. Life onboard consisted of long periods of drunken idleness, punctuated by brief periods of violent action when the men's tempers flared like cannon fire—shooting out and striking whoever, or whatever happened to wander within their range. More than once, Mister Clarke had been called upon to relieve himself of his private pantry—an area he now guarded more tersely than even his medical supplies as food supplies began to wane—and tend to one of the men. During the worst of it—around the time the wine ran dry and the last of the rum and brandy keys were tapped—I spent a few uneasy days concealed in Winters' cabin pretending to work on texts I had already deciphered. I was convinced that the constant threat of other pirates, or storms, or even the Royal Navy not withstanding, the men aboard might very well be the cause of their own watery end. If their tempers were not soon satiated, we would never reach the disappearing island of Bracile at all, much less find the vanished Mistress Dahl.

And then, just as suddenly as a shift in the winds might bring about a new tide, several changes fell upon the *Riptide* in rapid succession. None of them were terribly major, but still they were of number and significance impactful enough that, as a result, many things were very different now than they had been only a few days before as our steadfast vessel made her way toward the Old World.

The first change to come about the daily minutiae of the *Riptide* was the reemergence of Captain Winters. After his period of long, self-imposed seclusion he resurfaced and began to spend most of his time roaming about the decks of the ship, top deck to hull, stern to forecastle. In fact, now that he was free of the sanctuary of his own quarters he rarely returned to them, preferring to eat and work alongside the rest of his crew as much as drink and gamble. Winters himself inspected the canvas and the sails, as well as the rigging and other various aspects of shipboard maintenance. He spoke, sometimes in harsh whispers and other times in even harsher, clipped orders, in turns with Tom Birch, Brandon Dunn, Domingo Diaz, and even Jomo the cook—for whom he produced a lovely red stone in exchange for one of the chickens. His presence had caused a noticeable turn in the atmosphere about the vessel. The men seemed to work harder and quarrel less. Even Gregory Nip forced himself into a pair of breeches and could now manage himself through a few games of liars dice without declarations of treachery. Mister Clarke had remained undisturbed in his quarters with his medicines and meats and not performed so much as a single stitch. I was not sure if this change in the men was for fear of the captain, respect, or if they simply understood that our journey was reaching a pivotal point and were anxious to make preparations. Like Dunn's avoidance, it mattered not.

Once he seemed satisfied that all was in good order and re-turned command of such matters to his officers, Winters made his way to Rabbie, the navigator, and took up residence on the quarter deck. For the past several days the pair, sometimes joined by Mister Dunn, had been locked in private conference at the ship's helm. With pages of parchment and maps unfurled between them and bottles of various liquor used as paperweights throughout all of it, they endlessly examined charts and other instruments of navigation as they made small but important changes in our course at the captain's direction. It was a curious sight to be-hold—the reedy Dunn locked in a perpetual, sour grimace, the much larger Scotsman towering above all with the same heavy bulk as a highland bear, and the captain, slighter than them both but his presence still by far the largest of the trio.

Such was the view on one beautiful, cloudless day as I watched the three men speak in hushed voices for the space of a few moments before turning my attention back to my task at hand. The captain was holding a scrap of parchment that I had noticed a handful of times hidden alongside Evangeline's por-trait. I had guessed a hundred times over what was written on it, and though I never found out for sure, I had a mostly clear idea— and it was not good. I wondered how the other two men would react when he opened it. For now, the secret was clenched in the captain's fist, as safe a place as any. It was the last remaining bit of knowledge from his years of research, and he had kept it for himself until now.

The completion of our long study of every book and map aboard the ship, and the captain's exodus from his quarters, had marked another change, although it affected none but me. Not only had he abandoned his quarters, but he had expelled me from them as well, refusing to allow anyone to exist unwatched around his valuables. He had turned me out onto the decks, and as he had no further use for me, had left me in the employ of Mister Tom Birch, an assignment that had delighted and frustrated me. So far, however, with the ship in top condition, the boatswain had left me largely unbothered and I had been free to be idle about the ship, accompanied only by my thoughts.

Just as I was considering this, his lanky shadow appeared on the deck beside me. His shadow was stretched even longer in the setting sunlight so that it announced his arrival before his feet reached me.

"Oi, 'ho there, Rivers," he said now in his usual way, joining me against the deck where I sat on an upturned crate, preserving what I could recall of Captain Winters' texts in my leather-bound journal. When he wasn't working he was eating, this mast of a man, and he offered me a piece of bread with one hand while he held his own pinched between his teeth. The long, spindly fingers of his free hand reached out and tugged gently at the top of the book, pulling its pages downward so that he could have a look. I paid no concern as my secrets were spilled into Tom's view; I had learned weeks before that he—like most of the men onboard save Winters, Dunn, Rabbie, and myself—could not read. He had asked me three times to teach him, but time had not yet permitted, nor had I been eager to spend so much time alone with him.

"Nothing of interest really," I answered, which wasn't completely true but close enough. I closed the book and returned it safely to my pocket, then accepted the proffered bread. It took a moment of biting and tearing, but eventually I freed a chunk of the stale stuff into my mouth. It was barely edible, but at least with my mouth occupied with chewing I didn't have to say more.

Talking to Tom was dangerous; more than once I had already almost confided things to him that I shouldn't.

Tom's blond head bobbed good-naturedly, reflecting streaks of golden sunlight as it did. "It's not as dry yet as it will be," he mumbled around a mouthful of hard bread. "Think Jomo's been mixing it with bone broth to loosen the dough. Figured I'd get my lot while it's still worth eating, try to fatten up a bit so it doesn't hurt so bloody bad when all we've left to eat is seaweed. By the looks of it," he stopped to inspect the rock that resembled bread, "it ain't too far off from now."

He patted his hand reassuringly against the solid granite of his stomach and I tried not to look as he did. Nothing good had yet to come from me gawking at that man's skin, not that it ever would.

The freshly stocked stores of the ship's galley I had seen on my first trip below deck had diminished over the passing weeks. The goat had died, as had the chicken Winters had paid for. What hadn't been already had by the rats, Jomo had used in the pot, although it had not gone far on a ship of hungry and usually inebriated men. Now, when they weren't busy drinking, or sleeping off their rum, the men spent their time fishing to provide fresh meat for Jomo's use. A dish called salmagundi, a highly seasoned stew which was made from any meat available—currently mostly fish and a few remaining scraps of goat—pickled herrings, hard boiled eggs, vegetables, and liberal additions of wine, oil, vinegar, and salt, had been our new staple. It was not delicious, but it was filling, and more palatable than turtle meat (a muddy, mushy affair) when those poor ancient creatures had been caught and hauled up from the water. The rest of chickens would soon be next for the plate, once their eggs ran sour from lack of decent feed.

"That what you're trying to do, then?" I teased, waving the half-eaten chunk of ship biscuit in my hand at Tom. "Fatten me up to, is it? So's you're not the only one with a lump living in his stomach?"

Tom had the decency to look embarrassed, but only for a second before he laughed loudly and pushed his boot against the edge of my crate. It wobbled easily and he laughed harder. "Someone's got to do it, mate. If I didn't know better, I'd think you were trying to waste away to skin and bones. Eager to join ole Bullet's sea ghosts, are you?"

His eyes swept across my figure, causing his previous look of embarrassment to return. Tom diverted his eyes as he reached my chest, and I watched his cheeks turn ruddy with a color not caused by the sun.

Such behavior marked the third change that had recently passed over the men of the *Riptide*. At first I had thought it a figment of my own imagination, perhaps a result of reading one too many myths of beautiful women of the sea who could command the hearts of wanton sailors, but I had noticed recently that everyone seemed to look at me a bit differently—Tom Birch, Mister Dunn, and Jomo included—though none had yet to say anything to me directly. Even Domingo had reduced his deadly sneer to a more hostile frown, which was, somehow, a more frightening adjustment because on no less than four occasions I had seen lust behind his eyes. My own eyes had not been immune to the sudden transformation of my appearance, although I hardly thought the change striking enough to warrant such attention, which was not of the variety I had hoped to earn. Yet, it was undeniable, though I could not put my finger on exactly what *it* was. I had never been a homely girl, but neither had I been beautiful. Still, the past several weeks had seen my hair become a richer shade of coffee brown, the waves fuller and the whole of it longer and thicker so that I'd had to find a longer piece of ribbon to tie it back. My lips were larger and more red—rosebud, Claudette would have called them, and the type that needed no rouge to define them. The curves of my figure, too, were now more distinctly womanly than they had ever been before. This last I noticed perhaps more than anything, as had the men around me. Claudette and Mrs. Emery had often teased me about my boyish figure though its narrow frame was the impetus for my disguise as a sailor. Still, it was too slender and flat for their liking, and both women had encouraged me to wear one of those troublesome corsets to mold the skin of my chest into something round and full that might resemble breasts and pinch my waist so that my hips would swell out beneath it. Now, such a device was hardly necessary. Instead, I had to wrap bandaging around the plump devils to try and flatten them back into place, and I'd had to readjust the placement of my belt, as I could no longer wear a knife as low as I had before. If I did it simply swung about like a seductive pendulum and drew too much attention. I had also taken to rubbing gunpowder and pitch on my face to downplay the shine of my skin, and I'd stopped bathing all together.

None of it seemed a suitable fix, however, as when I'd cured one area another become more apparent, like this odd transformation simply insisted upon itself. I could think of no reason for it. I was far past the ripeness of early womanhood when most girls' bodies swayed and transformed. It must have been all the fresh air breathing life into a husk of a girl who'd spent years locked away in the kitchens of a brothel. Luckily, while it had brought a certain degree of new, unwanted attention from the men onboard, none had challenged me on it, and I kept more to myself than ever, hoping to fade from their interest—particularly Tom's.

A RUSH OF ANGRY WORDS STOLE MY ATTENTION AWAY FROM TOM Birch, our rocklike lunch, and my newfound femininity and to the quarterdeck, where Captain Winters and Rabbie were locked in heated debate.

The captain had not raised his voice, nor did his body language give any indication that anything was amiss. He simply stood with the same predatory poise that he always did, leaning placidly backward against the ship's railing with his arms crossed rightly over his chest and a piercing look in his eye as he stared at the Scot. Rabbie, quite the contrary, was neigh on belligerent—waving and flailing his arms about his head. He was yelling loudly, swearing I presumed, although the words were all smashed together in an incoherent jumble and may not have even been English. It was a foolish thing to do, in my opinion, to so openly challenge such a man as Erik Winters, who was studying the hysterical man with a look that said he was not at all concerned about dispatching the rare and valuable commodity that was a navigator. Winters, I was quite sure, could helm his ship. The navigator had only been a convenience, and, I suspected, since the captain wasn't keen on sharing his plans with anyone, perhaps even an expendable one.

"What's that about then?" Tom wondered out loud, only barely interested as he ripped another chunk of bread into his mouth and began chewing again. He swiveled on his crate to watch the men behind him, and I promptly ignored the way the movement pulled at the muscles in his back.

"I'm sure I have no idea," I answered, although I did. I stole a furtive glance over Tom's shoulder, and when I did I noticed the telltale slip of paper was no longer in the captain's fist.

Beyond Winters, and now Rabbie, I alone could guess at the heading to which the captain was instructing the ship's navigator to make way, even if I didn't know the full details of it. If Dunn—now missing from the quarterdeck—had been aware, his reaction might have been similar, although he was wise and cautious enough to have voiced his concerns in private. My own insight was a result of careful cobbling. I had studiously kept note of the passages of deciphered texts that captured the captain's attention, and stolen swift glances at his personal maps. Sometimes, when he was in heavy, rum-deepened sleep and I was sure he would not wake, I'd dared to lift the cover of his log slightly and try to memorize his writing.

My knowledge, however, was incomplete and biased greatly by the myths I had read and what I had gleaned from Dunn's chatter when he spoke to me. Still, were such a place as had been described real, and had I not cared for my own life, then quite probably I, too, would have flailed my arms about the sky and cursed. Instead, I was eager to change course and sail straight for it.

"I'll nae risk life an' limb tae sail intae th' heart ay th' sea. It can't be dain," Rabbie was ranting in surprisingly clear words. "Yoo've tint yer min', Winters, ye hae! We'll aw be th' bottom ay th' brine if ye hae yer way, an' fur some damned hen at that. Yoo're bludy radge!"

I saw a sharp glint in Winters' eye as Rabbie insulted Evangeline. In one single motion and without so much as a sound, he pulled a knife from the folds of his belt and slid it hilt-deep into the other man's heart. An expression of shock flooded Rabbie's features and then his face froze, locked in its final stare—one of shock more so than pain. Without bothering to look at him, Winters stood, as still and silent as a statue, as the much larger man fell forward, dead, to the deck. Then, with a quick survey of the crew, some of which were stunned while others didn't seem to notice, he removed the knife from the fallen man and let it hang in his hands. He clasped a bloody hand on a handle of the ship's wheel, and as he turned to face the crew his eyes landed on me, staring wide-eyed back at him.

"Rivers, man the wheel," he commanded, vastly overestimating my capacity at navigation. Then, "Hoist the sails," he called to the men at the rigging. Finally, he nodded at Mister Dunn, who returned the action, as if the nod were code for something more. "We sail for the heart of the ocean."

PART II

VIII

FOR THE NEXT SEVERAL DAYS AND SEVERAL NIGHTS, LIFE aboard the ship was quiet.

Before Rabbie's body had grown cold, Mister Clarke had attended to it, wrapping the heavy, leftover husk in mostly rotted linens, and then binding it tightly with ropes weighted with smooth stones. Together with the aid of a few other men who had assisted with the task as though it were a common chore, the doctor hoisted the body over the railings and committed it unceremoniously to the ocean deep. It bobbed for a moment or two, a strange mummified buoy drifting alone amongst the current, and then sank beneath the tide. Someone had been dispatched by Tom Birch to scrub the deck where the corpse had lay to prevent the spread of stench and disease, and then the matter was done.

No one seemed to have known the navigator well, and thus no one seemed to mourn his death terribly. In fact, most seemed to barely notice it at all. The few who had been friendly with the man had claimed his few meager belongings for their own with Tom Birch and Mister Dunn presiding over the affair. Later, the quartermaster had gathered up all of Rabbie's navigational instruments and relocated them to the captain's quarters where they had since been stored amongst the other charts and maps in his library. Meanwhile, word had spread below deck that the crew had been relieved of its navigator and that the captain was not in a state to be trifled with. Then, someone opened a new keg of rum and life moved on.

Death was not uncommon or unexpected in the life of a pirate. Even on the sunniest of days it was a shadow over their shoulders. Most of these seafaring men could enjoy only short, violent lives before they found their inevitable finish at the end of a sword or a rope, or at the bottom of the unforgiving sea. As such, so normal was death that it did not arouse the need for much attention or discussion. For the most part, the unspoken consensus amongst the men was that the whole thing had been justified, although normally such disputes were addressed on land—a practical matter meant to avoid the spread of corpse plagues while at sea. Being that there was no land in sight, however, the captain had been well within his rights to slay the man where he stood. Some were even of the opinion that had the captain let such a thing go unpunished, then he would have appeared weak and unworthy to lead. Rabbie had not only refused a direct edict during a time the men agreed the captain's orders were absolute, but he had also insulted both the captain's command and Mistress Dahl's honor—a woman that the crew unanimously either respected or adored or both—and had sealed his own fate. This had left Winters with only one avenue of recourse, and he had carried it out dutifully. Jomo had muttered something violent under his breath, noting that the captain had been too merciful on doling out the other man's end and suggesting with his fanged teeth and galley knives what he might have done instead, all of which Dunn had nodded in furious agreement. I had expected at least Tom Birch, who was typically grounded in fairness, to show some sign of upset at what had occurred, but he also seemed unperturbed that his captain had just sliced a man through the heart and spilled his life on the deck.

"I suppose it had to be done," the boatswain had said

dismissively when I'd inquired on the subject. Taking notice of my chagrin, he'd finished tying a monkey fist in a length of rope and draped his palm amiably over the curve of my shoulder. I tried to appear indifferent to the gesture, but my heart raced inside of me. "We take to a code, Westley, though it ain't perfect that's for sure," he said gently and familiarly, using a name I didn't recognize at first and then remembered was supposed to be mine. The men onboard referred to me so often by my false surname that I'd forgotten I had given a proper name as well. "Honor is the most important part of that code. We live by it, and sometimes we die by it, too. Aye?"

For my part, my naivety had left me shocked that death could be handed out so casually. I should have—and did—know this myself, of course, having resided in a place as wild as Isla Perla. There I had seen man and beast alike perish more times than I could count on both my hands four times over. Still, I was surprised to find that beyond a morbid sort of curiosity about the whole thing I felt nothing for the navigator's loss. Nor did the evidence that my captain was capable of such dispassionate slaughter distress me. The whole episode faded into memory so quickly that it seemed that the lumbering Scot had never been there at all. On the rare occasion it did reenter my mind I, like the rest of my new brothers, also felt that the captain had been justified in his actions, no matter how I tried to reason it out. Still, I did wish that I had allowed the big brute to tell me the story of Cygnus, the man who had been transformed into a swan and sent to live among the stars. Perhaps Rabbie joined him there now.

I had avoided looking at the stars since the navigator's death, worried I might see him reflecting downward knowingly at me.

With Rabbie departed, I alone was the only other soul

onboard besides the captain that I knew to be aware of the totality of our new heading. It was secret I held closely and silently though none had asked me of it. Not even Mister Dunn, although I was certain I saw the knowledge lurking in his eyes whenever I caught him looking at me, which was often. He seemed pricklier than normal, shorter of temper and quicker of suspicion, and permanently riddled with anxiety though I was unsure of the cause. We rarely spoke, the quartermaster and I, but he was always nearby, constantly watching with his sharp, black eyes fixed on me as I moved about the ship, or spoke with the captain, or Tom Birch. On these occasions his wiry shadow was especially close, trailing mine as if it were an extension of my own. I waited for more of his legends, more of his sailor's nonsense, but he was quiet and observant in a way I found most unsettling.

Winters himself said nothing about his slaying of Rabbie and had not attended his brief burial. He had simply wiped the smear of blood from the blade of his dagger and, using his own compass and the navigator's maps, had proven to be more than capable of handling the *Riptide*'s helm. He stood confidently at the wheel, adjusting our course under the gaze of Rabbie's stars. He let no one else near the helm, and now spent his nights staring at the sky, much like Rabbie had done, but instead of searching, wondrous eyes, his were cold and calculating and expectant. He was waiting for something, what I couldn't tell, but I imagined it was for the moment that the ocean would swallow us whole and lead us to an island that was not charted on any map and could never be found in the same place twice, and had never returned any man that had sailed for its shores.

And so we sailed on, no longer with our bow pointed across the ocean, but with a heading that, if real, would soon see us sailing within it. Our new course was beyond the boundaries of manmade maps and discovered oceans, and into the territories of the gods of the sea.

"It's not an island of gold as it says in the story of Odysseus," Winters' deep voice explained, rumbling into the darkness one night as he watched and waited, staring out into the blackness off the bow of the ship. "Not a haven of lost Aztec jewels or a fountain of youth, nothing so trivial as that. Doesn't matter what the stories say, there will be no riches to be found in a place like where we sail. Not the kind that most are searching for anyway."

There were no stars shining from the heavens that evening, and so the sky and the water were of such a similar shade of black, and the waves so glassy and still, that it was virtually impossible to tell where one ended and the other began. Even the ashrays were at peace, their absence only adding to the emptiness of the night. It felt like we were sailing into a grave. The only light for miles came from the flame of a single lantern set by my side. It cast vague shadows against the walls of the deck as I captured the day's notes in my journal. The time was nearly at curfew, and soon the order would be called for lights out and then the candle flame would, too, be gone and blackness would envelope the rest of the world until morning.

The sound of Winters' voice shook me from my writing and I looked around, uncertain at first that he was speaking to me. The man had not uttered so much as a word in days, to me or anyone else, and never had I heard him say so much at once. I swept my eyes about the decks, expecting to see Dunn lurking nearby even though I knew the captain and I would be the only two awake on the quarterdeck at this time. It had not been intentional, but it had become a habit just the same. The rest of the crew would be either sleeping on the main deck, huddling for warmth under the cool ocean breeze in the waist of the ship, or disappeared below to eat and rest. Still, it was just as likely that the captain was speaking aloud to the water as it was that he would bother to seek my company, and so I waited for him to say something else before I risked interrupt his thoughts. My quill hung suspended in midair above the page, providing a focal point for my eyes as I did not dare look at him, the man standing like a shadow in the dark at the edge of the ship.

Finally, he turned to face me, peeling his eyes away from their watchful vigil with noticeable effort so that his body turned first without the rest of him with it. Once his head had followed he leaned back against the railing and crossed his arms so tightly across his chest that the leather of his coat made a wrenching sound in the quiet. He bent one knee backward, anchoring his foot against the wall of the ship with a thud; the candle illuminated in his eyes so that the steel in them glinted in the darkness.

"I'm sorry, Captain?" I answered at last, unsure of what to say. I had been a member of Winters' crew for months and still hadn't grown accustomed to the weight of his full attention. "I don't catch your meaning."

"Where we're going," he answered in his gruff tone, not bothering to elaborate further. He walked over toward me, and then squatted down to crouch on his heels at my side as if we were speaking confidentially. His bent form absorbed the small circle of candlelight, and his scent, a wash of gun smoke and salt, filled my nostrils. I could see every fine line of his tanned flesh in my peripheral vision, could perceive in vivid detail the way his auburn hair shone like copper as it hung about his head and crawled across the sharp, unshaven cliffs of his face. It was unnerving how he could be so still even when he was moving. Even when he spoke he barely stirred, as if the sound simply pulsed from him. He tapped his finger against the cover of my journal. "Don't write it down wrong, Mister Rivers."

"Yes, sir." The words stuck like pitch in my throat.

"You aren't required to always agree with me," he snapped. His eyes were leveled with mine, and razor sharp. "Have I ever shown you any harm?"

I winced, and then was forced to agree again, this time with a note of apology both for the agreement and for saying it, "Of course not, Captain."

Winters rolled his eyes, and with a contemptuous look upon his face he pulled my journal from my hands, gently but firmly, and I could not resist. Panic rose in my throat and threatened to spill out of my mouth. I expected him to read what I'd been writing, to disclose the secrets I'd hidden from him and everyone else aboard this vessel, but he did not. Instead, he closed the book and flipped it in his hands, studying its cover intently. He ran his hand lightly across the leather, his fingertips caressing the fine, round edges of the sand dollar on top. It was a tender, almost sensual movement, as if the symbol meant something more to him than just a common shell. With every breath my fear mounted, panicked by the way he studied the book, and then, just as I could feel the fear crawling its way into my throat, he handed the journal back to me. Rising to his feet, he returned to the rail.

"She was the most beautiful creature I had ever seen, first time I laid eyes on her," he mused into the black night air. The thunderous quality of his voice had lowered to a rumble, so that the words mingled with the thumping sounds of the waves licking the sides of the ship. He needed not say her name. For other men, such a sentiment could have referred to a prize, or a ship, or even the ocean itself, but for Winters there could be only one *she*. "A woman of surpassing beauty in every way. Golden hair and eyes the color of the sea in the morning, neck like a swan. I had never seen anything as enchanting as her."

He pulled a rolled cigarette from his belt and, striking a match against the railing, lifted the flame to his lips and breathed life into the paper. After flicking the match into the water, he touched a finger to the bit of stone dangling on the cord around his neck. Silently my hand made its way to the secret fold of the inner pocket of my own coat to touch the ring that held the stone matching his. I listened, enrapt, as he continued to speak.

"But even more than she was beautiful she was fierce. Terrifying, actually. The only person I ever met that was capable of scaring me." He made a noise which might have been a laugh if he could have made such a sound, but I didn't think he could. "I knew from the moment I saw her that there was no going back. She owned me. Never doubted for a second that woman, if you could call her that, would be the death of me."

"You really mean to take her back then, even if she is … Even if it means …" My voice trailed off, unable to speak into existence the specifics of the legends we'd both read. Winters and I both held knowledge that the riddles in those ancient texts hadn't been able to share, though neither of us gave voice to them.

"Aye. I do."

"And then what?" I asked, my voice barely a whisper. "What happens after you find her? If we find Bracile, there's no certainty any of us will ever leave its shores again. We'll be as trapped as she is."

He was quiet for a long time, staring solemnly out into the

darkness until the glowing red ember of his cigarette shortened all the way to lips and fizzled out. "Doesn't matter," he said finally, pitching the scrap into the sea. "The sea stole her from me. I will have her back. Nothing else matters."

IX

I WOKE NATURALLY SEVERAL HOURS LATER TO FIND THAT WE were sailing uneasily upon a wintry ocean. It should have been first light, later even perhaps, but the day was still as dark as the night before it had been. A soft, otherworldly glow filled the space around me. It illuminated the shape of the ship with hazy pale blue light as the remnants of a foggy dream evaporated from my thoughts. Briefly I was convinced that the watery ghosts trailing in the wake of our ship—*ashrays*, Dunn had called them—had lifted themselves from the sea to walk amongst the crew still slumbering about the decks. This they had done in the dream from which I was still struggling to wake, these ghosts that looked oddly familiar and might have been remnants of my own past. With wispy arms which were deceivingly strong, they clung and dragged; their pale, shimmering forms had tried to pull me down below the waves, riving me from this world and forcing me unwillingly into the next. It had been dark, and frozen, and even knowing it was a dream I had feared it would never end, like an omen that needed only time before it would come to pass. As the dream mist cleared from my mind I worried that I had awoken inside of my own miserable dreamscape, carrying the ghosts with me to the waking world, but was comforted by the sounds of life stirring around me as other men awoke. I loosed a puff of breath into the frigid air in relief, and watched as it hung and then dissolved above me.

There were no ghosts aboard, but neither was there any

source of light responsible for the silvery sheen that turned day into night. I craned my head upward and saw that no moon hung from the sky, nor would there have been room for it if did. Instead, the dark canvas was filled with a host of a million stars, each shining as bright as Sirius and twinkling of its own accord like a net of diamonds had been cast over the heavens. Their combined, glittering light reflected off of a patchwork of freshly fallen snow that hovered like clouds atop the ocean waves and shaped itself into the petals of frost flowers. It made the light fragmented and fickle as it flickered against the ship, our vessel now a glowing prism where it slid amongst the current. Glittering white flakes fell from the sky and disappeared into the water. Icicles grew and hung like fingers off the railing of the deck. It was frigid and frozen, spectacularly beautiful and deadly with thick white rocks of ice floating and bumping against the hull. Someone had hoisted our colors while I slept and the black was a smear against the silver sky, the red and gold of Winters' marks bright and distinct and alien.

As my eyes adjusted to the strange light around me I stood, pushing away the thick linen I'd used as a blanket while I'd slept. It was cold, ever so much colder than it had been on the blacker, emptier night that I had fallen asleep. Colder, even, than my dream had been. The captain was nowhere to be seen, and for a moment I thought that our conversation might have been just another figment of fantasy, but then I saw him, standing still as freezing ocean spray decorated his bare arms in the starlight, and I knew that the time he'd been watching and waiting for would soon be upon us. I thought I saw a slight smile pull at the corner of his mouth, but then the stars flickered again and it was gone.

I pulled the heavy cloth back over my shoulders, bundling it against me as tightly as I could manage over the lumps of awkward clothing and weaponry I wore to hide my increasingly womanly figure. Men slugged about me on the ship, many cocooned in similar fashion with blankets and scraps of old sails wrapped around them. They moved about stiffly and gracelessly, frozen pupals covered in a thin layer of frost, gathering in small groups. None had been able to coax a flame to light in the icy air although many of them held tinderboxes uselessly in their hands. One of these bundled figures, taller than the rest, stood alone on the bow. The shimmer on my cheeks blurred the bottom portion of my vision, but even through that handicap and the disguising effect of the cloth I could recognize Tom's form. I made my way to him as slivers of ice stung the exposed skin of my face.

"I didn't know it could snow at sea," I said as I arrived beside him. I sidled up to him as closely as I dared, leaving only a deep breath to separate us.

"Not often," he responded without looking at me. There was a twinge of uncertainty in his voice. He scrunched his nose as a cold spray hit his face, and then used his forearm to wipe it away. "Although I don't think I ever seen it quite like this." He paused for a moment and contemplated the scene before him. "Must be the captain has found the way after all, and we be sailing to stranger tides than we have before. Can't think of no other explanation for such as this."

"That's a good thing, then?" I left it a question. I had never actually bothered to ask what the men truly thought of Captain Winters' mysterious heading, not that I would have dared to approach most of them with such a question, save for perhaps Dunn, but his feelings were already clear if not confusing. I wouldn't have asked it now if it had been anyone other than Tom. The memory of Rabbie's death flashed before me.

Tom Birch sucked his teeth consideringly and thought a

while before he answered. "Aye," he decided finally. "Though I don't think none of us knows what to expect from here. Might be good, might not." He shrugged and the cloth fell away. One of his taut, muscular arms reached out to pull it back closer against him. He shivered. "Either way, I figure we keep sailing 'til we find out, or 'til something makes us stop."

Knowing him as I did, I hadn't really expected Tom to say anything different, though there was comfort in the familiarity of his words. I made a sighing sound of agreement as I gazed out over the glittering carpet of midnight blue and silver water that unfurled endlessly before us. Some might have found Tom's predictable behavior tedious and dull, but I admired its simplicity, finding his unwavering loyalty and even-keel temperament a testament to his honest and true nature that made him, somehow, profoundly beautiful despite the physical features that had already decided him handsome. At least in my experience, men like him—*people* like him—were hard to come by, especially in a place like Isla Perla where most would slit your throat for nothing more than the coins in your pocket. Such honest men were doubtless a rare breed anywhere else for that matter. Tom rose above them all, in both the literal and figurative way.

"Can I ask you a question, Tom?" I inquired timidly a few minutes later. It had been slowly burning inside of me for weeks while I gathered the comfort to ask. We had spent so much time together I felt I could be forthcoming with this man, even it were an honesty tempered with deceit. "It's more of a personal one, this question."

He arched his eyebrow and looked at me out of the lowest corner of his eye so that the brilliant green of his eye shone above a crescent of white. He bowed his head to listen closely. "Aye?"

"Do you think it's worth it?" I gestured toward the wintry ocean with my elbows under the fabric. His eyebrow lifted into another question as if he wasn't following, and I realized I was being cryptic. "All this. Sailing into the middle of the ocean, to a place that only maybe exists and is said to be guarded by a monstrous beast? No charts, no prizes. Rabbie. All this to find a woman who he's been looking for for years but no has seen so much as a trace of?" I looked again to the bizarrely frozen sea, asking Tom a question I already knew the answer to. "Is it worth it to you?"

Several minutes passed in silence, and I regretted asking. "You don't have to answer. My apologies, Tom. Didn't mean to overstep." Small hot circles of embarrassment blossomed on my face despite the cold.

"Not that." He gave a small laugh. "Not at all. Just not an easy one to answer, mate." He clicked his tongue the way he did when he was thinking. "First part is simple enough. I go where he goes." He jerked his head backward in the direction of Winters, who was still standing resolutely at the wheel. "Been sailing with him and Ole' Bullet since I was a boy, I have, don't even remember life without those men. They're the only family I've got. Wouldn't be worth my time to let them leave me behind, so it ain't no matter where the captain wanted to sail—I go."

This I hadn't known, and it challenged many things I thought I knew about the two men. They had been decent enough to me, that much was true, but neither seemed the sort to serve as caretaker of a young boy, although to them that was exactly what I was, even if I wasn't a young boy in the traditional sense. I was still young and inexperienced, and very much out of place on this crew. Further, both of the men, with the assistance of Mistress

Dahl, had nursed a broken and battered Jomo back to health after he'd been rescued from the slaver—Winters had set the rest free rather than trade or sell them. Perhaps the two weathered pirates possessed softer hearts than I had assumed.

"About that last, well …" Tom shrugged and kept his eyes on the water, "the way I see it, there be worse things to sail for than a woman. Of course, I ain't never been in love, Rivers, so I don't rightly know how I might be about it. But if I ever was, I can only hope it's a kind that's strong as what the captain has, he and Miss Dahl. If that were so, I believe I'd rightly sail to the end of the world for her, too. Worth more than all the gold I could carry, I expect."

I smiled, but kept it hidden beneath the brim of my hat. With that I knew for certain, that if I were to ever put my heart in the hands of anyone, it would be Tom Birch.

TOM AND I CONTINUED TO STAND IN COMPANIONABLE QUIET AS the *Riptide* inched slowly forward. Eventually I lost track of what little sense of time I had. I knew it was not night, but neither could it be morning, nor midday. We were in a place without time, I thought, somewhere in between, and as we sailed onward time seemed to slow even further until it felt like we weren't really moving at all. The occasional noises of the other men stirring about the decks of the ship hushed, and the few audible sounds that did come were thick like they came from beneath water until they, too, ceased into silence. The only evidence that time had passed at all was from the frost itself, which had begun to thicken and increase in intensity, the cold coming to life in specks of white that swirled down in thick dust from the stars laying in a snowy white blanket on the edges of the ship. It covered my eyelashes, coating them in thick white down that made my eyelids droop under their weight while the air seemed to turn even colder. I shivered despite myself, the cold seeping into the hollow tunnels of my bones.

Spurred by my trembling, Tom Birch came closer, sealing the inches that remained between us as his body pressed firmly against me. He angled sideways and lifted one arm around my shoulders, letting his blanket fell heavily atop my own as his long fingers wrapped around my arm, holding me tightly to him. The movement was instinctive, a gesture so natural that it felt like one he'd performed a million times before, and yet so new and unexpected that a different sort of coldness instantly froze the blood flowing in my veins. I turned slowly to face him, lifting my head as his moved downward, mirroring mine. The embrace had been quick and instant, but now things moved in slow motion, the descent of Tom's eyes so slow that I saw the thick lush of his eyelashes touch as they blinked in the darkness. By the time his eyes met mine my head and heart had become engorged with more questions and emotions than I had ever experienced at the same time, all swelling up and demanding space at once, and I completely forgot that I was still on the verge of freezing. It was wrong, this way he stood holding me and looking at me, and yet nothing else had ever felt so right. The oxygen in the air ran empty, and I could not remember how to breathe.

"Who are you, Rivers?" he asked, his words slurring out of parted lips as if spoken in a trance. The words were his but his voice sounded distant and hollow. The green of his eyes shone brilliantly in the silver starlight, emeralds on a background of diamonds, but they were slightly out of focus so that the man looking at me was both Tom Birch and not him at all. One of his fingers rose to my cheeks to lightly brush snow from my eyes, and when this was finished he rested his hand against the side of my face, cupping my ear in his palm. The heat that pulsed from his skin amazed me as his thumb traced the length of my lower lip. It should have been cold, but it was not. His touch thawed the ice from my skin, and my entire body melted along with it, the specks of ice running to water and then turning to sweat that beaded on my flesh. It was odd and unusual, and just as I made to remark it I became aware of another heat against my skin, this one throbbing from within the layers of cloth wrapped around me. It started dull and increased in intensity with each thump, and it seemed to come from the pocket that held my ring, though that couldn't be possible. It was warm, hot, almost burning, and it felt alive. The longer Tom's hand lingered against my face the hotter and more insistently the ring pulsed, until it felt like it might burn through the layers of fabric and brand my flesh. At last I could withstand it no more and I let the bounds of my canvas sheath fall open as I pushed away from Tom's hold, desperate for cooler air.

I could breathe easier outside the reach of Tom arms, and I watched as a frost-tipped wave crested behind him, rising upward and waving in my direction. For a moment I forgot him entirely, staring instead into a black, snow-specked ocean that looked warm and inviting. The whisper of a hundred voices rose from the water, all calling and beckoning to me. I took a tiny step backward, out of Tom's grasp, and the canvas cloths gave way and fell to our feet. The overwhelming urge to leap overboard washed over me, and I placed a hand on the rim of the ship's wall, and sucked in a lungful of cool, sweet air. The voices called again, all mixed together and unclear, but before I drowned in them Tom's hand was on my cheek again, warm and heavy. Gently, he returned my gaze to him. "Who are you really?" he repeated, his voice was even thicker now as he stepped into me, his body pressing once more against mine as the ocean voices calmed. It was warm against him, and his lovely green eyes were soft and heavy and welcoming, like bathwater just begging to be stepped into.

"I ..." I breathed, my lips unable to shape words as Tom came closer, promising to touch mine. I would tell him. I could tell him anything, and we could go together into the warm, waiting water. My knees began to give way beneath me, but his arm looped around my back and held me upright. I opened my mouth to speak, to say my name, but no sound came out. The ring calmed, lying heavily as it hummed against my chest.

Just when I thought I would fall, sinking into the heat and darkness of my own desire, a man's voice called loudly somewhere outside of me, somewhere that sounded far away. "Get her below! Now, before the sea claims them both," it cracked like thunder in the quiet, and while the sounds were still echoing in my ears I felt a firm hand wrap tightly around my forearm. It pinched my skin and pulled me rudely back to life.

X

THE HAND BELONGED TO DUNN, AND IT WAS TEARING ME farther and farther away from the consuming eyes of Tom Birch as it pulled me behind him, his coif of white hair guiding us like a flickering white flame in the starlight. Cold wind blew suddenly from nowhere and buffeted deafeningly around us. I was still holding the canvas blanket in my fist, and I pulled it as tightly as around me as I could, tucking my head against my shoulder so that my hat would not fly away. My steps were shaky and uneven as my feet struggled to keep their footing on the deck that was barely solid beneath me. Glancing over my shoulder, I noticed that Tom made no move to follow us though his haunting green eyes tracked our retreat, shining with eerie, unnatural light. Their gaze did not break until we'd descended the short flight of stairs to the main deck and moved out of sight toward the back of the ship toward the captain's office. Then his shadowy figure turned its back to me and shifted its focus to the ocean. My heart sunk as his eyes left mine, like a piece of me had been ripped away with them.

Even with the strength and bluster of the wind, the ship was abnormally still, and I noticed as we made our way across the deck and hurried toward Captain Winters' quarters that Tom was not alone in his unusual behavior, although he seemed to be the only one to have any semblance of life in him. The remaining men above deck, nearly two dozen in total, had, in turn, each become a figure in a band of statues placed ornamentally about the ship. They stood like pieces on a chessboard—no more human than waxen ice ornately carved and decorated with the stylings of men. Some looked as if they had been rubbing their hands together for warmth, or attempting to light a fire, or even lifting a flagon of ale to their lips when they had simply paused, locked their eyes like magnets on the sea, and frozen solid. Others appeared as though they were staring up in wonder, their eyes blank and dark and unseeing. I gasped and nearly fell when I noticed Jomo, face turned upward from below the grating on the floor of the deck so that he could also see the sky above. His form would have been completely concealed in the dark had it not been for the silvery sheen of his scars reflecting the moonlight as they, too, faced skyward.

The sea had similarly transfixed each and every one of the *Riptide's* men—including those in the lower decks, too, I assumed, remembering Jomo—transforming her into a ghost ship manned by a frozen crew as it sailed on water obscured in thickening snow and roaring winds. With that new perspective things seemed much less magical than they had before, and I felt the first tingling of fear. It was too cold. The dust falling from the sky could just as well have been ashes rather than snow. I was reminded of ashrays, ghosts, and other less than kind things that Dunn had said occupied the depths below the ocean's surface, and thought again of the voices I had heard calling just moments ago from the waves. A shiver ran down my spine that had nothing to do with the temperature.

As Mister Dunn continued to pull me stumbling toward the door to the captain's cabin I stole a last glance at the helm. The only exception to this frightening icy stasis, I saw, aside from the ship's quartermaster and myself, was its captain—the embodiment of winter himself who faced the sea unaffected. He was still standing with both hands clasped sternly on the wheel, but his face was more animated than I had ever seen it. His eyes were alight with blue fire as they stared wildly out over the water from beneath his brow, and an anticipatory snarl lifted his lips so that deep rivets were carved in the folds of his skin around his mouth. His teeth were bared, and his long, auburn hair had come loose from its hold so that it billowed madly in the air around him in a glowing red mane that left a fiery blaze about his head. The fragment of stone at his throat burned white hot like the ground glass in a lighthouse's lamp. All combined, it was a terrifying sight, and my heart leapt in my throat as his eyes darted quickly to me and then off as Dunn pulled me farther away.

My last glimpse of Winters saw him with one fist raised, yelling a battle cry into the air. I was too far away and could only barely hear the sound of his voice, much less make out his words, but still I could feel the determination of it. He yelled again, and as if in response a fierce gale of frigid wind slammed into him. It knocked him backward but he did not fall, only steadied his feet, snarled harder, and yelled again. The thought struck me that his very name might have been given to him just for this—a sort of divine providence that a man so cold on the inside would be the one to fight against a night afloat on frozen sea. If it were to be a battle against frost and ice, then Erik Winters, the mad and ruthless pirate captain, would prevail.

Dunn did not release his grip until he'd sequestered me in the quiet solitude of the captain's office and bolted the door securely behind us. I rubbed the sting of his hold from my arm as he dropped me into one of the high-backed wooden chairs in the small sitting area of the cabin. Cold numbness began to fade and in its wake my body felt sore and bruised, like the wind had battered my flesh without my knowing. My arm throbbed where Dunn had gripped it, and I could already see purple smears forming where his fingers had dug into my skin. I watched wearily as he bustled wordlessly about the cabin, first procuring a tall candle from the captain's desk, and then quickly striking a match against its wood top. He held the flame against the wick until it caught fire and brought a glimmer of pale orange candlelight to the dark cabin. The icy wind, infuriated at his success, banged loudly against the door, but Dunn only cocked one ear briefly in its direction and then disregarded it. Cupping the flame in his hand, he dragged a stool along with his foot, returning to where he'd left me, still trembling in my chair and nursing my arm. The old quartermaster looked like he'd aged a decade as he seated himself with noticeable effort on the stool beside me, his throat producing a small, aching groan as he adjusted himself. He reached forward and tested the temperature of my skin with the back of his hand. It was surprisingly soft to the touch—warm, solid, and vibrating with life.

Apparently satisfied, he withdrew his hand, set the candle on the floor between us, and fixed me with his small, black eyes. As I met his stare I expected to find him shocked, furious perhaps, or even frightened, but the expression on his face was not at all what I anticipated. In fact, it looked like sympathy. A brief search of my memory could not produce an instance where I had ever seen an expression of this sort on Dunn's face. His characteristic look was sometimes a glower, sometimes a grimace, but always stern. Never had I seen him seem so much as tired or dismayed, and only on one occasion could I recall seeing him something akin to content—when we'd been moored in Isla Perla and he'd learned that I could read. In contrast, the closest to a match that I'd ever seen on the man's face to his current expression had been the one he'd worn the night he'd told Tom and me the story of Mélusine, but then it had been forlorn and diluted with brandy and madness. All of this made his current countenance more disturbing than any other might have been, although I was too exhausted and sore to care much at the moment. Even the bruises blossoming on my skin felt dull and far away. My head swam from pain and exhaustion, and I worried I might lose consciousness.

There was warmth even in the single light of the candle's small flame as it beat against my face, and while I stared into it I felt my eyelids turn heavy and begin to sag. After a few meager attempts to keep them open I allowed them to fall closed, but when I did, the image of Tom's eyes boring into me—bearing down into my soul while the sea called in its ghostly whisper—snapped me awake. His eyes had been so strange and bright, simultaneously Tom's eyes and not his at all. They held none of his normal mirth but were hollow and distant, the eyes of a ghost. The memory was cold, as if an arctic breath had blown through my bones. I felt pale, solid, and empty like the men on deck—a shell of a person in place of a real one. And it was maddening, how much I both wanted that look in Tom's eyes and feared it. I didn't even know what it meant. I didn't even know if it had been real. For the first time since we'd left Isla Perla, I was genuinely afraid.

Mister Dunn's hands were back on my forehead, feeling around for signs of distress. "Come on, now," he was saying in a gentle tone that matched the look of pity still hanging on his face.

It should have been a simple thing, for my eyes to adjust to the room that had been my home for weeks, for my body to warm and my mind to stop spinning here in the calm of the cabin, but it wasn't. I was cold again, so cold, even though the ring had begun to pulse warmly again with heat from my coat pocket and the room was a harbor from the wind gusting on the other side of it. My teeth chattered and I burrowed deeper in the linens. My hat had come loose atop my head and I pulled it down tightly over my eyes. I wished I could see the dusty streets and boring taverns of Isla Perla—that I could lay in my scratchy hammock in the brothel's kitchen. I longed for Claudette's company, for her sweet and pandering laugh, and for the balmy heat of the island that had been my home.

Dunn removed his hand from my forehead and pulled a flask from his breast pocket, and then without a word he forced it between my lips and tipped it into my mouth. Although I didn't want to, I drank, hating the way the liquid burned against my lips. It tasted bitter and sickly sour, like goat's milk that had spoiled but thinner and slimier than even that, medicinal and salty. I gagged and tried to expel it from my mouth, but Dunn held a hand firmly against the back of my head and continued to pour until I had no choice but to allow it to pass down my throat. When he finally removed the flask, I forced the last swallow down and tried to blink the taste away, but already I could feel sensation slowly returning to my limbs. It came over me like a rising tide, filling the hollowness that had carved out my insides and restoring me. Once I was whole and warm again, I felt weak—incredibly weak—and tired, as if I had not slept for days or more. I strained to hold my eyes open long enough for them roam around the cabin, forcing them to move around the small quarters and study it as if seeing it for the first time, concentrating on the details as best I could. I saw the captain's books, his desk, the soft blue hammock where I slept. It was familiar, this place. It was safe. The frozen ghosts and the icy water outside—the doppelgänger that had taken Tom's form—these things could not claim me here, and I was not alone so long as Dunn played guardian at my side.

"Wh-What is that out th-there?" I stammered finally. My voice cracked painfully from the cold and I cleared my throat and tried again. "Where are we? What's happening? It's so c-cold."

Mister Dunn shook his head slowly from side to side. "Don't exactly know how to explain it," he admitted with one his typical, infuriating shrugs. "We be sailin' on the boundaries between this world an' the next, and that be a haunted place—"

"Will they ..." I interrupted. I took a deep breath, forcing my eyes to stay open as I did so that Tom's face would not reappear behind my eyelids again. "Will *he*, Tom Birch ... will he ..." I couldn't find the right words to ask if they would survive this trek between two worlds. I wasn't even sure how I would, and it never occurred to me to doubt Dunn's words.

Dunn sighed heavily. "Aye, they'll be all right, once we sail through this." The wind banged noisily against the cabin door again and he muttered something I didn't catch under his breath. It sounded foreign and guttural, like an ancient chant, but I wasn't sure and didn't ask.

"If you don't know, how can you be sure?" The frozen statues on deck has been so damned unnerving; I didn't know if I could face them again.

The quartermaster sipped from his flask, taking in the bitter fluid with a satiated sort of grunt. "I told ye before we left Isla

Perla, there's a lot you don't know about life on the water. Life *in* the water, be a more fittin' way of puttin' it, though I don't think 'life' be quite right neither." He paused and sipped, and when he was ready he spoke again, attempting something close to an explanation. "The men, well, right now we be passin' through a place where the livin' ain't meant to be, you see. Place where old souls linger, and some things ain't which ne'er been alive to begin with make their beds. Makes the boundaries between things a little *thin*." He put emphasis on this last, narrowing his eyes for emphasis.

"What's that mean then?" I swallowed forcefully, pushing down the nausea that bubbled in my throat as I watched him drink. "Thin?"

Dunn loosed another deep sigh. "Just means that we best be movin' through quick as we can is all."

"And then what?" I was afraid to ask, and desperate to know. I was convinced there was more to this than Dunn was telling me. "They just go back to the way they were?"

"Aye, something like that. So long as we make it through, they'll be fine."

I nodded in acceptance. It wasn't much in the way of comfort, but still the sickness swirling in my insides calmed, if only slightly. I had seen the expression on the captain's face—that look of furious expectation—and found solace in the thought that if anyone could steer the ship through this frozen purgatory, it was Eric Winters. And with that I remembered that not all of the men were under the spell of this *thin* place. The captain, Dunn, and I seemed less affected—myself being the weakest of our trio while the other two men might as well have been immune—and Tom had spoken to me. He'd done more than speak to me, but Dunn had not mentioned his strange and intimate behaviors, and I thought better than to call attention to it.

"Why aren't we—you, the captain, and me—we're not …" I didn't know how to put it into words and so I motioned uselessly in the space between the quartermaster and myself and then upward in the direction of the quarterdeck. "Frozen, I mean. And I was talking to Tom Birch, least I think it was Tom Birch …"

"Listen." The sympathetic look fell off Dunn's face as he leaned forward, his elbows planting firmly on the tops of his knees as a cloud of darkness passed through his eyes, dulling their shine to shark-like bleakness. He let the silence grow heavy until it became so dense that it even forced his lips into what resembled a thin red slice across the lower half of his face. "Most men, when in the presence of things that pass between, they freeze, they do. Shut up like oysters hidin' their pearls. That's all that is goin' on out on the deck. When we come out of it, they probably won't remember nothin' ever happened at all. But some, well, some be different—more open, like. More sensitive to things that pass between one world and the other, you might say. They be pulled to the sea, and more agreeable to everythin' that be a part of it. Rest of us, we already be claimed by it."

I swallowed Dunn's ominous words, although I didn't grasp their meaning. "What does that have to do with me? And what does that mean, 'claimed by it'?"

Dunn blew out a breath and seemed to search for the right words. After a while he gave up and hung his head in his hands, but when he lifted it again there was newfound resolve in his eyes. "I don't know no other way of sayin' it, so I expect it be abou' time you find out who you really are, *Merrin Jones*."

Surprise slammed into me, and the nausea I had levied inside of myself broke free. I turned my head to the side and vomited, and then the room turned black as the floor of the cabin rushed up to meet me.

"THAT'S A GOOD LASS," DUNN'S VOICE WAS SAYING WITH UN-characteristic kindness when I came to. My hat lay on the floor beside me, far beyond reach, and my hair was spilled out in incriminating tangles on the floor. The wrinkled backs of the man's hands were tender as they pushed my hair behind my ears and then pressed lightly against my face. "Didn't mean to give you such a shock. Sorry abou' that," he said apologetically. He pushed the flask of sour liquid against my lips and again I tried to refuse it. "Have a swallow and you'll feel good as new."

Lass.

His word echoed horribly inside of my head as he pushed the flask firmly against my lips. The bitter fluid trickled across my tongue and I spat it out. It tasted like metallic saltwater. *Lass.* He knew—possibly *had* known all along. And he had called me by my name, or at least part of it.

"Lass," I repeated in a mumble. My words were garbled and I felt half-drunk from the amount of whatever it was that I'd swallowed. My head ached miserably; it must have hit the floor when I fell off the chair. The room was spinning without me. "I'm no damned lass," I said, trying to sound haughty and failing as I pulled myself upright. "Mind your tongue, you old drunk."

My threat fell flat.

A quick flash of anger blinked across the old man's face before he let out a sudden bark of laughter and clapped his knee, his beady black eyes glinting with unexpected merriment. I widened my eyes at him. "Aye, that be the damned truth," Dunn exclaimed, and waved his flask in my direction. "And even less a lass than you might expect yourself, I'd be willing to bet!" He barked again, and it sounded distinctly unlike any man's laughter I had ever heard—more like the sound an animal might make.

I'd barely so much as seen the man attempt a smile, and now he was laughing so hard that his great chest heaved with the force of it. I gawked at him, and let my mouth hang open under the weight of a thousand unanswered questions. I struggled to catalog the consequences of the current events. It was no use denying my sex; that much was done. Had the cunning old quartermaster known my secret this whole time? If so, why had he kept it? What other knowledge might he be in possession of? I felt foolish and scared, and could not fathom a reason as to why Dunn might have chosen this moment to disclose a truth I'd thought so smartly hidden. For weeks now I had taken great aims to disguise myself, carefully concealing my voice, my hair, my ever voluptuous form. On the few occasions I had dared to bathe I had performed the ritual quickly and under the cover of the dead of night. I slept fitfully light lest someone cross my bed at night, and avoided showing any flesh beyond my hands and arms, a strategy that had more than once almost ended me with heat and sunstroke. Even more troubling, though, than him knowing my sex was that he had *named* me. Perhaps a shrewd and discerning person could have cobbled together the first with months of careful study, but how had he learned my name?

I had lived in perpetual fear of being discovered, and yet I had been known all along. The voice I had heard on the deck echoed in my thoughts. *Get* her *below*, it had bellowed, stark as sunlight in a sky of darkness. It had not been Mister Dunn's voice, but nor had it sounded like the captain's, though I couldn't really be sure. Perhaps I hadn't heard anything at all. Everything felt murky and ambiguous, as if I'd been trapped in a long dream. For all I knew, those words might have come from the sea itself so loudly had their call be in my ears.

Once I'd recovered enough to find my voice, I asked, "How long have you known?"

This was an easy one for Mister Dunn, and another source of surprise for me. "Oh, e'er since you was a wee little lass." He winked after another sip of the vile fluid, and then laughed again at his own cleverness, so hard this time that he put his hand over his stomach to quell the ripples that passed through him. He smoothed his other hand, flask still pinned to his palm by his thumb, over the wave of his white hair. It flattened and then buoyed back into place. He clicked his tongue thoughtfully. "'Fact, I was was the one who be takin' you over to Miss Emery's house for keepin' when you first arrived in Isla Perla."

My oldest memory flashed into my mind, this time slightly different than it had replayed before. I saw, again, Evangeline's golden hair in the Caribbean sunlight as she waved at me from the door of her tavern. The man beside her was still eclipsed in shadow, but for the first time the memory loosened, and as it gave way I noticed that there was someone else at my side, fingers entwined with mine. In this edited version of my memory I saw myself looking upward at the man whose hand was wrapped around mine, and then I saw them staring down at me—eyes that were black and round and kind, and as unmistakably those that belonged Brandon Dunn as was the coif of hair that rose above his head, still white even then. There was something else, too— another new addition I hadn't noticed before. It was unclear, but

I imagined I saw, gripping Dunn's other hand, a boy child with seawater green eyes and a mess of dishwater blond hair. And then another memory, this one newer, broke through as if it simply insisted upon itself: Dunn speaking to Claudette and Mrs. Emery in the shadows the day we set out to sea. I had thought it odd then, but now it all seemed so obvious. He had known, and so had they.

A second wave of shock washed over me, this time erasing all of my pending questions and leaving blank, cavernous headspace where they had been. I started half a dozen attempts at questions, each one failing and dying silently on my lips while Mister Dunn stared back at me wearing an expression of patient amusement and sipping from that damned flask. There was an odd gleam to his eye, one that suggested he'd been waiting to have this conversation for a long time. Finally, my tongue wrapped around a thought. "You've known—" I nearly shouted. My vision swam from the effort and I gasped for air. Unconsciousness threatened again. "You've known who I am all this time, and still you've said nothing? Done nothing? *Why?*"

"Aye. Well, that's not entirely true," he scoffed, apparently offended. His voice was raised with agitation. "Let you sail, didn't I? Kep' you safe, didn't I? I ain't allowed no harm to come to Jones' daughter."

It felt like a bullet had ripped through me—again. I forgot everything else—the frozen sea, the cryptic comments, the surprise that he'd known my identity this whole time. None of it mattered suddenly; he'd given me the first hint to a parentage that I had ever had. He'd called me Jones, not Smith, the surname assigned to orphans like myself. "You knew my father?"

His face settled back into its normal frown as a dark thought passed through him, and then he squinted his eyes, snatched the flask from my hand, and took a final swig. He tossed it, empty, to the floor, and passed his palm over his head again. "Aye, I knew 'im. *Captain* Jones," he stressed the title, and there was reverence in his voice. "He weren't always what he be now. He was a good man, he was, 'for his greed got the best of him—greed and fury from the sea and women, too. Now he be cursed to sail the seas with ne'er making port. He's out there somewhere, sailin' between this world and the next. Sold his soul to sail, he did, but not in the way the stories say, not tha' it matters. Some things can't be undone."

"Captain Jones?" I repeated, racking my memory. I had heard the name before, and the story that went with it. There was only one man called Jones who had sailed the seas to Mister Dunn's description, and he was as much as a legend as the others the old man loved to tell, though the tragedy of Captain Davy Jones was one that had passed through the lips of every sailor I'd ever met. "You can't mean Davy Jones?" I couldn't help the skepticism that had found its way into my voice.

"Aye," Dunn confirmed without the slightest hint of irony. "Captain Davy Jones. Knew 'im a long time ago, I did." I shook my head, trying to recall the lore that I'd read on the doomed pirate captain from Winters' books. The story went that Davy Jones had found himself in trouble at sea after taking on the greatest treasure ever found. He had hailed to the sky, calling out to whatever god that answered with a pledge that he would sail the ocean forever if they would spare him his death. Something dark had taken control of the ship, and as a price for granting his request, had sentenced Jones to an eternity spent on the sea—one without life or love or land. "Davy Jones is not but a legend," I argued. "Traded his soul to the devil so that he could sail the ocean forever on a ghost ship crewed by the silent spirits of dead men. He's no more real than—"

"Than what, girl?" the old man countered. His eyes glinted devilishly in the flickering light of the candle. "Than a magical island that be disappearin' and reappearin', trapped in a place that only exists e'ry few years? Than sailin' on a sea between two worlds with men frozen over?"

He had a point.

"These legends might have faded into naught more 'an old stories, lass," he continued. "But they be startin' somewhere in truth, and the versions you heard sometimes be twisted. I think it's time ye stop worryin' on old pirates' tales, and start thinkin' 'bout what your part be in all this, Merrin Jones. On my honor, you be the daughter of Captain Davy Jones and another I don't dare be namin' while we be a-sail on these dark waters, and it ain't be no accident that you be joinin' this crew."

Before I could speak again the wind rapped loudly against the cabin door once more, only this time it wasn't the wind. With a loud crash the door of the captain's quarters flung inward, squealing on its hinges as a bolt of lightning ripped across the sky and illuminated the darkness on the other side. Winters was standing in the doorway, wild-eyed and covered in a layer of frost. He looked fierce, like some sort of spectral spirit, his eyes still possessed with strange blue fire. His long tresses had become so frozen that their ends were tipped with icicles that made a clinking, metallic sound when the wind blew through them. His gaze slid from Dunn to me on the floor, at my exposed locks and the dazed expression on my face, and it was impossible to see him as anything less than another actor in the legends of the mighty sea.

"Captain," Dunn greeted him with a sigh of relief. He clapped his palms against the knobs of his knees and made to stand. "Seemed it be abou' time to be tellin' Mister Rivers who she really is."

"It'll have to wait," the captain growled. "We're here." The same anticipatory snarl he'd worn on the helm crawled across his face as the ship pitched violently forward, sending books and golden trinkets and Dunn's empty flask flying about the room. I watched as the candle that sat on the floor between Dunn and me fell over, broke in half, and rolled between Winters' booted feet, disappearing out of the open cabin door behind him. The ship rocked again and I searched for something to hold on to, but found nothing on the floor other than Dunn's weathered hand. I gripped it tightly as a roaring noise shook the ship, sending the debris of empty rum bottles and broken candlesticks scuttling across the floor beside me.

XI

I HAD NO TIME TO DIGEST THE REVELATIONS THAT HAD JUST taken place, much less unravel them. For now, whether they held any truth or not, whether I was the daughter of some ill-fated pirate captain or just the bastard of some drunken sailor, Dunn and his legends would have to wait. None of it would matter anyway if I died at sea—something that as I looked out toward the writhing mass of wind and water outside I decided to be distinctly possible.

Whilst we had been discussing the fantastical roots of my genealogy, the ocean had come alive again outside of the captain's cabin. The previously tranquil sea was now furious and black, boiling in angry waves that rose in jagged cliffs and crashed down in white-tipped fangs that bit savagely into the hull of the ship. The ghostly sheen on the water was gone, but the unyielding cold was not. Even with my blanket still wrapped around me, the frigid air beat forcefully against my body like the breath of an angry ocean god, freezing the blood flowing in my veins until it chilled so deep it slowed even the marrow of my bones. Darkness had consumed the sky again, with only a sparse spattering of stars left to decorate the black canvas, and most of them were dulled and hidden behind thick nighttime clouds that warned of a storm brewing over the water.

Even though the air remained just as devastatingly cold, the strange trance that had wasted the men into icy statues had thawed. As the waves rushed and pounded upon the ship so, too, again did the crew, roused from their frozen stasis to combat a suddenly violent sea. Spurred into action, they worked with the same single-mindedness of a colonized whole, moving frantically above and below the decks with the precision and speed of the citizens of an ant bed that had just been kicked over. It was not the first time this analogy had come to mind. The *Riptide*'s men moved in a synchronized accord that required no command or direction, laboring quickly and agilely and without so much as a shiver, the linens and sail scraps they had clutched against themselves just moment's ago now cast away in forgotten heaps on the deck. Even in my mounting dread of being sucked into the sea it was impossible to ignore the beautiful choreography of their movements—brawny men moving about on nimble feet made confident from years of sailing, leaning from side to side as the deck rocked ferociously beneath them. I observed how in quick, practiced actions they handled the sails; there was much heaving on ropes and the guns and cannons were secured to anything that didn't move. The most practiced of all, Tom Birch, simultaneously shouted orders while he tied knots and adjusted sails, moving from task to task without the slightest amount of hesitation although his eyes still had a dazed look about them, as if he'd been caught off unaware by the storm.

Otherwise, if the men had noticed anything amiss they did not show it. Their mannerisms gave away no knowledge that they had just been possessed by the ghosts that lingered between sea and air—just as Mister Dunn had predicted.

IT TOOK MORE EFFORT AND AFFORDED LESS DIGNITY THAN I WAS proud of, but eventually I managed to crawl my way on all fours to the doorway of the cabin and join Mister Dunn and Captain Winters. I was pulling myself up on wobbling legs beside the feet of the two men in my company when a sudden thrash of water collided against the starboard side of the ship. Salty sea spray rose over the edges of the hull and drenched everything in its path, some of it finding its way into my eyes and mouth so that for a split second I was blinded by the smell and taste of the ocean. Then, just when I could see again, another crash of water came, this time so roughly that it sent the ship rocking. Her bow and stern seesawed as they took turns pointing toward the sky. The motion nearly sent me flying backward into the cabin, but I grabbed hold of a length of rigging just as my legs flew out from beneath me, and I more or less remained upright.

Through all of this the captain and Mister Dunn stood on anchored feet while both watched the activity on the decks with oddly placid expressions. The older man lifted his nose skyward and inhaled deeply, a wry smile creeping through the staunch set of his jaw. "Aye," he agreed to no one in particular, his throaty voice barely audible over the crashing sounds of the water and the rumbling thunder overhead. Another flash of lightning tore across the sky, and he eyed it approvingly, as if he'd been waiting for it. For now, all talk of sea-ghosts and legends was forgotten, and Dunn and Winters observed the impending storm as if it were any other day at sea. "We be here all right, Erik. Just a few more minutes and then it be time. Best make ready."

Winters, who I had never heard referred to by his first name, nodded and then was gone. He strode calmly through the throngs of men rushing busily about the deck, and when he arrived at the waist of the ship he rooted his feet and tilted his head upward, hands at his sides as another bang of thunder shook the sky. A bolt of lightning cracked overhead, so bright and white hot that it left behind a pale streamer of green trembling against the black. Winters cast a backward glance at Dunn, and then me, and there was madness in his eyes.

"Not long now," his voice was disembodied by the wind as he called back, heading quickly toward the forecastle of the ship and drawing a cutlass from his belt while he did. He wrapped his fist around a length of rigging from the foremast and stood with his back to us, staring dead ahead, his mane of red hair flying behind him so that he looked for all the world like a lost Viking god readying for battle.

If it was to our deaths that we sailed, then I wanted to meet it in full view. Another wall of water hit the ship and my boots slipped beneath me again, and I cursed my feet as I clung to the rope and gritted my teeth, trying vainly to pull myself through the cabin door and out into the fury. All around me, men yelled and scrambled about the decks, working with ropes and sails as if they could outrun the storm into which we were headed— or perhaps they were racing toward it. I wasn't familiar enough with outrunning storms to be entirely sure and, frankly, either would have been just as likely. The sounds of the sea and the thunder crashing into each other were deafening and impossible to separate, and the wind buffeted violently around me. A white bolt of lightning scarred a starless sky and the water rumbled like the growling, hungry belly of a great beast. The ship jerked again and a man whose name I had never learned let out a sudden wail as he was pitched overboard. I saw Domingo reach an arm out after him, but it was of no use, and so he quickly pulled it back and resumed his work, his lips moving in what I assumed was a parting farewell to the mate just lost at sea.

It was the second death I'd seen in my time aboard, and somehow watching a man plummet to his end over the side of the ship was more disturbing than when I had watched Winters slice Rabbie through the heart. My sense of adventure failed instantly as I took in the enormity of the scene before me, leaving me too scared to give a damn about where we had finally arrived or what these two pirates saw when they watched the sky break apart over the churning ocean. In that moment, staring into what I was convinced to be the very watery end that my dear Claudette had warned of, I surrendered myself to the ignominy of disappointment and fear.

"We're sailing straight into a storm," I screamed frantically at Winters' back, at Dunn's eager scowl, at any of the men who might hear me as they clambered about the deck securing the ship. "We have to turn back. We have to turn back *now.*" I nearly choked on tears of shame and of sorrow that welled up in my throat. I would die without ever reaching Bracile and I would die still an orphan, and I was not sure which was worse.

"No, lass," Dunn yelled in correction when he leaned farther out of the cabin door, his scowling face refiguring into a sly smirk as he braced himself to its frame, seemingly unbothered that the ship was rolling beneath us like a leaf in a drain, or maybe excited by it. "Ain't no turnin' around now, and it ain't no storm we be sailin' for neither. We be nearin' the heart of the ocean, we are. Few more minutes and we be right in it."

"The heart of the ocean?" I called back as I pulled myself upright and found my footing. Using the rigging as a pulley, I dragged myself to where Mister Dunn stood solidly, smiling at the storm. "I thought was just some poetry, not an actual place. What is it, exactly?"

Dunn laughed, and the sound matched the madness I'd seen in Winters' eyes. "No, lass, it be real. It be where the very gods of the sea live. Where we be tryin' to find for many years. Some be callin' it the heart of the ocean, others call it ole Davy Jones' locker itself. Others have names even older and more teriffyin' than that."

When I didn't respond, he nudged his elbow in my ribs and said in a lower growl, "Helpin' him reach this place be the reason you're onboard this ship, Miss Jones. It be where we findin' Evangeline, it is. Might be that Jones himself be waitin' there, too."

Bracile.

I had wanted more than anything to find that mystical island, to find Mistress Dahl and myself in the process, but that was before I'd learned of Dunn's legends and had seen the secrets of the oceans made real with my own eyes. Perhaps the mysteries of my beginnings were too dangerous to ever be known, or perhaps I was not as brave as I had wanted to believe.

"We'll be dead before we reach Bracile if we try to make it through this storm," I argued as another wave racked the bow of ship so forcefully that it twisted her around clockwise. Dunn didn't respond, and I was not sure if the old man could not hear my warnings, or if he simply did not care. "We need to find another way."

"There not be another way, lass," he said, and in the flashing light I thought I saw him wink at me. "Either way it's no matter now. Look."

He pointed the stub of his thumb toward the fore of the ship, where far off in the distance Winters was shouting orders to his men, cutlass held high in the air as he aimed it in the direction of the lightning that continued to rake claw marks in the heavens. The few remaining stars had been snuffed out and the storm clouds had narrowed, sharpening into thin, skeletal fingers that reached down, their tendrils grazing upon the surface of the swirling ocean. It was a storm well and proper, and unlike any I had ever seen or heard of before; the sky and sea melded together to form a never-ending tempest and we were sailing straight for it. For the first time since we had left Isla Perla, I worried that I had given my allegiance—my life—to a madman and his crew. Perhaps there was no such place as Bracile. Perhaps Mistress Dahl was well and truly lost and no amount of mythical legends of seafaring folklore would bring her back.

Perhaps Merrin Smith was all that I was, and whatever answers I hoped to find to my identity and my past were lost along with Evangeline, for surely nothing could be so absurd as that she and I would both be connected by legends of the deep.

I shook my head in disbelief. "No man who's ever sailed for the island of Bracile has come back to tell the tale. No matter which story it is, it ends the same."

"Aye," the old man agreed, still infuriatingly unruffled. "Dead men tell no tales, that they say." His meaty hand clasped the knob of my shoulder, and he pulled me into the swirling mass of men and wind and water competing on deck. "But this time we not be sailin' just as idle men, are we, searchin' for an island that can't be found? We be sailin' with the daughter of Davy Jones." Then, as if to drive his point home, he tapped a finger against the imperceptible lump in my breast pocket that held the ring, which was growing hot again against my chest with every flash of lightning overhead. "And what's more 'an that," Dunn continued, motioning toward the captain, who, satisfied with the preparations done by his crew, had resumed his perch on the forecastle where he was speaking to a dazed looking Tom Birch, "yer count be off, Miss Jones. There be *one* man who's been to Bracile and back ... and he be onboard this ship."

I watched as Winters spoke and wondered how much history the ever-brooding, enigmatic man held locked away within, but I had no time to dwell on what adventures the *Riptide*'s Captain may have endured. With both hands Dunn brought my hat back down atop my head, forcing my dark curls beneath its folds. "Put your hat on, *Mister Rivers*," Dunn said, adding emphasis on the last as he held the brim of the hat so that I was forced to meet his small, shiny eyes. "Now migh' not be the best time to go introducin' yeh just yet. Be best to let the storm pass first." He directed a look of meaningful punctuation in the direction of Tom Birch, who had moved away from the captain and was now standing at the edge of the ship with his fist wrapped in a knot of rope. He alone had a mist still lingering in his eyes, and he was blinking in rapid succession as wind and rain pelted mightily against him. Unlike the rest of the men, the strange trance still had its tendrils in the ship's boatswain.

The warning in Dunn's words had been obvious—a command to keep my distance from Tom Birch—but I couldn't help myself; with Tom in my sights, my unsteady feet finally found purchase on the slick wooden planks beneath me. I heard the old quartermaster's voice calling from behind, telling me to stop, but this only made me charge harder into the storm as I made my way to Tom. It was like trudging through sand, and I had to run hunched over to avoid being barreled over by the gusting wind, one hand firmly holding my hat atop my head while the curls that broke free whipped around in the air around my face and stuck unpleasantly to my skin like soggy seaweed. Whether it was out of desperation to know if the longing I'd seen in his eyes on the sea water had been for me or the water, or if it was only to speak to a man not entrenched in lore and mystery, the only thing I knew for sure was that if we were to drown I wanted my last words to be shared with this man and not that damned, riddle-ridden quartermaster. The storm seemed to sense my passion and responded accordingly, the sea swelling up another notch in its intensity, and I slid across the deck, taking hold of anything solid enough to hold on to.

When I finally reached Tom I clenched my fists at my side before they could reach up and wrap around him of their own accord. "Tom," I yelled, my voice barely breaking above the roar of the sea. "Tom Birch! Are you all right, mate?"

"Oi, Rivers," he called back as he bent his head downward, his eyes blinking rapidly. He looked down in my direction but the water that washed in small rivers down his face and dripped off his eyelashes obscured his vision. He tried to lift a hand to wipe at the salt water pouring down his face but it was caught beneath the heavy weight of the wet canvas he'd tied around his neck. This he wrenched away from his body, looking bewilderedly at it as if he had no idea why he wore it, and then dropped at his feet. "I had the queerest dream," he shouted over the storm as he swatted away the water from his face. He looked at me blearily at first, and then a glimmer of recognition sharpened his gaze, and behind it a look that might have been shame. "You were in it, but only you weren't, well, you." I wished I knew what it was he wasn't saying when he shook his head and rubbed his face roughly. "I must have been dreaming, but I thought I ..." He stopped and stared at me again, letting the end of his sentence trail off.

"You thought what, Tom?"

Before he could answer, lightning split the sky high above our heads, and the ship surged forward under our feet, like it were beginning to slide down a drain. Tom yanked a spyglass from the inside of his coat pocket and held it up to his eye. Even in the darkness I could see the color drain from his skin. What he saw in the distance absorbed his attention immediately, and he hoisted himself up the rigging, hooked a foot in the rope, and swung backward, waving the branch of his arm frantically as hailed the captain. "Maelstrom," he yelled, "Straight ahead, Captain."

The word stopped my heart as the ship fell out from beneath me.

Then, "Bear down," Tom yelled to the men scurrying on the deck without waiting for the captain's reply. "Brace abox!" It was a command to stop immediately, and to turn the ship. The boatswain, believing he had been first to see what was waiting dead ahead, signaled again at the captain, who was staring eagerly in the same direction that Tom had pointed his spyglass.

"Belay that." Winters' voice was even more powerful than the wind's mighty roar as he turned and faced the crew. "It's not a maelstrom that waits for us."

He took a step down the stairs, and then with one hand still gripping the rigging of the foremast he leaned into the wind above his men. All eyes met his expectantly, and his vibrant blue eyes were shining more fiercely than ever I'd seen them. He looked ferocious, all pretenses of cautious command gone. "It's Charybdis," he announced triumphantly, as if that was enough.

And it was.

It started soft. One man began banging the flat of his cutlass against the rail in a slow, purposeful rhythm, and then another, and then a third began to beat two lengths of iron chains together. Their call was picked up by others, and soon all around, from Jomo—who had emerged on deck and was standing with his array of jagged knives tucked in his belt—to Domingo, the ship's carpenter, who wielded an axe, and even Dunn, who stood with half a dozen pistols in his baldric and the grips of two more held in each hand, the men's voices rose together in a chanting, thunderclap of sound, rising in a horrifying chorus as they pointed their weapons toward the sea. Even Tom had loosed a gleaming sword from his belt and twisted away from me to stare into the storm, his face contorted into a look of intense determination.

The captain yelled loudest and most terribly of all as every man of the *Riptide*'s crew flocked to the rails of the ship from bow to stern, quarterdeck to forecastle, and clung, screaming, chanting, and beating the sides of the ship with their swords, cutlasses, and even cannonballs clenched firmly in white-knuckled fists. They pummeled their feet on the decks of the ship around them, the noise steadily increasing in volume and rhythm until it grew so loud and fast that it became even more furious and frightening than the storm itself.

XII

IT WAS CALLED VAPORING, THIS SORT OF HIGH-PITCHED, CLANG-ing cry formed by the combination of the men's voices, and fists, and feet. It was a throaty, pounding, terrifying sort of racket, intended to simultaneously hearten the crew for a bloody battle and to strike horror into its adversary. Since we had avoided confrontations with other crews who might interrupt our voyage or follow in our lead, we had not yet faced another ship in combat, and so I had yet to experience the effect of vaporing for myself. Still, I had heard of it often in the relaying of old terrors from pirates and sailors alike who had become too old or too injured to take back to the sea. Whether from the side of victim or tormentor their tales of the phenomenon had been the same, all told with the pale ghosts of fear still haunting their faces. The harsh tremor of this jarring sound was said to be a noise that commanded nightmares in those who had witnessed it and lived to tell the tale. It was a noise that had the ability to worm its way into your core, and upon having heard it, left one forever scarred.

It was the sound of impending death.

As it swelled around me, the sound of the pirate's vaporing—of my own voice as it raged forth from the very depths of my soul—rose fierce and raw and horrible, but it did not fill me with dread. Rather it was a deliciously potent cacophony of bolstering, brutal energy that burned black the tender spots that endured inside of me, hardening my resolve as if what remained of my courage had been brought up like silt swirled from the pit of a deep pool. Without any conscious decision to do so I, too, loosed my cutlass from its place on my belt and held it aloft, gripped tightly in my sweaty palm, while my empty fist pounded against a length of railing seemingly of its own accord. I had made no conscious decision to join them, but the sound had quickened me and I yelled and stomped my feet alongside my brethren, my voice joining theirs and my eyes transfixed on the storm brewing ahead so that we faced it as one united, writhing mass.

Had the storm before us been born of mortal flesh and bone, it would have crouched in fear, halted in awe or in terror of the sound and sight that greeted it as the *Riptide* brazenly bared its mighty broadside and its crew before it. But as it was not mortal it was unaffected. Instead, it continued to churn angrily before us as it pulled the ship into the glistening teeth of water that rung the edges of the deep funnel, tightening in a coil that burrowed into the heart of the ocean.

As I stared forward into certain doom, my thoughts raced backward, flashing in brief, half-formed glimpses at the memories I'd earned in my short lifetime. I saw Claudette's face first, my oldest and dearest friend, her caramel skin and smoky chocolate eyes smiling at me above a coy, smirking mouth. She was a delicacy of a woman, too beautiful and too smart to spend her life as nothing more than a whore in a dirty quayside brothel. I saw Mistress Dahl, Evangeline, the same in my last memory as she had been in my earliest, with tumbling golden curls and bright, gemstone eyes that taunted me with the promise of secrets and knowledge still unshared from the porch of her tavern where she presided over the island. These women, whose countenances were carved into my heart, were joined by the faces of the men I had grown to love, despite their hardness and their flaws.

Brandon Dunn with his scowl and wraithlike white hair, alternatively my guardian and antagonist. The unlovable, unmovable captain, Erik Winters, a man formed as much by his iconic auburn tangles and steel grey eyes as he was of growls and granite and other things just as hard and merciless. I saw Jomo and Rabbie, the glaring, one good eye of Domingo "Left Eye" Diaz, and even Gregory Nip, strangers who had become my peers, and my brothers.

The last face to pass through my thoughts was that of Tom Birch. I saw him now as I had when I'd first laid eyes on him, scaling the full six and a half feet of his tall height from beneath the brim of the hat I'd claimed from the forgotten artifacts of one of Claudette's clients. I had never been able to define what it was about this man that had the habit of speeding my heart and slowing it down at the same time, but I had long ago accepted it. What's more was that I had come to depend on his companionship onboard as much as I had Claudette's on land, although it caused my heart to flutter every time I dared to look into his saltwater green eyes or watch the disheveled crown of his sandy head high above the rest as he moved about the deck with a gentle quality not typically associated with a man who'd spent his entire life in the company of pirates. He was kind and unassuming, but loyal and dependable, and I was startled to find that even though I'd barely known him two months, I felt as though somehow I'd always known him. Now, I was unwilling to live even one day of a life without Tom Birch in it.

With my thoughts filled with the faces of the first family I had ever known—one I was not eager to lose so soon—, and my throat raging with the vaporing, I scaled a swatch of net at the base of a mast and lifted my body upward in challenge to

THE ISLE OF GOLD

the thrashing waves. Awash in the voices of my brothers and the power bestowed by a full heart, I faced the blistering, icy wind and the swirling, consuming sea, but I no longer did so as a dubious coward who feared her own end. I faced the storm renewed—the proud, determined woman who'd had the courage to disguise herself as a pirate and join a notorious and ruthless crew helmed by the mightiest man I'd ever known. Whether I were Merrin Smith, the brothel-dwelling orphan of Isla Perla, or Merrin Jones, daughter of the fabled Captain Davy Jones who sailed the seas immortally cursed, I would not be undone by the storm that formed the boundary between one world and the next.

I took a deep breath, pumped my blade as high as I could reach, and screamed into the sky. If the sound of vaporing were to be a scar, then it was one I would proudly wear as a mark of honor for the remainder of my days.

I would wear until it my bones laid with those of my brothers at the bottom of the sea.

XIII

WHEN HE HAD FIRST SET EYES UPON IT, WINTERS HAD named the storm that spun and bucked in the sky and seas, tossing the ship like a twig in the water as we were swept into the spinning currents at it crest. He had not just called it any name, but had given it the name of a goddess—one that I remembered well from my research.

Charybdis.

A daughter of Poseidon, Charybdis had been stolen away by his brother, Zeus, after she'd helped her father in combat against her uncle. As punishment, Zeus had chained her to the seabed and cursed her with an uncontrollable thirst that could never be quenched. To abate her thirst Charybdis drank the ocean whole thrice times daily and then vomited it back again, alternatively gulping and belching the water and giving rise to both whirlpools and tides that flooded and drowned the ships who sailed above where she lay. When Odysseus had faced her, he had said that Charybdis seethed like a cauldron on a blazing fire, swallowing the saltwater down so completely that the dark sands of the sea's bottom were visible in the depths of her throat.

Dunn had said the heart of the ocean was the home of the gods of the sea. By my estimation that meant that if such a place existed, it would reside in the belly of Charybdis, housed within the space of seabed exposed by her funnel. Incited with the energy from the vaporing, fury gave way to curiosity and anticipation to face this great, raging legend made real before my eyes. I returned my cutlass to its position on my belt and swung free from the net, moving nearer to the mainmast and into the throng of the men who had gathered at the rails in the waist of the ship. The captain was standing with his hands locked on the rail while Dunn waited nearby, scowling unpleasantly as though the sight disgusted him, and so I took my place beside Tom. We did not bother to waste words that would have gone unheard in the booming winds. Instead, the two of us stared overboard, down the bottomless gullet of the cursed daughter of Poseidon as she raged just off the starboard side of the ship.

Perhaps it was a consequence of her curse, but goddess or not, the maelstrom was unlike any I had ever heard of before. I had expected it to take the usual appearance of shaken saltwater, blue and frothy, but as I stared into the whirlpool's mouth I saw that it was black and speckled with jagged chunks of swirling, icy rock, same as the sea around it had been. Words failed me as I studied its funnel, which was describable only as a sharp fang of ice that narrowed in a thin, serrated ribbon as it spun in wild, twisting motions toward the ocean floor. It was a violent cone of water that sucked, and pulled, and swallowed everything into its downdraft to crush it within a churning spiral of death. Upon closer inspection I saw that some of the shards I had thought to be ice were in fact not ice, but splintered remains of wooden planks, the broken corpses, presumably, of other vessels that had fallen victim to Charybdis' unending thirst.

Staring, hypnotized by the spiraling depths of Charybdis' throat, I was so entranced that I barely noticed the first flash of blinding green light that lit the sky above me. It was vivid and bright, and it cast a hue over the sea, recoloring the black water an eerie shade of ethereal green that was brilliant enough to glow behind my eyelids when I blinked, like I had stared into the flame of a candle too long. Behind this strange light came a deafening shudder as a second bolt of the green light seared the sky, and then a sharp crack like the sound of a tree snapping in half shook the ship. It tore my attention away from the water and I jerked my eyes in the direction of the sound, not even bothering to shield my eyes from the pouring rain. About halfway up the height of the topmast I saw where the sound had landed: the tall pole bore a zigzagged wound where lightning had raked its claws into it. I watched as it toppled and began to fall.

It came down heavily, purposefully, and rushing along with it came a host of smaller pieces of heavy debris—bits of rope and iron. The sail tore away from the mast in shreds that were instantly whipped away into the wind and lost before they could begin to drift downward. I followed the fall with widened eyes, watching as wood and rope plummeted with surprising velocity toward the waist of the ship. I observed their fall, projecting their path with morbid curiosity until my eyes landed on the man standing directly in their path. I had not felt Tom move beside me, but there he stood—ignorant of the danger rushing down above him as he worked with his head bowed, securing something to the base of the mast.

"Tom!" The name tore from my throat in a screech so high and tight that it felt like I had swallowed splinters of glass. The boatswain could not hear my voice above Charybdis' roar. "Tom!" I called again, waving my arms frantically while I rushed toward him.

I watched in horror as a thick knot of rigging plunged downward, falling faster than the rest of the debris like a bullet aimed directly for his head. I ran faster, barreling through the other men who were just as oblivious to the danger while they worked to brace for the inevitable impact of the storm ahead, but I was no match for the speeding weight of the rope. Time slowed as I watched it bear down at Tom's head, and then I screamed another mouthful of glass as I watched it collide against him, the impact instantly erasing the consciousness from his eyes as his body crumpled lifelessly to the slick, wet planks of the deck at my feet.

As if it sensed my despair, a blast of thunder boomed overhead in a mocking howl of laughter. I put my hands against Tom's chest and then his neck, feeling for his pulse while the rain pounded down upon me, obscuring my vision even more as tears joined the raindrops pouring down my face. I pushed desperately at the places where it should be—wrist, neck, wrist again—but felt nothing. I would not believe he was dead.

"Help," I called out, grabbing at the pant legs of the men who passed by within my reach. "Mister Birch is hurt. I need help moving him out of the way of the storm."

"Ain't no way out of the storm," Domingo, owner of the scrap of breeches in my fist, sneered at me as he jerked out of my grasp. "Pull 'im to the side of the—"

Another crash shook the ship and I threw my body over the limp expanse of Tom's, using as much of my smaller form as was possible to shelter his unconscious body from the items that continued to rain from the sky as the ship edged closer to the mouth of the swirling, swallowing maelstrom. A hunk of rusty iron landed at my side, missing me by no more than three inches. It clattered away when the ship lurched severely on its keel, one side rising as the other rolled beneath it. Everything that wasn't tied down skidded across the deck, Tom's body and mine included. I dug my fingers into the fabric of Tom's coat and burrowed my head into his chest, clinging to him so tightly that it felt like the bones of my fingers might break from the strength of their own grip. The ship pulled again, and we were slammed into the opposite rail of the ship with such force that it knocked the breath from my lungs. In the clamor around me I heard the screams of men as more were lost, flying over the edges when the *Riptide* fell on her side. The sky was lost and all that was left to see was water.

Vaguely, I hoped the scream had been that heartless bastard Domingo's.

If it hadn't, it might soon be. One final sip of the mighty Charybdis and the ship would be sucked completely into her greedy gullet. The cold breath of fear crept like frost along the edges of my heart.

Dunn's voice reached me over the noise. "It be time, *Mister Rivers*, for ye to take off your disguise an' reveal who you really be."

Lifting my face from Tom's chest, I looked for the older man. I found him, standing in the waist of the ship with his hands crossed over his chest. Despite everything he seemed calm, almost serene.

"I am no one," I screamed at him over the roar over the storm, while, as if heeding Dunn's words my hat blew away from my head and was lost in the wind. My hair whipped wildly around my face, covering my eyes before being matted down in place with sea spray. I could taste the salt from my tears as they slid toward my lips. "An orphan left behind like waste on an island. Who cares that I am not a man when the ship is about to be swallowed by the ocean?"

"Aye," Dunn shouted in agreement, eyes on the water as the deck began to fill with puddles. "But names have power ... 'specially yours." He said this as if it meant something. Brandon Dunn would be cryptic 'til the end, damn him.

"I am no one," I repeated, fresh, bitter tears stinging my face as they fell from my eyes. I looked at Dunn, whose eyes were soft, encouraging, and infuriating. "I am a woman without a name, and no story about legends and—"

"Speak your name, damn you!" Winters interrupted to issue an impatient command from somewhere behind me. A flash of green light lit up the sky, this time so bold and blazing it could not be mistaken, and the urgency in his raspy voice increased as he ordered me again, "It is time! Speak your name and by the gods, deliver us all."

"No name has the power to save us from this beast," I started, but even as I said the words I wasn't sure I believed them. Once a string was pulled from the fabric of what one considered reality, the entire thing quickly came unraveled, the boundaries of things real and imagined blurred together in a tangled, indistinct truth. I had seen frozen, ghostly seas and the soulless eyes of possessed men, and was at that very moment waiting to be consumed by a goddess turned monster.

With those as my final thoughts, I sat myself on the deck of the ship and, pulling Tom's unconscious, unbeating body into my lap, I prepared to address the sea. "I am Merrin Smith," I whispered, taking one last look at the swirling waves that tightened closer and closer around the ship like the glittering blue-black scales of a constricting python. I stared at the consuming emptiness which would swallow the ship whole, that would suck, chew, and tear it into scraps of wood and canvas as it consumed us all in one final gulp. Then, I blinked the image away and once more I set my eyes on Tom Birch's face, taking in his face one final time, slack-mouthed and sightless as he lay in the nest of my crossed legs, unaware that they would never again see the light of day. Unaware that the image of his face would be the last beautiful sight I saw.

I closed my eyes, preserving this final view safely behind my eyelids. "I am Merrin Smith," I began, my voice as weak and shaky as the name. I swallowed and took a deep, steadying breath, and then started over once more, this time with my eyes opened and facing the storm. Dunn's words and Winters' demand echoed in my head. "I am Merrin *Jones*," I said with a voice as loud and powerful as I could manage, loudly enough for the men nearest me to notice, to see their eyes widen in shocked recognition upon hearing the infamous name that Dunn had insisted was mine, and to see my hair blowing freely and tellingly in the wind. I saw them see *me* for the first time, not Westley Rivers, and I thought perhaps I saw a hint of relief in their eyes. "I am Merrin Jones," I yelled again, strengthened by my own words. "I am the daughter of Captain Davy Jones, and we will not be taken by the sea!"

These words were my last as the nose of the ship tipped into the fury, hovered, and then dove headfirst into the throat of the storm.

PART THREE

XIV

I DO NOT KNOW WHAT HAPPENED AFTER WE FELL INTO THE swirling throat of Charybdis' maelstrom, nor for how long I slept, if that is indeed what I did. I awoke in a place that was warm, quiet, and not my own—and for that matter not any room I knew to exist aboard the *Riptide*.

The first clue to my strange new surroundings was the bed in which I lay. Rather than the thin, worn canvas of my familiar hammock in the captain's quarters, my body rested comfortably on a soft, down mattress stacked high with dozens of silken pillows. There was a heavy blanket draped across me, soft and supple and made perhaps of seal fur, and as I pushed it away I saw that the torn, sea-soaked rags of my usual clothing had been removed. Now, I was dressed in a thin cotton damask shift that wasn't mine, and which was laced in eyelets sewn up and down the front and studded with tiny freshwater pearls. Another pair of beaded eyelets marched down the lengths of my outer arms until they rounded the curves of my elbows and reached my forearms. It was by far the most feminine item I had ever worn and it seemed like it had been sewn just for me, with a fit tailored to hug my figure as if a soft corset had been sewn invisibly within it, and of a quality more rich than I had ever seen or imagined. My hair was loose and dry, and it tumbled down my back in long, lively curls that were fuller and of a deeper shade of brown than I had ever seen it, as if my hair had been dyed the color of chocolate and styled by a fine salon in the Old World. It was longer than I remembered it to be, but I had worn it tied back and bound for so long that it was impossible to truly tell.

I felt refreshed and at ease, as if I'd slept soundly for days and was now struggling to wake, held captive in the embrace of a temporal, dreamlike fog. The feeling was curious and slightly surreal—*thin* almost—and I ran my hands over myself, raking my fingers through my hair and running the tips over the delicate eyelets to see if I could discern the source of the odd feeling in my bones. All was as it should be, but then it wasn't, either—the body simultaneously mine and not mine at all. I paused when I reached my left arm and did not feel the dull throb of bruises I knew to be there. As I looked at my skin I saw that no trace of the purple smudges left by Dunn's fingers remained; my arm was as blank and perfectly white as if the mark had never happened.

Alarmed and dazed, I sat up sharply in the bed and looked around the unfamiliar chamber in which I had found myself, unsure if I should search for a path to escape or enjoy the stunning view of this dazzling and unusual place that overwhelmed all of my senses in turn. The room was a bedroom chamber, but not like any I'd ever seen; it was still, and dry, and appeared to have been carved in the cavity of a cenote. The walls and floors were made of sea-green tinted limestone, and stalagmites of carved calcium ran in columns from its top to bottom, providing conduits for the distant sound of rainwater that echoed softly in the otherwise quiet room. The trembling flames of what must have been a thousand candles of varying size reflected brightly, their flames lighting the room in the reflections of blazing mirror mosaics and dancing across the gilded surfaces of more treasure than would have filled the *Riptide*'s holds if she had the space of a ship five times her size. The air was scented, but not salty like the ocean—a scent like lotus, powdery and sweet. The room flourished with the wealth of beautiful trinkets, each more lovely than the last, but none were as beautiful as the woman who I discovered sitting at a vanity at the far end of the room, nestled like a crowned jewel amongst her treasures.

Her back was to me as she studied her own image in an ornate golden handheld mirror, held slightly tilted to the side so that her reflection was hidden from my view. A second, larger mirror hung on a wall of stone beside her, entwined in gold, but its glass was clouded and foggy from age so that her face was obscured. Still, I could see that her profile had a familiar quality to it, as if I had seen it somewhere before though I was certain that I had not.

Seeing her now, I was not sure how I'd missed her in my initial sweep of the chamber. I surely shouldn't have—there was nothing about her that was common or *unnoticeable*; in fact, it was difficult to do anything other than stare in amazement at a woman who looked as she did. Besides Evangeline, this lovely creature was the most stunningly beautiful thing I had ever seen, though as I regarded her from behind there was something distinctly unsettling about her that made her appear less than entirely human and utterly devoid of Mistress Dahl's warmth. I wasn't sure if she were a creature to be adored or to be feared, nor why I had awoken in her presence. The latter unnerved me most of all. I should have been fighting a storming sea, or lying somewhere at its bottom. And then I remembered the gods at the heart of the ocean, and thought that perhaps I had arrived after all.

It was near impossible to put the woman's description into words. She was overwhelmingly feminine, as if she were a flower transformed into flesh—regal and fragile, ethereal but still so strongly tethered to the earth that she might have governed it. An orchid perhaps, or a yawning calla lily. Her busy movements about her vanity were graceful and precise, and she conducted them silently as if they were for my benefit. Of all of her qualities, most striking about her appearance, I decided finally, was her hair. It was not of any shade I'd seen before, save for atop the crown of a figure carved of shell and stone. It could only be described as the color of pearls if they had been spun into tresses as fine as glass; silvery-white with hues of blues and purples as it shimmered illusively in the flickering light the same as abalone under the sun. A line of scalloped seashells that were still pink from the sea offset the gleam of her hair. These adorned the length of her profile on one side, sweeping in a waving line from her forehead to the nape of her neck. The rest of her magnificent mane had been combed into a long twist of glossy curls that swept over her opposite shoulder and were clasped by a mother of pearl clip. An expanse of the milky white flesh of her back was exposed and it had the same shimmering, spectral quality as her hair, like it were all made from the same substance. A dainty gold chain interrupted the solid perfection of her skin as it wound itself around from her waist, up and around, and ending as it circled the base of her tall, swanlike neck. She wore a wrapped dress of crinkled red silk that clung to her slender form, tight and tucked and ending in golden tendrils that reached back over her bare shoulder like the pale tips of a many-fingered crab claw.

She laughed softly as I completed my memorization of her unearthly form. The sound tittered about the echoing chamber like a bubbling brook if the water had been too cold to support life. "Welcome, Merrin Jones," the echo of her voice said as it arrived where I waited on the bed.

"Who are you?" I asked of her back, although I had a guess. There was only one woman born of the sea who could have matched her description, although she had been called by many names in stories as old as the sea itself and it was impossible to tell which one may have been the first, or correct. "And where am I?"

"A friend," she replied lightly, her voice lilting in a way that made me uneasy but not fearful. "And you are safe, dear. There is no need to be troubled here. I mean you no harm." Her voice might have warmed on the last part, but the heat was fleeting.

With a flick of her wrist she sat the mirror down on the table, baring a surface inlaid with mother of pearl and a perfect, crisp sand dollar. Her long, slender fingers lay atop the mirror's face, lovingly stroking the outline of the sand dollar, but still she made no move to face me.

Despite her assurances of friendship and peace, I pushed my feet to the edge of the bed and slid with them until my toes touched the cool stone of the floor. I pulled myself upright, enjoying the sensation of the curls swinging against my back as I sat lightly on the edge, wishing I were in my familiar clothing, even if it were so much less lovely. There were knives in the worn folds of the garments, and it would not be an easy thing to defend myself in a shift, even it was such a lovely one that I hated to be rid of.

"You're Mélusine." It was a statement, not a question, although it was one I spoke tentatively and without accusation. I was not sure how one should address a goddess.

She sighed and there was sadness in it. "No," she said, and her voice sounded like cold crystal. "I am not."

"Then who are you?" I asked, but she answered only with

silence. It hung in the air between us. "Why am I here?" I questioned. Then, remembering the storm … "What has happened to the ship? Where are the others of my crew?" Each of my questions grew louder, and more adamant, and I could feel the urgency of them in my chest as each was left just as unanswered as the one before.

There was a rustling of silk and a sound like rushing water, and the woman stood without turning. Around the narrow pinch of her waist I could see that she held something in her hands in front of her. She bent her long, perfect neck so that her face was lowered when she turned to me. I noticed two things at once. First, was that even though she faced me, her gaze was hidden by a thick ribbon of red lace the same color of her gown. All I could see of her face was its shape: a long, narrow nose like a downward arrow over a strong jaw with the slightest hint of a dimple in the chin, and the curve of smirking, deep red lips. The mask complicated her beauty, but did not diminish it, and her smile would have been pleasant had it not been for the concealing effect of the lace, which made it alternatively cruel and kind depending on the blink of the chamber's candlelight as she slid toward me over the limestone floor.

The second thing I noticed was the thing she held clasped in front of her, a round edge of its worn leather brim grasped in each of her long-fingered hands. She was in possession of my hat, the same one I'd seen blow away and be lost into the storm.

"Charybdis." Like Winters, I named the storm.

She laughed, a soft, breathy sound, and extended the hat in one hand toward me. "No, dear," she cooed dismissively. "She lost her form a long time ago." She held the hat in her outstretched arm, waiting for me to take it, but I was hesitant. I

THE ISLE OF GOLD

reached forward, but then my hand stalled halfway between us, afraid to touch her or take anything from her hand. She tittered coldly again, and this time it was unmistakably a frightening sound. The expression of her face remained hidden behind the lace, but I couldn't dismiss the feeling that her eyes were cruel above the smile she wore while she spoke, making otherwise kind words completely sinister. "Don't worry, dear, I won't bite."

Said the snake to Eve.

My hat toppled out of her fingers and into mine, and I held it tightly, like it was a protective shield. A satisfied chitter came from behind her still-smirking red lips, and the strange being turned her back to me again and began to glide back to her vanity. I could not see if she had feet to carry her beneath the flowing red silk, but it didn't seem that she did.

"I just wanted to see you … just once. For now," she said in clipped words spoken over her shoulder as she moved farther and farther away. Her voice had stopped pretending to be human and the tendrils of her gown waved good-bye over the curve of her skin as if they were floating in water. Her face seemed frozen as she cast one final backward glance at me, the image of her faltering slightly, and then she gave a tight, unpleasant smile before leaving me with her final words: "You have your father's eyes, Merrin Jones."

My eyes snapped open to the sounds of men yelling and the ship swaying violently beneath me, jarred from the tranquility of what had obviously been a dream by sensations that were becoming all too common. I thought, at first, that we were still in the storm, but then my hands gripped the edges of my hammock as it swung abruptly and then slowed to a stop. The familiar view of the captain's cabin filled my sight, and the feeling of my scratchy clothes and limp, sea-hardened hair brought me great comfort. My body relaxed in the wrap of my bed, and for a moment I thought that maybe I had dreamt it all—the frozen sea, the ashrays that walked amongst the men on deck, the cetone chamber and the strange, beguiling woman—but I knew I hadn't. Such idle fantasies were the stuff of those who could only stare at the water and imagine its secrets, but did not belong to those who had lived them. The memories of these were now as much a part of me as every other I possessed.

Now, the sea cove was gone and I was relieved to be in familiar surroundings, but unsure of how I had come to be in the captain's quarters. My last memory was of the storm, and Tom Birch's unconscious body sheltered beneath mine as we braced for the impact of the maelstrom's fury.

Tom.

What had become of him, and the rest of the men? It made no sense that we had survived the storm, but it was apparent we had. As the haze of sleep cleared and the remnants of the dream faded, I could make out the men's voices more clearly, funneling in through the cracks in the walls above board. They were yelling, not in panic or in manner intended to build confidence for oncoming battle, but in a sound that sounded almost merry, like celebration. Grey sunshine, the result of an overcast sky, filtered in through the edges of the curtains hanging over the cabin's sprawling windows. The burden of night and storm had passed. The ship stalled and then heaved sharply to one side, like she, too, was resting herself, and then all was still. I could hear the sound of men's voices in agreeable chorus, and then the scuttling sounds that suggested that each man had claimed for himself a piece of the deck to rest and drink and gamble in a well-earned reprieve after the past night's adventure.

Over my months at sea I had perfected the ability to rise upward from the folds of the hammock without allowing it to sway awkwardly, and as I sat forward to see the room fully the first thing my eyes landed on was Tom's long, lean body on the other end of the cabin. His skin was ashen, and his long limbs draped limply over the edges of a makeshift cot brought up from the crew's quarters. At first I thought him to be surely dead, but then I saw the shallow rise and set of his chest, lifting and falling with short, uneven breaths. Anchored in place beside him was the squat lump that belonged to Mister Horace Clarke, the ship's doctor. He attended to Tom in quick, fidgeting movements—snaps of fingers and jerks of wrists—that had a distinctly rodent-like quality to them, befitting of the round little hoarder who existed almost entirely in his little cowardly hole of seclusion, joined only with the company of his medical instruments and bibelots and whatever stores of his private pantry he had left. I guessed this could not have been much; of late he and Jomo had regarded each other with suspicion whenever they crossed paths, like neither fully trusted the other not to steal the precious remaining bits of food aboard the ship.

When his gaze met mine, his beady eyes were leveled over Tom's sleeping form and drilling into me with such intensity that they might catch fire and burn like sunlight pointed through glass. There was obvious accusation in them, and disgust. Most pirates, I knew, even those who were more lax in their adherence to Bartholomew Robert's pirate's code that decreed penalty of death to those caught sailing with women, still believed it mighty bad luck to have a woman onboard, even if she were a member of the crew. Worse still, in our circumstance, men like the ship's doctor might not only consider my presence a consequence of poor luck, but the reason for it. It had been my name called when we plunged headfirst into the storm.

He glared at me until I had no choice but to acknowledge it, swallowing his distrust as I met his stare. Then, satisfied that he had made his distaste for me known, he returned his eyes to his charge, fussing with bandages and ointments that seemed unnecessary. There were no obvious wounds on Tom's body, no justification for the condition in which he lay. He looked like he was only sleeping, and if it had not been for his unnatural color I would have guessed he'd wake any moment. "You be needing anything, missus?" Mister Clarke asked in a raspy voice that cracked painfully on *missus,* as if it carried a sour taste, and I realized with a start that he was addressing me.

The thought occurred that perhaps I should apologize, or introduce myself, but I had sailed with the man for months and still did not feel like I owed him anything. "No," I decided, both in response to Mister Clarke's question and to the possibility of a new introduction. Nothing I could say would erase the look in his eyes anyway. "How is Mister Birch?"

The doctor grunted in a manner that did not inspire confidence. He ran a bloated hand stemmed with sausage-fingers over the bald slick of his thinning hair and shrugged. "To be honest, I don't rightly know," he admitted with an exasperated tone. "Man's just *stuck* in sleep. Pulse is beating, but it's weak and faster than it aught to be. Can't find nothing else wrong with him. I tried bleeding him, tried resuscitating him … hell, I tried every damn thing I can think to try." He shrugged, then sunk his palms into his knees and pushed himself upright. "Best to keep him comfortable and see if he wakes up on his own, I guess. I've done all I can for him."

"*If*?" The word stuck in my throat as I digested the horrors of what he'd done to Tom's unaware form—bleeding and bandaging and covering it in foul smelling ointments. Even for a pirate's crew, the doctor's methods were crude.

Clarke glared at me at again, not even trying to hide the scorn in his eyes. "Tom Birch be one of the most respectable men onboard this ship, *too* damned good for the life of a pirate if I'm being honest. It be a damn shame if he be lost to this place."

"What—"

I had more questions for the surly doctor, but before I could ask them he pushed himself heavily out of his seat and stomped out of the cabin without inviting further conversation, pulling the door open roughly and shutting it just as roughly behind him the second his bulk cleared the narrow opening. There was the sound of harsh whispers behind the closed door in voices too low for me to recognize, and then it opened again and Captain Winters entered, followed closely by Jomo, who had apparently shed his role of the ship's cook and was now robed in a layer of leather and steel like a warrior prepared for battle. I had assumed that the doctor had provided an update on Tom's condition, but both men passed only quick, unlanding glances in Tom's direction as they came to me instead. Their swift and direct pace to my bedside was unnerving, and for a moment I feared that I was about pay dearly for my deceitful act as the young sailor Westley Rivers, but then Jomo, the fearsome warrior with eyes made kind by friendship, tipped his head in his usual curt nod, and offered me his hand. The captain, less genteel, fixed me with piercing, resolute eyes.

There was a sense of anticipation in the air around them, like they'd been waiting for me to wake. I could see it tremble in Jomo's hand and behind the icy exterior of Winters' gaze. After a moment of hesitation I accepted Jomo's proffered hand and allowed myself to be pulled out of the hammock. My feet were unsteady and they wavered beneath me, my knees wobbling and clanging together like a newborn calf as I tried to stand. I would have fallen, but the captain's hand shot out suddenly and clenched me in a firm, yet surprisingly tender grip and held my arm steadily and patiently as I righted myself. I made a sighing sound of gratitude as the deck became solid beneath me, and Winters retracted his arm with an expressionless face while Jomo kept my hand locked in his grip. I could not decide if there was any emotion in the captain, or if the gesture had been automatic. His eyes remained unchanged as he crossed his arms sternly atop his chest in a position that suggested both curiosity and disapproval, like one a parent might give a misbehaving child before dispensing judgment. His hand on my arm reminded me of the dream I'd just had and I checked my arm again, hoping to see Dunn's purple fingerprints still blotchy and real on my skin. I found them where they'd last been, but they were no longer the vivid purple of freshly forming bruises, but instead had faded largely to hues of black and yellow, with pale, sickly green edges that indicated they had already matured to their peak and begun to heal.

"How long have I slept?" I asked incredulously, sliding my hand out of Jomo's and using it to rub first my forearm and then the sleep from my eyes.

"Two days," he answered, again without the pesky inflection of emotion—as if losing days to sleep was no more unusual than was waking up in a vastly different place than the one you remembered last. "Maybe more," he added in a loose of smoke from a freshly lit cigarette. Its sour scent accosted my nose, which was still full with the powdery scent of lotus. "Hard to tell what's what now that we aren't on familiar tides." He narrowed his eyes into hardened steel and puffed on the length of paper between his thin lips without saying more.

Bracile.

"Did we make it?" I asked excitedly, forgetting my concerns about bruises and lost time, even about Tom Birch's precarious condition. I took a step forward but my knees buckled again, and again a supporting hand reached out to steady me from falling. The movement made me nauseous and my vision swam in front of me. In the blur I could just make out Jomo's strong, dark arms as they reached forward and then around me as he guided me to the captain's chair and helped me to sit. After pulling a canteen from the folds of his shirt, he poured water into a mug, and handed it to me. I accepted the water and swallowed it down, but wasn't certain why the fearsome man was bestowing upon me such royal treatment. It was an unfamiliar and foreign thing to be treated like a lady. I had seen men, even pirates, use such gracious gestures when courting other women on Isla Perla and always thought it must be a lovely feeling to be regarded as something precious, but now applied to me I found that I did not like it. It made me feel uncomfortable, and fragile. I considered noting it, or asking Jomo why he held my hand and helped me situate myself as I could regained control of my body, but thought better of it. Even more taciturn than Winters, Jomo traded in words like they were a valuable commodity and rarely spent more than was necessary. It was likely he wouldn't provide an answer even if I dared the question. Besides, as I needed his help at the moment I dared not complain. I made a mental note to repay him for his kindness the next time I found something beautiful and red.

The captain made it clear in his own fashion that he was not interested in answering my questions any more than would Jomo. "You spoke as you slept," he said instead. "What was it you dreamed?" There was no curiosity in his voice—this was an inquisition, not a request.

The memory of the strange woman came to mind and I struggled to put it into words. "I dreamt that I was in a strange chamber, one that appeared to have been carved into the belly of a sea cave. There was a woman there—if you could call her that. She certainly manifested as a woman, but she … wasn't." I shook my head and sipped down another mug of water, then did my best to describe her physically although no words I could think of did her image justice.

I kept my eyes on locked on Winters as I described her, but they were hard and cold and gave away nothing. "She said she just wanted to see me, and that I had my father's eyes. Does any of that mean anything to you? Do you know who she might have been?"

"No," he said, but I didn't believe him. He offered no further explanation, but in his countenance I also saw something else—that the dream struck a chord of fear in him.

He turned on his heel to leave before I could ask, and Jomo's thick hand wrapped around the top of my arm, urging me to rise. Winters opened the door and glanced backward over his shoulder at me, wearing a look of anticipation mingled with antipathy.

"Come," he ordered, and he was clearly not happy about it. "There is someone you should meet."

XV

D AWN HAD BROKEN ON THE BOW OF THE *RIPTIDE* AND MY
heart swelled as I beheld it. Following behind my captain,
I exited the dark cabin and came out into the light of the upper
decks, adjusting my hat back atop my head to shield my eyes
from the sun's bright glare as I did. We had been enfolded in dark
and cold for so long that it felt like ages since the last time I had
seen the sun, or the expansive deep blue waters of the daytime
ocean, or felt the sunshine beat hotly upon my skin. It seemed a
lifetime ago, the last time I filled my lungs with the sweet, salty
scent of warm ocean air, or watched the rippling of the waves as
the ship passed through parted waters like a torch blazing across
the water, sailing unencumbered and alone on still, peaceful seas
that were brimming with life. On this long-anticipated morning
the sun shone down through a sky full of wispy white clouds to
light on crisp, turquoise waters that were still adrift with gleaming hunks of solid ice. These were not the same hard, cold masses
that we encountered in the frozen sea, but sparkled like floating
diamonds glittering atop a bed of blue silk. I sucked in a lungful
of sweet ocean breeze, filling my senses with fresh saltwater and
flushing out the heavy, intoxicating scent of the woman's chamber until the sea, and sun, and salt made it seem no more than a
distant, unpleasant dream.

On this morning, the sight of the ocean was even more enchanting than normal, and not just because it was unlike any
expanse of water I had yet seen. This new view was beautiful,

yes, and warm, but of a distinctly otherworldly appeal that was inexplicably older and less predictable than the seas charted in the land of men. The water was a little too green and the sky a little too orange, and I when I looked overboard I saw unsightly, misshapen shadows that did not resemble any creature I'd seen before gliding about beneath the waves.

Besides that, for the first time since setting out to sea, I now embraced the new day as I had dreamt it when I had stared out into the harbor from the dusty quayside streets of Isla Perla's humid shores. It was the moment I had longed for most, and thought least likely to experience, besides the hope of finding Evangeline herself. This morning I stepped onto the deck for the first time no longer concealed as the young sailor Westley Rivers, but as Merrin Smith. No, not as her either—not the orphan drowning in a million questions who had timidly joined the crew of the pirate ship *Riptide* and spent the past several months lurking in the shadows, reading through stolen, water-damaged texts and trying to avoid the scrutinizing gazes of every man on the crew. She, that Merrin, had been left on the other side of ocean, in a realm where sea myths and legends were reduced to little more than stories in old books. I faced the open waters this morning as Merrin *Jones*, a daughter with a name as tied to the ocean as those of Mélusine and Charybdis themselves, and sailing boldly upon a sea where no man had yet sailed, and perhaps no woman either. The newfound freedom was in perfect harmony with the new break of light outside the ship.

The long length of my hair was let to hang out freely from beneath the brim of my familiar, well-worn hat, and I enjoyed the feel of the wind as it swept through, eagerly blowing the strands into salty tangles. More than anything, in all my months at sea I had craved the sensation of the wind blowing within my hair the same as it did against my face, but had been denied this simple pleasure as I strove to blend in with the men of the crew. Like my hair, this day my body was also free, as between my sudden awakening and being pulled out of the cabin by Winters and Jomo, I had not had an opportunity to apply the bandages I'd worn to conceal my figure—not that they were necessary now. My sex and my identity were known, even if I was still coming to terms with the latter, and I had not yet been pitched overboard because of either. I would have abandoned the hat, too, but it had become too much a part of me to let go—though it did give me a chill to remember it in the grip of the strange creature in the cetone chamber.

Still, finally, and for better or worse, such drudgery was over and I had never felt so comfortable being myself in my entire life as I did right at this moment. The sudden urge to remove the ring from my coat and put it on my hand overwhelmed me and so I did, admiring its sparkle in the sunlight on my hand as I walked. The stone, as if knowing it had been freed, hummed warmly against my skin with an undeniable life force of its own.

AS I FOLLOWED BEHIND THE CAPTAIN AND JOMO, I SAW THAT I had been correct in my assumptions of the *Riptide*'s men. Those I could see were relaxing about the deck, drinking away the rest of the ship's stores or playing dice. Gregory Nip was among the latter, as he would likely always be, laughing and slapping his knee as he joked with a man whose back was turned toward me. Still other men were curled up fast asleep on piles of old cloth or empty sacks that had once been filled with flour in Jomo's kitchen.

The rest were just staring wondrously at the water, grateful to be alive, perhaps, or considering the strange sea on which we now sailed. All of the men had a look of edginess to them, and all stopped what they were doing as I passed, alternating between nods of acknowledgement to amiably raised mugs, and some that pulled off their hats and were silent. Few met my eyes as I moved between them and the rails along the waist of the ship, save for Domingo whose one good eye met mine briefly, a hint of challenge in it, and I stared boldly at him until he averted his gaze and stepped aside. I wasn't sure if the men's distance was for my benefit or the captain's as he marched purposely through his crew with Jomo and myself trailing behind him. It did not feel like a respectful distance, but rather like a sort of hesitancy, and once or twice I though I saw something akin to fear in their eyes.

What did trouble me, however, was the single obvious absence on the decks. The only man not present in the throngs of men relaxing or enjoying themselves, I was painfully aware as I took into account the face of each man as I passed them, was Tom Birch, who laid in unwaking sleep on his rickety cot in the captain's quarters. I wondered if he would ever wake again—if he would ever see this place or me as I now was free to be, and what he would think if he did.

I must have paused, thoughts of Tom's fate dulling the edges of bliss I had allowed to selfishly color my thoughts. Perhaps I had played some part in our survival of the storm, but it had come at a cost that none had paid more dearly than the man who had owed it the least.

"This way," Winters growled impatiently, as if escorting me to this unknown person was a distasteful task that he was anxious to complete. He cast a backward glance over his shoulder as he and Jomo led me in the direction of Captain Winters' favorite perch on the quarterdeck. The taller, darker man said nothing and regarded me with a deadpan face that I could not read through its scars and studs. One of his heavy hands reached back ad wrapped around my forearm and tugged me gently but not unkindly forward, and I quickened my pace.

AT THE LANDING OF THE STAIRS TO THE UPPERMOST DECK MISter Dunn sat perched atop a barrel, smoking one of his cigars he reserved for special occasions. I had seen many expressions pass across this man's face over the course of our time together—sometimes scowling, sometimes stern, and usually in between. Even in his most drunken stupor he had never worn an expression such as he did now. It wasn't a smile, exactly—I don't think the rigid lines of his weathered face would have allowed such a thing—but his eyes were gleaming and he blew soft smoke rings that lit lightly from his tongue as he flicked them into the air. If I hadn't known better, I would have said he looked positively radiant.

In days past I would have thought better of opening my mouth to inquire on the source of his happiness, but this time I did not. Such timorous things were behind me, and after our conversation in the captain's cabin I felt we were passed playing at formalities. "What is it that has you in such good spirits today, Mister Dunn?" I asked. The edges of my words were chilled with suspicion. I ignored the way the side of his mouth not busy with the cigar curled into a smirk. I never cared for it when he made such faces. They were usually at my expense. "In all your stories I don't believe you've ever told me what it is that Bracile means to you?"

The quartermaster fixed me with his black eyes. "Home," he said simply, and his eyes shone like onyx. He pulled again at the cigar without another word, and tapped his heels against the side of the barrel.

Before I could respond, the captain and Jomo halted in front of me, and Winters locked eyes with Dunn in a look that clearly said, *enough*. Dunn smirked again, but his eyes left mine so that he could give his concentration to another smoke ring he let to float in the air between us.

The word—*home*—rung in my ears while the ring thumped on my hand.

Winters remained beside his quartermaster and motioned that I should continue on my own up the stairs that led to the upper deck. Jomo, likewise, stepped aside so that I could continue. Not knowing what else to do, I followed the path cleared before me, stepping up the wooden stairs to the landing above with an ominous feeling tossing in my stomach.

A MAN I DID NOT KNOW SAT UNACCOMPANIED ON THE UPPER deck, seated in the heavy oak chair that had previously resided at the head of the captain's table. His head was cocked to the side and his eyes were watching the water with an obvious weariness as I approached. He was not one of the *Riptide*'s men, of that I was sure, but I had no clue as to from where he had come or how he had arrived on the ship, nor how long he might have been onboard. There were no other ships whose sails could be seen on the horizon, and no rowboats were tied alongside the *Riptides*'s hull. No land was visible in any direction. Perhaps he had arrived in the missing space of time I had slept. This was, of course, the only possible scenario, though if he had been on this side of the seas that would have meant that this stranger had been here all along, and none had ever been said to survive the swallow of Charbydis' throat

At least none had arrived in the heart of the ocean that were human, but as I observed the man more closely I began to suspect that perhaps he was not a mere man after all. There was something odd about him—that much was plain to see as I observed his appearance from where I stood on the edge of the landing. But it was not a frightening sort of difference—not at all like the woman in the cave—though there was something certainly that marked him as *other*. He did not look at me as I approached, but kept his face turned to the sea so that the details of his face were hard to discern. I wished I could see the expression on his face.

The man seated in the captain's chair on the upper deck was grey—grey boots, grey hair, grey skin, and there was a slight transparency to him, like he were not entirely solid, but the shape of a man bound together by fog and shadow. The golden glow of the sun did not light on him, but shone through him. He was spectral, yet solid; I could easily see the sharp edges of his cheekbones where they pushed through the thin skin of his profile. Likewise, his form was so rich in detail I could even see the dark smear of sand beneath his fingernails on the long fingers of his hand where they tapped against his knee. He sat with one leg crossed atop the other, a tricorn hat dangling loosely from the fingers of his other hand at his side.

The edges of his clothing, also grey, floated of their own accord in the still air around him. He wore the trappings of a pirate, all guns and steel. His brocade buccaneer coat hung past his hips, with wide cuffs and a fold-over collar that folded over a grey linen shirt and cotton breeches. He wore boots that were similar to those worn by Captain Winters and which reached nearly to his knees, laced intricately by a material that looked more like seaweed than leather string. Judging by the roots of his hair it had once been rich brown, almost black in color, but even without the effect of its strange colorlessness had faded largely to grey with age, darkened in streaks that wove through it to give it the appearance of aged silver straw. It had the appearance of hair that had been windblown for decades, so long uncombed that it had rolled into spun lengths of cordish, rope-like hair that sprung from his head in a host of uneven tentacles, at least ten in number. Hair the same shade descended along the length of his jaw, past a grey ear featuring a grey stone, and then parted to cover both the top and bottom of his mouth, rounding at the point of his chin, and then curving upward again. The weathered skin of his face marked him as older, older than the captain but not nearly as old as Dunn. He was lean but not frail, pulsing with an ethereal vitality as he sat with surprisingly stately posture, like some aged king waiting boredly on his throne.

"Miss Jones," he said without turning to me. His voice was as deep and rolling as the boundless sea itself. It was not raspy like the captain's, but it thundered with the same powerful tenor that could command men and sea alike. It was a captain's voice, and the most familiar voice that I had never heard. "I always knew you'd find your way to this place, love."

"You know my name," I said. My voice shook and I cleared my throat. "But I do not know yours."

"I am happy to see you," he continued as if he hadn't heard me. He rose to his feet, tossing the hat in the seat of the chair as he stepped to the railing, which he gripped so tightly with both hands that his grey knuckles turned white. He bowed his head and the cords of his hair rushed forward, writhing in their own current above him. I had never seen a sword as long as the one he wore, and was not sure how I hadn't noticed it before. It was almost like another appendage, extending from its hilt rose at his ribs until the blade reached well past his knee and hovered only an inch or two off the ground. "Though, of course, I would have wished it were not under such conditions." He sighed with a sound like resignation and relaxed his grip on the railing. "I would have wished so many things different, love. None of this is as I would have intended it to be. I had only wanted to keep you safe."

"Who are you?" I asked again, although I felt I already knew. I took a step forward. "Who am I to you?"

He didn't answer, but turned at last to face me, and at his throat I saw a gleaming piece of white shell—the same as the one on my hand—strung on a length of grey leather. I saw, too, that dozens of spirally coiled shells of sea snails were encrusted in his rope-like hair, and that the skin that was visible beneath the edges of his sleeves on his forearm and at the collar of his throat had a slightly scaly texture to it. His face was gaunt, and he had a thin nose and even thinner lips, but then I met his eyes, which were the only thing of him that were not grey. They were large, kind, and full of life, and as I looked into them I found that I was looking into hazel eyes the same as mine.

I was staring into the eyes of Captain Davy Jones. I was staring into the eyes of my father.

XVI

You're Davy Jones." "*Captain* Davy Jones, aye," he corrected me with a self-depreciating smile, spreading his palms upward with a slight flourish as he turned and leaned backward against the railing. I watched as the tails of his coat followed at their own pace behind him, the ends swirling around his legs with a languid, water-like motion. His hair swished lively and then settled in the air above his head. The twisted cords never quite stopped moving, but continued to wave in place independently of each other like a host of grey tentacles against a backdrop of cloudless, copper sky. Taking in his full height I saw that he was tall, by my estimation as tall as Tom Birch, nearly six and a half feet or close to it, and his frame was fashioned with the same commanding posture that built Winters or even Jomo, though his movements were markedly different. His were loose and calm and contained none of the pent-up fury so uneasily kept by the other men. Liquid, that was the word that seemed best to describe him—liquid and grey, like the ocean on a foggy day. "And you be called Jones, too, I believe," he said in a knowing sort of way.

"Aye," I agreed, my voice barely above a whisper as I tried not to stare at the gleaming white shell around his neck. I could not bring myself to meet his eyes that were so similar to mine, and so I fixed my gaze on his grey coat instead, scrutinizing the embroidery at the lapel. The chaos in my heart had not yet decided if it wanted to laugh, or cry, or scream. I pushed the feelings away, and tried to focus on what the grey man had said, still struggling to accept that he was indeed a man and not a figment of my imagination or worse: another temporal dream that would soon evaporate into nothingness like the woman in the cove. "That's what I've been told."

He laughed, and it was a dense, musical sound—a rumbling of percussive beats that seemed to have a direct line to my heart, which itself was still beating wildly and without rhythm. He touched a long finger to the bridge of his nose as if he were thinking, and then said in a good-natured way, "And who was it told you that? It was Bullet, that clever sold dog, was it not?"

No one besides Tom Birch had ever called the quartermaster by that name, and so it took me a moment to realize whom he was referring to, shocking me when I did. This strange captain, my father, trapped on the other side of the ocean from which no man had returned—a place the old quartermaster himself had called home—had spoken the name fondly, referring to Mister Brandon Dunn not by his rank or his proper name, but by the name of a friend. I wondered what strange story might connect these men. Dunn had said he'd been the one to deliver me into Mrs. Emery's care at the House of Swallows, but he had never hinted to anything more that might explain his connections to these legend made flesh. There was a mist over the whole thing, a murky veil that covered everything in a substance that was not quite real, and not quite dream, but something else—something *thinner*, that word again—that somehow made up the fabric of my life and the events around it. How long had it been that these men had sailed upon the seas, and in what ways had their paths crossed and interwoven so that their connection with my own was a result of inevitably rather than consequence? What strange secrets was I left to still discover, what other revelations that would shake the very bedrock of all that I had assumed real in my life? I could not remember when I had arrived at Isla Perla any more clearly than I could know for certain how many years had passed that I'd been there. A dozen, two, more, less. Each was as likely as the other. My infirm grasp on time was much the same as that of the men onboard the *Riptide* who could not seem to count how many years they had sailed under Winters' command or—save Jomo, whose life and sanity would have been forfeit without the aid of Winters, Dunn, and Evangline Dahl—where they had come from before they had found themselves a member of his crew. Such questions of time and sequences of events were great, winding mysteries that tangled up with each other and grew tighter each time I tied to unwind them. However, undoing such mysteries would hold until another time and so I set these questions aside for now.

"Aye, it was Dunn," I confirmed, not able to bring myself to speak of him so familiarly as Jones or Birch would. "He told me so only a few days ago, when we sailed on the frozen sea on the other side of the ocean, though why he kept such a thing a secret for so long I could not guess." The Captain Jones lifted a well-defined grey eyebrow but did not say anything, waiting, perhaps, as I summoned my courage to ask the single most important question I had ever asked. After a few moments, I did. "Is it true? Am I … well, am I a *Jones*?" The word was heavy, as if it were so much more than a name, and it was.

He gave a small smile that looked half-apologetic and half-proud. "Aye, love. It is true, that you are."

We looked at each other for a few moments, letting unsaid words pass between a father and daughter who were barely more than strangers. There were so many things I wanted to say—so many things that I had planned to say if ever I found this moment—and now that it was here, nothing came. There were too many, and not enough, and none of them felt quite right.

"Don't hold it against the old sea lion, love," Davy Jones said, returning to our mutual friend Mister Dunn who had kept my father's secret and mine for all those innumerable years. "After all, it wasn't his secret to tell. I would have told you myself as soon as I had the occasion, but I expect he had a reason to tell you before we had the chance to meet."

I didn't know what to say to that so I said nothing. Instead, I pursed my lips together and tugged the brim of my hat over my eyes, shielding both the sun and Jones' permeating gaze. I was glad to have known my true name that night on the frozen sea, even if it had come from Dunn and under such circumstances. The knowing alone had given me strength, and courage, and had renewed my spirit at a time when it had been nearly broken. Without that name, I might not have made it through the storm, much less made it here, and here on these unfamiliar tides I was unsure what the consequences might be now that I had led us all to a place that would not let us leave.

When Davy Jones spoke again his voice was softer, kinder—the same patient tone that one might reserve for coaxing a frightened animal out of hiding, though I was not an animal, nor was I scared. I was sad, really. In fact, I was overwhelmed with a deep, guttural, longing type of sadness about what I had known and not known, and the price others might have paid on my behalf—on Erik Winters' and Brandon Dunn's and mine. Had we condemned them all in our quest to reclaim the pieces of our hearts that had been stolen from us?

"What's your given name, love?" he asked now, halting my own inner monologue. "What do they call you back on Isla Perla? I never had a chance to know it."

"Merrin," I said, swallowing down the pain that rose with it. "Formerly, Merrin Smith it would seem."

His smile was warm and there was a glint in his eye, like I'd said something that sparked his interest. "Lovely name, that is. Merrin." He closed his eyes and repeated it, "*Merrin*. Suits you, it does. Do you know what it means?"

Shrugging, I averted my eyes. "It doesn't mean anything. It's just a name. I don't even know who gave it to me." *It was an orphan's name,* I almost said, but didn't. It was a petulant comment, I knew, and an unfair one. It was also untrue. Mrs. Emery had given me that name, and although I had my quarrels with the strict mistress of the island's brothel, she had been the only mother I'd ever known. Still, it broke my heart a little that my own father did not know my name, even thought that was perhaps unfair as well. After all, I had only just learned his. Jones made a *tsk*-ing sound and swept his hand graciously in the air before him, again demonstrating that eerie, noble-like quality that marked him as more than a simple pirate, even one who held the title of captain. "Aye, love, but names hold power, whether you know it or not. It is still there, underneath, waiting all the while like a great sunken thing, waiting to be found. That's a lesson you've learned more than most. It was the power of a name that brought you and the rest of your crew here," he swept his arms open in front of him, "that brought you back to me at last in a place where no man has yet sailed."

"It was, and I have," I agreed, thinking again on the strength the name Jones had given me, and the strength it had not. Still,

THE ISLE OF GOLD

there was a deep bitterness seeded within me, and I could not help the sharp edges that crept into my voice. My next words were high and harsh, each one a small, poison-tipped arrow that flew from the bowstring of my lips. "But I've also learned that to not have a name is to rob someone of their power, to steal from them a part of their very core, and that is a lesson I've known even longer—every day for ever year for the past many years that I've lived without one, wasting my life away alone, and as nothing more than a nameless orphan kept as a kitchen maid in a filthy island brothel. I was left behind like a piece of unwanted cargo." I stomped my boot on the deck as if it were punctuation, and then as if propelled by the energy of my own anger I took one step forward, and then another, and another, until I was so close to my father that I stood in the place where his shadow should have been but wasn't—so close that if I had wanted to I could have wrapped my arms around him. I could have held my body close against his, embracing the only blood relative I had ever known, and I wanted to. I was desperate to. But I did not. Suddenly, I realized I was angry—angry that I had been abandoned, that I had never known my own name, my parents, and that they had never known me; angry that I still had more questions than answers, perhaps more even than when I had started. I was standing in the presence of a man who was more myth than real, of a legend who'd somehow become my father, and I wasn't even sure he was human or what sort of implications that might hold for me or what it might mean for the men who had become my brothers on this journey. As something more, perhaps, as my thoughts brushed as they always did past Tom Birch. I blinked the image of him, unconscious on the cot, out of my mind.

A spark of something that might have been remorse moved

across his face, and then Davy Jones, my father, sighed another deep, full-throated, sad sigh. "No, love, you were not unwanted. Never *un*wanted. I never wanted to send you off to Isla Perla, but I had no other choice to keep you safe. I was going to come back for you, but then I was trapped here." He motioned at the water. "Trapped in this damned place for more years that I can count by a being too bitter to ever let me go."

I ignored him. "And now here I stand, and you wish to talk to me about the power of names like it's some buried treasure."

He sighed. "No, not treasure. Names hold power, that's true enough, but power isn't always a good thing. Aye, I fear I've cursed you to the same fate as I, and for that I am truly sorry, love."

"What fate is that?"

He turned and looked back toward … into the deep greenish-blue water over the edge of the ship. It was still and smooth, like polished sea glass, but it was not clear. The color was thick and impenetrable, warning of dangers that lurked within its depths. "The same as that's reserved for all who sail under the name of Jones. The curse of the sea herself."

His words were heavy with a nameless agony. For as long as I had heard stories of the sea, I had heard men refer to it as a pronoun. Such was the manner of sailors who cherished nothing as they did their waters and their ships and their gold. For these men, *she* was their deepest love, and they spoke of her with the same affection as another man might speak of a woman. But Captain Davy Jones spoke of her as if she were indeed a woman flesh and blood.

"And what is that curse?" I asked.

With a last yearning look at the water, my father returned

to the chair, settling himself once more with his grey hat on his lap. He gestured to me, inviting me closer, and this time I went to him, lowering myself to rest against an overturned crate near where he sat. Up close I could see each of the lines in his skin; they appeared soft in contrast to the scale-like texture that glistened in patches at his throat and elbows. Without the glare of the sun he appeared more solid than I had initially thought. I resisted the urge to touch him, to verify that he was real. I could see now that he had once been a very handsome man, strong-boned with an expressive face, but time and age had hardened him and turned those features stiff and hardly recognizable. I could see my own countenance in his—the same eyes, yes, as well as the same cheekbones, the same curve of lip and thin nose.

He smiled at me as I rested beside him, and it was my smile I saw reflected in his face. "Once, long ago," he began, and his eyes went soft, glazed over by memory, "I fell in love with the sea. And I don't mean the shining blue waters of the ocean, nay, but the sea herself made flesh. The very spirit of the sea. She was beautiful and terrible, and I loved her for it, and she loved me, dreadful pirate that I was … that I am. Loved me so much she forsook the water for a life with a mortal man. But other gods cursed her for leaving her home and obligations to the tide behind, and it weren't no matter—being away from it made a hole in her heart that after a time turned her cruel and unforgiving. And while I was off sailing the seas, taking and bending it to my will, I became so consumed with the quest to free her from her own bitterness that I lost sight of the woman I loved, until she forgot me altogether." He paused for a moment, lost in a thought too painful to speak.

"I underestimated her, the woman and the sea. I made a

terrible mistake. And in the end I was foolish enough that I traded my soul to sail the seas forever, thinking it might redeem me in her eyes, might grant me grace. But the sea is a wild and unpredictable thing, and she does not suffer herself to be forgiving of the errors of men. And so now I am bound to it, this place that is both the sea and farthest from it, condemned to haunt these waters until the very sea herself sets me free. I had hoped that the daughters Jones would be spared. I did my best to keep you both safe, but it would seem my sins are enough to have cursed us all. It would seem that she be willing to forget she ever loved any of us."

"Daughters Jones?" I repeated, forgetting all the rest, emphasis on the plural.

"Aye," he said. "For we three be here now, locked together in this cursed place, the Captain Jones and his two daughters, Merrin," he placed a hand upon my shoulder, "and Evangeline."

XVII

I COULD NOT SPEAK. I COULD NOT BREATHE. MY ENTIRE BODY was numb with shock and disbelief as I took in my father's words, hearing them but not quite grasping their meaning as they reverberated against one another in my mind. Every time I received an answer to one question, a hundred more took its place, the mysterious coil that made up the truth of my existence ever tightening as things I thought I had known came unglued and contradictory, spinning and retracting like a giant, unbound top. I had always felt a connection between Mistress Dahl and myself, this of course, was indisputable. For as long as I could recall it had been an unrelenting bond, impossible to articulate but undeniably strong, though I could not say that it ever had felt familial, but more of a sort of reverence for a woman I had idolized as a goddess. I wondered now if she had been as ignorant to this knowledge as I had been, or if she had known all along, and whether she had felt the same unyielding pull to me as I had to her. I saw her again as she was in my earliest memory, golden hair reflecting the sunlight as she smiled at me across the sand-covered gravel of Isla Perla.

My sister.

How different so many things might have been, if only I had been privy to this secret. How I might have left the brothel and gone to her, how together we might have changed our fate so that neither of us would have ventured out into such strange and unknown waters. It was no matter now. I had left Isla Perla to find Evangeline, and now I had more of a reason for it than I had before—as much of a reason as Erik Winters himself. We sailed to find a woman we loved, and I had discovered so much more along the way than I had ever expected.

My father's hand was still on my shoulder and he squeezed it gently, reassuringly. He did not speak again, although I wished he would. There was so much more still that I needed and wanted to know, even if I did not have the words to ask.

This was just as well as the white flame of Mister Dunn's wild hair announced his sudden arrival on the upper deck, and then the rest of his wiry form appeared quickly below it as he scrambled up the steps. His movements were marked with agitation, and he made no effort to excuse his interruption. I knew at once that something had changed while I had been in private concert with Captain Davy Jones and away from the rest of the crew on the lower decks. Whatever it was had not been for the better, that much was plain to see from the look on the quartermaster's face. The smirk had been replaced with a pained expression that twisted at his features. His eyes, shiny before with anticipation, had darkened into impermeable darkness and his skin was been relieved of its flush so that it was nearly as grey as my father's.

"Jones," he said, addressing both of us at once with a scratchy voice that was not his usual tone. I pushed myself up off the crate so abruptly that it scattered away behind me. My father was instantly beside me, one hand on the hilt of his weapon and the other rested protectively against the small of my back. "Both of ye be needed in the captain's cabin, an' quick. Tom Birch has taken a turn for the worst, and it ain't be lookin' like he has much time left." His black eyes fixed on my father and there was a hint of knowledge in them that I was not party to. He was a man of sharp questions, and sharp solutions. "We act now or we lose the boy, Captain."

THE CURTAINS IN THE CAPTAIN'S OFFICE WERE CLOSED AGAINST the bright sun, blanketing the room in shadow except for the little flickers of light that came from the soft glow of a dozen or so candles stationed around the cot where Tom Birch lay. Winters had been sitting on a low stool beside the bed at Tom's side, and he rose when we entered the cabin, his icy eyes moving from Dunn's to my father's to mine in turn with a look that demanded in no uncertain terms that something be done about the boatswain's state. Then, he withdrew wordlessly to the other side of the room, walking solidly, heavily, across the floor. When he reached his desk he crossed his arms gruffly atop his chest and returned his cold eyes to Tom's body, staring so intently that if it had been possible for him to will the man awake he would have woken instantly.

In the time since I'd been away, someone—presumably the doctor, Mr. Clarke—had covered Tom's body in layers of heavy blankets so thick that all that was left to see of the man was the top of his sand-colored head where it rested on a bundle of soft cloth fashioned into a pillow at the edge of the cot. Even with his eyes closed, the unnatural stiffness of death had already begun to overtake his features so that a terse expression set across his face unlike one I'd ever seen on the boatswain in life. His color was a ghostly white and the pink of his lips had faded to a sickly, mawkish blue. The doctor was still bumbling about the bed in an unproductive, useless sort of way the same as he had been when I awoke, and was occupied currently with the business of tucking and retucking bits of stray fabric as if it had any purpose whatsoever. He was sweaty and distracted, and when his piggish little eyes finally lifted to see who had entered the room and he saw the great Captain Davy Jones, flanked on either side by Dunn and myself, his jaw came unhinged, the little pink hole hanging open amidst the company of several chins. He stared stupidly at us, his eyes stuck on my father like an animal bound for slaughter, and he attempted once or twice to say something, causing his jowls to waggle loosely in the space below his chins, but the only sound that resulted from his efforts was a hitch-pitched whining.

"Get out," Winters growled savagely from the other side of the room, and this was all the permission the little man needed to instantly abandon his charge and scurry out, ducking alongside the narrow opening of the thin cabin door as he stuffed himself through it.

The doctor gone, I crossed the room in three quick steps and fell to Tom's side, touching the backs of my hands to the skin of his face as I took my place on the stool where Captain Winters had previously kept watch. The flesh of his cheek was cool and clammy to the touch, like his body had been left to lie beneath a pool of cold water though it was dry and did not even have a sheen of sweat to cool it. It felt like chilled wax and I recoiled when I touched it, but only for a second. I studied the stack of blankets for movement but they were piled so high and dense that I could not tell if they rose with his breath in the dim light of the room, and I shoved them away so that they fell heavily to the floor. I pressed my palms into Tom's still chest and then my finger against his throat, but as I ran my hands across his body I could not find a pulse beating with life in his neck, nor could I feel the thump of his heart pounding within his chest. I leaned my head

THE ISLE OF GOLD

to his, and waited to feel an exhale that never came, and when I touched my lips to his I felt no breath and no life lingering with him. The stone on my hand flared with a peculiar, white light and then dimmed again, flaming hot and then cold where it sat on my finger.

"He's dead," I cried, the grief swelling within me, choking me, winding my heart so viciously within my chest that I could feel it tear as it ripped in two. "Tom Birch is dead."

XVIII

I LET OUT A SOB AND BURROWED MY HEAD IN THE FABRIC OF Tom's shirt, gripping the thin cloth tightly in each of my fists as my breath came in great racking heaves against the unnatural stillness of his chest. With each inhale I could feel his body growing colder; I could sense the indescribable substance of soul lifting and quietly vacating his form, leaving behind nothing more than the husk of a body that was no longer required. The protocol of grief was as unfamiliar to me as were the behaviors of love, but there was a sharp stabbing pain in my chest that I could only assume was the shattering of my heart. No tears came, but I wouldn't have cared if they did. There was no space for dignity when your heart was broken, and the fragments of what had been mine were being wrenched from my body with each anguished gasp, scraping and tearing at my throat as the noise of them filled the room.

"He's not dead," came a growl from the other side of the cabin. I thought it was Winters' voice, but I could just as readily been my father's, or Dunn's. It did not matter. Whoever it was, his words did not reach me. I felt a draining emptiness tug at me, sucking the life inside of me away in greedy pulls so that deep, hollow ravines were trenched in the recesses of my soul, and I did not fight against it, but let myself be emptied sip by sip, surrendering to sorrow. My father had spoken of the curse of Jones, and the death of Tom Birch was my penance, a price on the heads of men who loved women of the sea and for which everyone paid. Whether I willed it or not, I was to blame for his death, and that knowledge was more than I could bear.

A hand came down firmly atop my shoulder, but I ignored it. After a moment the hand's mate rested atop my other shoulder, both of them rubbing me in a supporting, comforting kind of way at first, then becoming more insistent and less consoling, until I became aware that the fingers of the hands were pressing into my skin as they attempted to pull me away from Tom's body. I strained against these cursed hands with all my might, gripping the fabric of Tom's shirt tighter as I struggled to relearn how to breathe in the wake of this new reality, the one that did not include the sweet, charming boatswain that had befriended me, perhaps cared for me as I had grown to care for him. If I were to be removed from his body, then it would be by force. I would not allow it to be dumped overboard like waste the same as the navigator's had been. Tom Birch deserved so much more than that.

The fingers grew impatient, digging painfully into the tender space below my shoulder. A stinging, bitter pain came then, the slicing of fingernails into my flesh as they bit through the cloth. The pain was sharp and immediate, but it cleared my head of the swirling torrent I'd been trapped in. To this was joined the un-mistakable voice of Brandon Dunn as it arrived against my ear. I felt the sensation of his head as his hair brushed against mine, his breath sweet with brandy and cigar smoke when it filled my ears.

"The captain be right, lass," he whispered edgily as his sting-ing fingertips pulled at me again, not bothering to clarify which captain he referred to. There was a tremor in his voice, a slightly uplifted twinge that caught my attention more than any words that could have been said. It resounded within me, this unbeliev-able note that sounded remarkably like hope. "The man ain't dead yet," he continued, his warm breath still sweet against my ear. He smiled and it was a bitter smile; I could not see it but I could feel the edges of it as they curved upward against my cheek from where his face hung above mine. "There may still be a way to save him."

At this, I pulled my face from Tom's chest, a matter that was no small feat under the weight of my grief. Blinking back the wetness that swam across my vision, I tried to focus my eyes on the men standing stoically about in the room wearing serious, unsympathetic faces—all except for Dunn, who wore an expression of apprehension and urgency that was a poor substitute for sorrow. How did they not feel this, this overwhelming grief? A life at sea was a harsh one, yes, but did they feel nothing, these heartless pirates? How could they gaze upon the body that had belonged to Tom Birch and not feel as I did, empty and broken? My eyes found Erik Winters and I stared angrily at him, forgetting for once that he was my captain, that he was the man I had watched with my own eyes as he'd run his blade through Rabbie's heart at the merest hint of insolence, the man I'd pledged to follow and obey, come what may in times of peril. This death was as much Winters' fault as it was mine—he who had his desire to reclaim Evangeline before the lives of his crew, who had known the storm into which we sailed and said nothing ... done *nothing*. He returned my stare, his cold, unfeeling eyes locked on mine. I loosed my grip on Tom's shirt and shoved Dunn aside, and then stood resolutely with my body between Tom's and the rest of the room. Fueled by grief, I rose to challenge the captain.

My hand found the hilt of the shell guard hanger on my belt and gripped the short handle of the short sword. I could handle a sword well enough, thanks to the men on Isla Perla who'd thought me boy enough to teach me the art of fencing, but my skill was piteously far below that of any of the men in this room. Even so, the look of amusement that crossed through the captain's eyes infuriated me and I used that fury to free the blade from its sheath, brandishing it in the air before me. It wobbled once or twice, but I gritted my teeth and planted my feet until both the glinting blade and I were steady. Meanwhile, Winters said nothing, but continued to meet my gaze, staring at me from his perch atop his desk. I watched angrily as he lifted an unlit cigarette to his mouth, and then in intentionally slow, unhurried movements he struck a match against the edge of the desk and lit a candle. This he brought to his lips, touching it lightly to the tip of the cigarette and inhaling a lungful of smoke that he pushed out of a slightly parted mouth with the small red triangle of his tongue—all without breaking his stare.

When he spoke only his lips moved. "Lower your sword, girl," he stated in a toneless voice.

I did not, but my eyes passed to my father, who was also staring at Winters. He was silent and unmoving, and if it weren't for the coils of his hair—which writhed in the air above him like a collection of small, angry grey eels jerking and snapping with sharp, pointed tips as they twitched uneasily—he might have been a statue in the corner of the room. His large, brown eyes had hardened into amber stone as he watched the other captain, and his hand was on his belt. It was clear that neither had any fondness for the other.

Once more Dunn had his hand on my shoulder again, pulling at me. However, my eyes had fixed back upon Winters and his smooth, expressionless face, and I would not be moved any easier now than I would before. "Put it down, lass," Dunn muttered softly in my ear, his voice hushed like it was only meant for me. "And listen to me. Birch ain't dead, not yet. But we be wasting precious time with this now."

"Take another look, Mister Dunn," I snapped, resettling both of my hands around the hilt of the sword, which was beginning to feel heavy in my grasp. I did not take my eyes away from Winters and I did not believe the quartermaster—I could not believe him. I had felt the stillness in Tom's chest myself, had heard the silence where his heartbeat should have been and knew death when I saw it. Even now I knew that coldness was creeping over him, transforming the softness of his skin to the icy stone of a corpse's shell. I shivered even though it was warm in the cabin. "If he is not dead, then can you be so kind as to explain what he is? There is no life within him. He draws no breath, his skin is cold to the touch. How can he possibly not be dead in a state as this?"

"He ain't dead," Dunn repeated flatly, his voice firmer this time as if there could be no disagreement. I studied the captain's face as I felt Dunn press closer, his body so close it nearly touched mine. His claim made no sense, but while I knew the quartermaster to be secretive and shrewd and even suspicious at times, I had never known him to be a liar. On the contrary, his words, often unbelievable, had been true thus far, and from Charybdis to Davy Jones, no one had contradicted him. I considered this as I allowed his hand to lie on the flat part of the blade and push it down until the point tapped the floor. I could not be certain, but I suspected I saw the captain's frozen eyes thaw as he glowered at me over the fiery tip of his cigarette. He did not speak, and my father did not take his eyes from him.

"Bullet is right. Young Mister Birch is not yet dead. He is

trapped in a place that passes between, love, a state that is worse than death," said Davy Jones then, stepping up in front of me so that he towered above Dunn and I like a grey shadow that eclipsed my view of Winters. His face was unreadable, and haunted, and I could learn nothing from his grey expression. "The sea has not yet claimed his soul. She is letting it wait here."

"For what?" I challenged, but lighter this time. Immediately I thought of *her*—the woman in the cove. She was connected to all of this, although I wasn't sure how, just that she was. She *was* the sea, and somehow she was holding Tom Birch's soul in ransom.

"You." Captain Winters' voice brought the answer from his place at the far end of the room. My father stepped aside with a noise like the frustrated rustling of sea grass, positioning himself by my side so that I could see Winters again. He stayed close, one of his grey arms rising protectively across me as though he did not entirely trust the other captain.

"This does not concern you, Erik," Jones snapped.

A lesser man might have cowered, but not Winters. "The fuck it doesn't," he returned. Throughout all of this, Winters had remained perched atop his desk, watching with his arms crossed tightly over his chest and chewing at his cigarette. Now he looked off to some point in the distance, and when his eyes returned to mine there was something in them I had not seen before. I could not name it, but it was a similar look I had seen in Claudette's eyes when she said her final good-byes outside of The Goodnight Mermaid. He touched his fingers together over the candle flame, snuffing it out so that he was lost to shadow. The piece of shell at his neck, the same as the one on my hand and around my father's neck, shone faintly in the darkness of the cabin as if influenced by its own inner light. He stalked toward me in the dimness of the cabin, the blue of his eyes catching the light of the stone and sparking fiercely, like steel scraped across ice.

"You can save him, Miss Jones," Erik Winters said, his voice a rasping echo that reverberated inside of me. "And you alone."

"How?" It was the only question that mattered.

"No," my father's voice cut in. I jerked in surprise but Winters did not as he advanced. My father inserted himself with the same protective posture as I stood in front of Tom between the oncoming captain and me, standing sideways between the two of us so that the pair of his hazel eyes could be divided to watch us both. The two men faced each other, locked in a silent debate of history and loyalties of which I had no part. I could feel the tension between them and it was suffocating. "I will not allow it, Erik. She will not bind herself to him. You and I both know all too well the consequences of such an action, and I will not allow my daughter or this boy to suffer it. No!" The last was a roar.

"What you will or will not allow means nothing." Winter voice was a low, predatory snarl as he stopped no more than a sword's length away. He was roughly the same height as my father, and so their eyes bored into each other as they faced one other, each of them just as fierce and unyielding as the other. They were two unearthly forces—my father as grey and cold as stony statue, and Winters, fire and lightning made flesh.

"She is my daughter," Jones said, his voice stern and definite.

"And this is my ship," Winters countered, and his voice stabbed heavily on the last. "I am the captain here, and she is a member of my crew. That boy is my charge. You know as well as I do the reason Tom Birch has spent his life on this ship, Jones." The captain's voice took on a jocular tone, but the look on his face was that of an unmistakable threat. "Or have you forgotten?"

Something flickered across my father's face, but he was not moved. If anything, he stood more solidly, more resolute in his decision. "None of that matters any longer. He belongs to the sea now. Merrin cannot save him."

"It has already started." Winters pointed an incriminating finger in Tom's direction. "You know it as well as I do. Look at him, and see it for yourself." He turned his eyes to me and looked at me intently with an expression that was as commanding as it was unsettling. I would have been made uncomfortable by his hostile expression had it not been for the growing passion that pushed itself urgently against the inside of my chest.

Dunn contributed a small grunt of confirmation. "I'm 'fraid it be so," he said in the tone reserved for moments of dire diplomacy. "She still be possess—"

"No," Jones snapped, and the word thundered in the small space of the cabin, the octave of his voice rising so loud that I clapped my hands to my ears in fear that they might shatter from the noise of it. He did not look at Tom, but I did, and I saw nothing more than what I had already observed before. Whatever these men might see, I saw only death.

When I returned to them, Winters was in Jones' face, anger seeping through the cracks in his stoic façade. "I will not allow the boy to die, Jones," he said in a venomous voice that paused between each syllable. "Not while there remains the power to save him."

My father brought himself to his full height, rising inches above the only slightly smaller man so that he stared down at him as if from a lofty height. "You are powerless to do anything about it, Erik," he replied with a snarl. "Or do you wish to condemn his soul to the same hellish fate as yours?"

"What do you know of hell?" Winters' voice was a deep, menacing growl. "You who have condemned us all."

A tension as thick as quicksand settled upon the room. For a moment it felt like my lungs were collapsing, and try as I might I could not find the strength to draw in a breath. The pressure continued until the edges of my vision blurred, causing the room and the men around me to become slightly out of focus as they breathed metaphorical fire at each other, each as unwilling to break as the other.

And then finally came Dunn's voice, breaking through the tension like a wave crashing down upon land. "Enough!" he demanded with an expression of pure exasperation on his craggy, sea hardened face. "It will no' matter either way if the boy passes while the two of you fight abou' it."

"Tell me how to save him," I demanded as I slid the blade of my sword between my two captains, putting myself between the two titans as best as I could manage. Three pairs of eyes—one blue, one black, one brown—turned to gaze upon me and they all featured different emotions. "Tell me how, and I will do it."

My father gave a strangled, rasping sound and red flared in his cheeks despite their ghostly pallor. He shook his head as if genuinely disappointed. "You know not what you do. The boy will die. I wish it were not so, but it must be this way. It is not your choice."

"In fact ..." I began, diverting my eyes from one captain so that I stared into the cold, blue eyes of the other. "In fact, it is very much my choice, whatever this *choice* be. If I am the one to make it, then the decision lies with me." I sucked in a deep breath and returned my short sword to its sheath, giving my back to the three men as I turned to face Tom's body. He had paled to a skeletal grey, nearly the same color that painted my father. "If it will spare Birch's life, then I choose it."

When Winter's spoke again his voice sounded proud. "You have the same spirit as your sister," he remarked, and I got the impression there was more to his words than what he said.

I had no clue how I might save him—what this *binding* was the men had alluded to—but somehow deep within my bones I knew that it began with laying my hands upon Tom, and so I made to do just that, reaching forward so that I could rest my palms on his chest. Ancient words that my lips had never spoken formed on my tongue, little more than phonetic imitations of their true form, and I felt my eyes close as I opened my mouth to say them. There was a scuffling sound of feet then, and a hand closed around my wrist as I reached to touch Tom's forehead. The hand that held me was grey, and flecked with glittering, iridescent scales. "There may be another way," Jones confessed, although he did little to hide his misgivings. "I can't save young Mister Birch, not exactly. I cannot restore him, but I can give him a place aboard my crew."

"What does that mean?" I asked. "What does it mean to sail with Captain Davy Jones?"

"It means that he will not die," answered my father, and there was resignation in his face. "But he will not live. He will be part of the crew, part of the curse, until such time that the sea decides to set us free. And if there be anyone left who can break this curse, it be you, love."

"That's not good enough," Winters snarled. "You cannot do this, Jones. You cannot consign Tom Birch to sail with the dead any more than you can your daughter to free them." There was movement again, and I could feel but not see what took place behind me. Whatever it was, Winters did not come forward again and I thought perhaps Dunn had managed to stay his hand though I could not imagine how.

"Jones," Winters barked again from somewhere behind my back.

"There is no other way," said my father as he knelt down beside the cot where Tom Birch lay. "If she binds him to herself now, we might lose the advantage we need to escape this hell. The sea will react without giving Merrin a chance." I looked once more at my father, and then over my shoulder to the other men, and to this I saw Dunn nod as Winters tightened his jaw, unconvinced but permitting.

Jones pressed the palm of his right hand, fingers splayed open like the points of a star, on top of the dead man's chest, and I watched in amazement as a pale green light erupted beneath his hand, spreading outward so that it washed over Tom's form completely. A swishing sound—like a soft ocean breeze—moved within the light, quickening Tom's body with conscious life as I saw his chest rise and fall with newfound breath. Color returned to his body, or it started to, the pale pink of living flesh blooming in the skin of his face, recasting the lifeless blue of his lips, and paling to a soft sandy yellow that encircled his hair before it dulled to a faint, watery grey, leaving Tom's body unfinished, like a charcoal portrait to which no color had been added.

While these changes were happening to Tom, I saw that changes were also happening to my father, as if the process affected both men in tandem, pulling life from one and passing it into the other. Where it touched Tom, the dark grey skin of my father's hand was lightening, the solid grey fading to a hazy, fog-like consistency that fractured and crackled, recasting itself from the smooth flesh of a man's arm and into gleaming silver scales.

By the time Tom's mouth opened to inhale a replenishing lungful of air, so many scales had consumed my father's hand that it looked as if he wore a glove made from the body of a fish. As I studied him closely, I realized more scales had also been added to the collection at his throat, and his tentacle-like hair was longer, the edges of his short beard curling in toward themselves to form new tendrils at the edge of his jaw. A row of acorn barnacles lined the side of his face.

"You did not tell me what this would cost you," I said as what was left of my father dissolved further into a relic of the sea.

To which he replied, withdrawing his hand as he did, "My fate is sealed, love. But perhaps there is redemption for me yet."

He stood and stepped backward so I could settle into the space he'd left. I wanted to ask questions about what had occurred, what sort of transmission had taken place that had traded life from my father into the man on the bed, but I did not. Instead, I took Tom's head in both of my hands, cradling him gently as I turned his face to me. His eyes were heavy and half lidded, the whites that showed glassy and shiny in the same way that a dead animal's eyes might gleam when they rolled upward, unseeing. His lips were parted ever so slightly, sipping small breaths too small and shallow even to raise his chest in a full intake of air.

I waited anxiously for Tom to open his eyes, to speak so that I could hear his calm, friendly voice saying *"Oi, Rivers"* as it was want to do, and I gasped, excited as he moved his hand to clasp mine. His eyelids fluttered and then breath caught and died in my throat as they opened fully, revealing not brilliant green eyes the color of the saltwater, but dull, grey, soulless eyes instead. Tom Birch, or the thing that had taken his form, stared at me, through me, and there was no recognition in his eyes.

XIX

I DID NOT SEE WHAT HAPPENED NEXT. I WAS USHERED QUICKLY out of the cabin by Dunn and Winters as they left the strangely silent version of Tom Birch with his new, unwilling captain. I had questions, innumerable questions, but as was becoming all too common had not the time or opportunity to ask them in the flurry of mysterious activity that continued to surround me since the moment we'd found ourselves on the frozen sea.

Winters, still angry, glared at me as he pushed out of our assembly and made his way in swift, furious steps toward the forecastle of the ship where he climbed the small flight of stairs and took watch out over the bowsprit. I watched him go, and then felt Dunn at my elbow. "Don't trouble yerself, lass," he mused, eyes affixed to some point far over the water, staring at something that I could not see as he peered hard with the same sightless stare of someone peering into their own thoughts. "Between Winters and Jones, I've always found Erik Winters to be the more reasonable of the two."

I wasn't sure if this was meant to comfort or terrify me. It had the effect of both. "And what of Tom?" I asked. "What is that thing he has become? He looks like a ghost still possessed with life, but not like the man I had known at all ... something else, something other, and it aches to my very soul to see him like so. Would it have been the same if I had done it—'saved him' as you said? What happens now?"

The questions came as a rush, and Dunn rubbed his palm

across his face in the way that I was only just now beginning to realize meant that he was troubled. "I don't rightly know," he admitted. "But what I do know is this: the sea does not give back what is taken from it lightly, no matter who it is that do the taking, and especially if they be called Jones."

"Why?" I demanded. "Why is this so? Everyone—you, the captain, even my father—speaks in riddles of curses, naming the sea as if she is some jealous goddess, and yet no one provides any answers or details to their stories. I am tired of this incomplete information, these tempting, partial legends." It was delicious, this speech as it came out of me, and Dunn listened consideringly, although he made no move to speak, still watching intently over my shoulder. He was always watching and waiting, and I never knew for what, and it infuriated me. "Tell me," I demanded. "Give me answers. I know you know."

"There is only one person who knows enough to tell you the whole tale," he said. "More than Winters and Jones and I, than the three of us put together. And if we ever reach her, aye, then I imagine she will." "Evangeline."

"Aye." A faint smile relaxed his face as he repeated the name in dreamy voice. "Evangeline."

"Who is she to you?" I asked. "A daughter, a sister, a lover— these things she is to the rest of us onboard this ship, but who is she to you, Mister Dunn? I'm not sure about the other men of the crew, but I understand enough to know that she is more than a simple island proprietress to you. How does your story connect with hers, and with mine? And with Tom Birch's?"

He opened his mouth to respond, but as he did a sudden shock rocked through the ship. It seemed to originate from the captain's quarters, and shuddered so violently that for a moment

I thought we'd run aground, though of course we had not. It had started and ended within the space of a single heartbeat, and I watched with mesmerized curiosity as the rippling effect of the shudder moved out across the water in small, purposeful waves, and when I had regained control of my thoughts, I drew the sword from my belt, prepared to fight.

"You can put that away, lass," said Dunn, and I noticed that a look of terror had seized his features as whatever he had been waiting and waiting for had finally appeared. "It's the *Caleuche*. The ship of the damned. She comes to claim her captain, and her crew, and let's hope that's all she be takin'."

THE NAME OF THE *CALEUCHE* WAS—LIKE THAT OF DAVY JONES OR of Charybdis—one I had only read about in legends of the demons of the sea or heard in terse whispers in the recounting of nightmares from old sailors who had seen the ocean at its most terrifying. And like these other legends, the story of the *Caleuche* was every bit as chilling, although there were rumors that it had not always been this way. It was said to be a beautiful, luminescent ship of no equal, with blood-red sails, and a gleaming white hull. The *Caleuche* was believed to be a vessel of its own sentience, a pet of some sea goddess who kept the ship as an instrument of her power and of her favor. In days past, so long ago now that it had mostly passed from memory, the ship had been said to be a merry one, allowing those worthy ones who had died at sea to sail in eternity. It sailed the world, ferrying those who had died at sea to their resting places as it traded, making merchants and buyers wealthy beyond measure. But the sea had grown resentful of men, and so she had given the *Caleuche* another mission. Now

THE ISLE OF GOLD

it sailed as a ghost ship, crewed with the souls of the damned and possessing of the abilities to glide across the surface of the water at impossible speeds or to sail beneath its waves, rising to gulp and swallow men with the same omnivorous, indifferent appetite as a whale. It kept, according to the tales, men it deemed of sufficient cruelty and evil desires to fill its crew while it spilled the others, driven half-mad by the experience, upon the banks of beaches as it passed.

The sound of music—a wailing, clanging sort of melody—announced the ship as she lifted from the water, rising to her full height beside the *Riptide*, a magnificent ship bearing three masts of five sails each, and all red as blood as described by her legends. She was fashioned in the style of a Spanish galleon, wide decked and with a thick hull made for bearing down on her enemies while they fired uselessly against her. She appeared constructed entirely of driftwood—beautiful, pale, gleaming driftwood if such a thing were real—that shone like radiant starlight against the deep green of the sea as the water ran from her masts and she settled lightly atop the waves, a drowned and shining thing freshly risen from where she'd sailed on some underwater lake. There were dozens of gun ports on her starboard side, so many that I lost count, but there must have been at least two dozen, perhaps three, each covered by a circular, copper shell bearing the shape and detail of a sand dollar. The effigy of a woman, more beautiful even than the likeness of Evangeline Dahl on the *Riptide*, adorned her figurehead, a painted stretch of red across where its eyes should have been.

A line of men stood at her rail, if one was bold enough to call them men. Indeed, they were of a similar hue and substance as what formed Captain Davy Jones, but he was solid and dense and whatever affected him did not touch the other men. These shimmery, spectral images had the shape of men but were brittle, fragile looking things that seemed as if they could be disrupted entirely with the passing of too much air, like loosely cobbled clouds of mist and ash. Their clothing and weapons were un-fixed, not glistening exactly, but stretched somehow so that they appeared thin and partially translucent like bits of canvas that had spent too much time battered by the wind and had begun to come apart at the seams. These strange apparitions were identical to what I had seen become of Tom, grey shadows imbued with life, but I noticed as I watched them that they had the tendency to take on the colors of the water and sky around them, even the red of the sails. So at first glance they might have appeared iridescent, even pretty in the right light if you could disregard their somber expressions and listless eyes. I could see how they might have indeed been beautiful if the *Caleuche* had ever really been kind.

These men, nearly fifty in all, stood shoulder to shoulder at the edge of the *Caleuche*, all of them with dull, unseeing eyes trained across the thin bit of water that separated the two ships. One of these mist-shaped men standing in the center of the line was cranking a hurdy gurdy, an unusual, clunky sort of wooden, stringed instrument that generated sound as the player cranked a rosined wheel which, in turn, rubbed against strings as might a violin bow. This misshapen instrument was capable of produc-ing melodies ranging from delicate, tickling percussion sounds and the melodies of wailing bagpipes, to deep, undulating drones with drifting, screeching, buzzing harmonics. I could easily see how such an odd and unpredictable arrangement of sounds could be mistaken for the cackles of demonic laugher from a vessel crewed by the damned, or the spellbinding music of an enchanted ship or a siren's call. Currently, the music pouring forth from the malformed wooden instrument was lively and celebratory, a queer juxtaposition to the silent, somber expression of the ship's ghosts, and I suspected this had something to do with the fact that a new member had been added to the crew of the *Caleuche* in the form of Tom Birch. Its call was loud, much louder than it naturally should have been, as if it were being amplified in some way so that it drowned out all other sound, not that there was any.

Not a soul on the *Riptide* moved as the large, hulking mass of the *Caleuche* completed its ascent above water, settling herself alongside the starboard side of the leaner ship as its ghastly crew stared, the sound of the hurdy gurdy the only noise heard on the otherwise silent sea. Though comparable in size, the *Caleuche* was, as Spanish galleons to English galleons were, stouter and more dominating than the *Riptide*, making her appear smaller in the shadow of the bulkier ship, but what the *Riptide* might lack in heft she made up for in speed, both in maneuverability and in the effective use of her cannons, a strategy that was vastly different than the tactics that would be applied by the gleaming, driftwood ship. The victor of a battle between the two ships would largely depend on the skill of its captain, which between Winters and Jones might have been equally matched.

Winters had reappeared at my side, eyes sparking ruefully as he took in the ghost ship before him.

"What do we do, Cap'n?" A large, hulking man rushed to the captain's side, clearly in a panic. His name, I knew, was Mister Elias O'Quinn, and he was the ship's gunner. He had a hooked nose and one of his eyes dragged behind the other, giving his face a sour expression that was perpetually darkened by a smear of ash and gunpowder. He skin was pallid and drawn, and his cheeks were rather gaunt despite his large size, giving him the look of a slightly rotted piece of fruit that had begun to pucker and concave upon itself. He was rarely seen above deck, preferring to remain below and in the company of his cannons and shot and gunpowder, and when he was above deck he was never without his powder monkey, a small, wiry boy of no more than fourteen or fifteen, called Bim, who followed him dutifully like a parasitic pilot fish. "We 'an run a shot across the bow?" He offered this with obvious excitement, either oblivious or undaunted by the fact that he was suggesting firing a warning shot at a ship piloted by the dead.

"No," responded Winters, who evidently took umbrage with the comment. "They mean us no harm. They have only come to reclaim what is theirs. We have no quarrel with them for now."

The gunner looked put out. "And what is that they be claimin'?" he asked, and then he and Bim stepped back as the hurdy gurdy hit a powerful chord and with it the door to the captain's office swung open, and Davy Jones walked out, followed closely behind by the brittle grey shadow that had once been Tom Birch. Neither of them said a word and spared not so much as a glance in our direction as they walked in lock step across the waist of the ship and then stepped up and over the railings, dropping into the water below as we watched. Their bodies made no sound as they slipped beneath the water, and in a blink of the same ethereal green light that had preceded Charybdis' swirling throat, the entirety of the *Caleuche* vanished, disappearing so completely it was hard to imagine that she had ever been there. Even the water was flat and glassy where she had rested atop the water. The sudden silence was deafening.

And then O'Quinn let out a bellow of startled sound, and then Bim produced a high-pitched wail, and this was joined quickly by the startled cries of the other men as they rushed the rail of the ship, looking over her edges into the deeps for a sign of the two men, or perhaps the ship. But there was no sight of them, and no evidence that any man had been there, alive or grey ghost or anything else. There was chaos then, as every man in the crew yelled and pounded against the ship, weapons clanging and feet stomping in frenzied, disorganized sound that was worse even than the vaporing. Winters, Dunn, and I stood, staring at the empty space left by the strange, sentient ship captained if only in title by the man who had once been Davy Jones. We said nothing, and did nothing, letting the rest of the men swarm around us as if they were no more than a cast of thumping, scuttling crabs until finally the Captain's voice boomed above the racket.

"Quiet," he demanded. He pulled a spyglass from his frog on his belt and lifted it to his eye, and when he lowered it a wrathful smile was spread across his face. He pointed his forefinger in the direction he had been studying. A mass had appeared on the horizon, a large, blurry bulk of mist and earth of indistinct shape and topography, but it was unmistakable nonetheless. *Land*.

"*Bracile*," he whispered beneath his breath. Then, "Land, ho!" he shouted, and the men instantly forgot what they had been upset about and clung again to the edges of the ship, this time with mouths agape in wonder. Winters said nothing but the smile stayed stretched menacingly across the space between his ears, and he kept his eyes fixed on Bracile in a manner that suggested total and complete anticipation, so fiercely intent and unwavering that it might, in fact, be a look not of expectation at all, but of insanity.

I thought of Evangeline, the source of both his anticipation and his madness. I thought of her waiting, trapped on an unreachable island, but beyond that the vision was unclear. "Did she know who I was ... who I am?" I asked Dunn, who was still beside me. "I expect you will soon be able to ask her yourself. If we e'er reach the island that is."

"*If* we reach the island?" I repeated.

"This island be guarded by a fearsome beast, Miss Jones," Dunn explained. "And she knows we be here. Question now be whether she will allow us safe passage 'til she be ready to claim us."

XX

ACH OF US KEPT OUR SIGHTS LOCKED ON THE BLURRY MASS of land ahead as we sailed along in soundless wonder, our worries over monsters of the deep or of demon ships crewed by the dead and the damned momentarily forgotten as we beheld the shape of what was surely the fabled island of Bracile looming before us. The ocean was so silent you could hear the soft, creaking sounds of the wooden ship as she swayed and groaned beneath us, moving so swiftly atop the waves that salty sea spray covered our faces like morning dew. Although the wind was still, we rushed forward at our maximum speed of about eight knots, the ship pushing ahead quickly despite the lack of any strong breeze so that she might have moved of her own accord, or of Winters', who stood staring ahead wearing the look of a starved man facing an oncoming feast. The men had abandoned their frantic pummeling and no one stirred on the decks other than the few who took turns managing the quotidian tasks of adjusting sails and pulling on rigging, exercising the same speed and thoroughness they would have if Tom Birch had still been onboard to direct them. The rest of us simply stared in anticipation—some mixed with looks of awe, others with dread—as we approached land ahead.

I gasped when the mist around the island cleared, pushed out of the way by the breath of the ship, and I saw her plainly for the first time. Even the brilliant blue waters of the Caribbean could not compare to the unrivaled beauty of the waters that lay at the feet of Bracile. The ocean around her was a rich tapestry of colors spun from the vibrant hues of jewels: deep emerald greens, brilliant sapphire blue, and crisp, luminescent turquoise, all of these mixed together and then fading into fair, almost crystalline waters of pure aquamarine as they touched the edges of the island. Even in the bright daylight sun I could see the glittering sparkle of bioluminescent bays that twinkled and turned to frothy white foam as they lapped against the edges as delicately as a bridal train.

The island itself, as far as I could tell, was a kludge of craggy, stone-grey cliffs and granite canyon walls that rose forth from the ocean so steeply that the island might have been an underwater mountain sprung from the seabed, the tips of her so tall that they were lost in the fog of low-hanging clouds. Water ran from their precipices in quick-moving falls, and streams of foamy emerald water fell like tears down the face of a glacial goddess to pour back into the bays below her. I could see no signs of earthy life on the island; no palms or other signs of green vegetation that might nourish land-bound life or nesting birds, nor fruiting trees or wild bushes to provide shelter or comfort for a living being. There were, as well, no beaches along the outskirts of the island, and thus no place to find safe harbor. Bracile was a fortress at sea, impenetrable and harsh but still relentlessly beautiful.

As we neared her shores a beautiful melody began to swell in the air, accompanied by a scent I could only describe as *feminine*. It was powdery and painfully familiar, and growing ever stronger as the song, too, lifted so that it was near impossible to hear anything else. I realized with a start that it was not music that I was hearing, but voices, and the smell was the one of lotus I had encountered in the sea cove. The sound was a lilting phantom opera, rising and falling in sharp crescendos and humming valleys that reverberated off the island's rocky walls. "Do you hear that, now?" a man mused beside me, more to himself than to me. It was the gunner, O'Quinn, who had spoken. He wrapped his fist around a length of rigging from the main mast and pulled it and himself sharply to the side, angling the ship roughly toward the cliffs as he strained to see the source of the music. I noticed that his eyes had a glazed, glassy look and that his lips were wet with the sheen of saliva as he licked at them. "Such a beautiful song, that is."

I looked about me and noticed that nearly all of the men were similarly affected, their preparations with the rigging and sails forgotten as the entire lot of them leaned over the rails of the ship or hung like upended crabs from the nets as they strove to see the source of the disembodied, musical voices. Only Dunn and myself were immune; even Winters had an odd, dazed expression as he stood with his eyes shut and jaw locked in a frustrated grimace. It appeared as though he were in pain and I made to go to him, but then Dunn was there first, ordering me to steady the ship while he leaned in close to the captain, speaking in hushed, rough words. Most of them were too low to make out, but I heard something of sirens and nearing the cave, and then these were followed by words in a foreign tongue that I could not understand but sounded like they were made from the same ancient language I had felt in my throat earlier when I hovered over Tom's body in the captain's quarters. Whatever the quartermaster said had a restoring effect on the captain. I saw his eyes spark and reanimate, and he shook his head in one stiff downward jerk, and then returned the spyglass to his eye and continued to study the island while the other man whispered a steady stream of information at his ear.

As Dunn continued to counsel the captain, I pushed O'Quinn out of the way and grabbed hold of the rope with uncertain hands. I had watched intently when Tom had piped orders regarding the proper management of the sails, but this had mostly been to watch him and not to learn the actual mechanics of sailing and so I had never handled them myself. I tugged at the rigging hesitantly, coaxing the ship off of her collision course with the cliffs as the sails turned and gave way. I felt the ship groan as if she, too, had been lulled by the siren's song, but eventually her nose straightened and the ship turned its broadside to the island that was suddenly much nearer than it had previously been. The craggy cliffs took on more definite forms, and I saw that sharp overhangs jutted out from their sides, and upon them—in numbers that must have reached a hundred—perched silvery beings, each open-mouthed and adding to the airy opus around us.

I had not seen them before but they were clear now, formed of sinewy upper bodies with small, rounded shoulders and small, rounded breasts. At their ends, thin, sickly green reptilian tails forked into two flatted fins and swished independently of each other. These were mermaids, that much was evident, but never had I heard a tale of mermaids that resembled such insidious creatures. Their skin was the pale blue of a waterlogged corpse, and their eyes were large and ominous, yellow in color and almond shaped so that they had a distinctly carnivorous look to them. Atop each of their heads writhed a mass of tentacle-like arms, all insipid though of different shades of green and grey, some even hues of blue or red, and none of which belonged to the natural world. Most frightening of all their features, however, were their faces below their eyes—two tiny slits for nostrils and thin black mouths from which came beautiful streams of sound that masked an undercurrent of fierce hisses and growls. I alone—or perhaps Dunn also, I could not be sure—heard these and the creatures seemed to know it. Gradually their feline eyes turned to focus on mine while the sound pitched higher and more insistent. The ring on my finger turned to ice, so cold that the chill rose up my arm and I shivered despite the intense heat.

"Never mind them," Dunn's voice, calm and unperturbed, came over my shoulder as the sound soared to a deafening roar. "They only be trying to scare us. If they wanted us drowned they'd have been in the water 'fore we ever reached this far, pullin' the men over one by one, the damned beasts." He was beside me then, and when I did not respond he snapped his fingers in front of my eyes. I blinked and the cold was gone and so was the music. He eyed the mermaids with a distasteful sneer and then spat on the deck as if their very image disgusted him, and perhaps it did. "Don't stare at them, lass. They keep you from seein' what you be lookin' to see."

"What's tha—" I started to ask, but I blinked again and then I saw it. Behind the twisting tentacle hair of a particularly vicious looking mermaid was a small break in the cliffs slicing upward from the water to the sky. In truth, it was little more than a narrow passage into which a stream of water fed, but now that I saw it I was amazed I had missed it before. A ship the size of the *Riptide* was far too large to fit through it, but it was deep and wide enough that a small vessel might be able to maneuver through the sharp curves and steep cliffs that carved their way into the belly of the island. "There," I announced, pointing in its direction. The shrieking noise of the mermaids quieted immediately and though I could sense the men freeing of the trance around me I did not dare to take my eyes off of the passage.

"Drop anchor," ordered Winters. It was done instantly as Jomo himself walked in front of me and untied the anchor lashing ropes and then removed the wedge that jammed the anchor chain. With a big clanking noise, the anchor plunged into the sea. The ship was allowed to drift until the rope was at full extension, and then she pulled to a slow stop. We were so close to the island now that I could have swam the distance easily, had I been brave enough to dare what swam below the water's surface.

Winters wasted no time. "Boats," he barked. "Miss Jones, Mister Dunn, Jomo," he listed, spearing us each in turn with blazing eyes before he marched toward the waist of the ship where the smaller boats were stored. He tossed a small rucksack into the bottom of the boat and stepped in, watching impatiently as the rest of us joined him. A small assembly of men whose names he had not called followed and made ready to let us down in one of the skiffs. He addressed them sternly. "We row the rest of the way. The lot of you keep a wary eye on the horizon. If we have not returned by first light, haul anchor and leave this place."

THE FOUR OF US DESCENDED INTO A SMALL SKIFF AND DROPPED into the waters below, Jomo and Dunn paddling while the captain and I sat in the middle row of the boat. We made for a quiet quartet, all of us preoccupied with studying the island as we entered the narrow space between striking cliffs that seemed to have no top, sliding uninterrupted over water so still and perfect it might have been made of glass. We wound through tall looming walls of granite the color of chalk, their endless heights accented by streaks of black flint, seeming to stretch endlessly on. There were no birds or waves to disturb the silence, and the

THE ISLE OF GOLD

only sounds were those of our breathing. Even the oars slipping beneath the water was quiet. I wondered how I might have explained such a vision to Claudette if she had been here with me now, what she would have made of this place.

Day melted into evening as we continued silently on, passing slowly along the current until so much time had passed that the moon rose and turned the glassy green waters into a rich shade of midnight blue. Finally, we rounded another bend and illuminated in the soft glow of moonlight, a giant conch shell came into view, its spikes slicing upward into the air as it stood on its end, tipped toward the sky. It was embedded in glittering black sands that sparkled like diamonds under the light of a million stars so that the beach was a perfect reflection of the night sky, strewn with large boulders of gleaming ice the same as those that had floated in the wider ocean waters. Winters stood as we drew near, standing with his legs shoulder width apart, and when we were near enough to the shore he jumped out and into the water, holding the boat still so that the rest of us could do as he has done. We followed his lead, me slushing through the water a pace or so behind the captain while Jomo and Dunn dragged the skiff up onto the bank of black sand. For the first time in months I felt the firm substance of land as it swelled beneath my boots. I stumbled from the weight of it, and one of the men's hands—I did not know whose—caught my arm as I relearned how walk on solid earth.

In the pink fleshy curl of the cave's yawning mouth stood a woman, waiting just at the edge so at first glance she was invisible against the white of the shell. The sight of her rooted us in place where we stood as we stared at her like she were a mirage in the moonlight. The curls of her hair hung long and loose, tumbling over her shoulders in waves the color of spun honey, and where her skin had been milk white before it was now dusted in gold that glittered in the starlight so that she appeared a living, gilded statue. Flecks of gold leaf encircled her eyes and covered her eyebrows completely so that the blue of her eyes shone like dazzling jewels in contrast. She wore a shimmering metallic gown of a slightly paler color, more bronze perhaps than gold. It wrapped the length of her long neck and then swept across her chest, clinging tightly to the slender narrows of her waist before billowing out softly and then stopping short at her ankles so that she could move freely in the glittering, black sands.

She was golden and she was beautiful and she was Evangeline. She did not come any closer toward us. In fact, she did not appear to believe we were real any more than we did her, and she stood staring cooly at us from across the beach. When at last her face finally softened, she seemed only to have eyes for Winters, and a small smile bowed the corners of her lips. This was a signal of sorts; Winters made a moaning sound and took a cautious step forward, and then another, and then he charged forward, his strides long and quick even as they sunk into the dunes of black sand. When they were less than an arm's length apart, he slowed to a stop and they stood facing each other, neither of them moving to close the space between them as they regarded one another silently from under heavy-lidded eyes. I could not tell what passed between them as they waited, barely breathing and contemplating each other as if they were staring at nothing more than a vision of their deepest desires.

Evangeline was first to speak. "Erik," she said, in a mellifluous voice that carried strong and sweetly on the wind, "you should not have come for me."

His face remained impassive as he reached out to gently tuck a strand of stray curls behind her ear. The tips of his fingers traced the curve of her jaw as he withdrew his hand and then it drop at his side. "What else could I have done?" he asked.

I could see Evangeline inhale, her face as smoothly inexpressive as his as she stared at him for a moment longer. Her lips parted and then closed, and then with a deep breath she lifted her arms and reached for his face, threading long, slender fingers inside the tangles of his hair as with a hand on either side of his face she pulled him desperately into her, rising against him in a golden tide of curls and cloth. Then his arms found their way around her waist and locked her tightly against him, and the three of us watching from afar turned our eyes away as they embraced.

XXI

WHEN AT LAST THEY PARTED AND TURNED TO US, IT WAS TO Mister Dunn they came first, walking hand in hand across the starry black sand as if afraid to let one another go. Evangeline was a vision in gold and smiling more easily than I had known her to, her eyes bare of the cunning glint I had seen when I studied her from afar from the balconies of the House of Sparrows. If she was bothered to have been trapped here in this unreachable place for the last two years it did not show. Instead, she appeared composed and contented, moving as gracefully across the black sands of Bracile as she had the dusty quayside streets of Isla Perla. Winters, too, had changed; there was a new peace to him, though the set of his jaw was as taut as ever and the sharpness of his eyes had not dulled. If anything, he was more tenacious now than he had been before. The madness that hung about him these past few years dissipated so that he moved about with the same kingly air I had seen in my own father when he had visited the *Riptide*.

"Brandon," Evangeline called, and Mister Dunn went to her immediately, the words "my lady" falling from his lips as he sank to his knees before her. She embraced him warmly, holding the white flame of his head against her breast as a mother might coddle a child. Words too low to be overheard passed between them. When at last she released him, he stood and she lifted her free to hand to stroke his face, and as she turned her gaze to Jomo I saw that she wore a ring on the middle finger of her left hand that was identical to the one I wore on my right. She smiled up at the towering, dark man, and then, releasing Winters' hand, allowed herself to be gathered up in his arms, her delicate form almost lost entirely in his hold as she clung tightly to him. "My warrior, Jomo," she murmured into the muscle of his shoulder. "I am so relieved to see you well."

I watched all of this curiously, surprised by the amount of tenderness that passed between the four of them as they reunited. The rumors that had passed on the island had been that Mistress Dahl was as cold and detached as Winters himself, and just as prone to violent fits of temper that had been the death of men who crossed her, but I did not see that same woman now. This version of Evangeline was kind and genteel, and she embraced her friends warmly. I knew so little of these people, I realized, and would not have anticipated that Dunn and Jomo would have been received into her arms with such obvious affection. A jealousy rose up within me, and as it did, I could feel the warmth of my ring on my finger as I pulled my hat down over my eyes. My heartbeat drummed in my throat as Jomo unfolded his arms and Evangeline stepped out again, this time with her eyes set on me.

"Merrin," she said, and my name had never sounded as sweet on anyone's lips. She held out both of her hands to me, and I accepted them, enjoying the feel of her hands in mine as my anxiety and envy melted instantly away. "I have waited so long for this, my sister. I am so sorry that we have lost so many years together, but there will be time for that later." She smiled at me, and without meaning to do so I was smiling back, and I saw in her face the same smile I had seen on our father's, fond and inviting, but I saw something else in her face, too. My pulse sped as I recalled the woman in the cove and her sinister smirk. Evangeline's face was rounder, her nose less severely thin, but the likeness was undeniable, down to the same subtle cleft in her chin. "I know you must have many questions, and I will answer them all in time as best I can, I promise it. But, tell me, where is Tom Birch?" She squeezed my fingers and then let go of my hand, reaching for Winters as he approached from behind and touched his palm to the small of her back.

I struggled to find the right words, too enthralled by the sound of her voice and the feel of her skin to answer plainly. She stepped backward and something hardened in her eyes. A look of cold impatience washed over her features and again her face took on the same imperious countenance that belonged to the proprietress of The Goodnight Mermaid, and not this trapped goddess awaiting rescue from an enchanted island. "Where is Tom Birch?" she demanded, turning so quickly to face Winters that her skirts swirled around her in a flurry of spinning gold.

"He sails the *Caleuche*," explained Winters, his voice gruff and without inflection. He did not elaborate further.

"No," she gasped as if this had been the last thing she expected to hear, and she shook her head as if the news has stung her. She spun back to me. "That cannot be," she said, searching my eyes under the brim of the hat for confirmation.

"It is, my lady," Dunn affirmed, bowing his head slightly as he came forward. He did not look at either of us, but kept his face apologetically downcast. "He fell as we sailed int' the heart of the ocean, and when we arrived in this place your father took 'im aboard rather than let him die. Merrin very nearly bound herself to save 'im she did."

"No," she repeated, and there was horror on her face, as well as anger.

I saw unspoken knowledge in both of their eyes, and thus an

opportunity. "Is there a way to save him?" I asked, passing my eyes from Evangeline to Dunn and back again, avoiding Winters. "Is there a way to free him from the *Caleuche*? Or to free its captain?"

"I believe so," she admitted, although she sounded hesitant. There was irritation, too, in her eyes as she looked at Winters, but about what I did not know. Something passed unsaid between them, but she took my hand and squeezed it reassuringly. "But the cost will be high, sweet sister … higher now than before."

"Come," Winters cut in briskly. He took her by the arm, ignoring her glower. "The sky grows light." I had not realized so much time had passed and was surprised to find that it was true. Already the dark black of night was fading into a pale, purplish dawn and there was a sliver of the sun's orange eyelash visible on the horizon. "We must return to the ship."

At his words, Evangeline was visibly mollified, but she made no move to allow herself to be removed from the island. "She will never let us leave this place, Erik" she said, her voice reduced to barely more than a whisper. "You know she won't."

Winters pulled her tightly against him, riving her hand from mine as he took her into his arms. He touched a crooked finger to the underside of her jaw and forced her eyes to his, his face equal parts intensity and resolve. "She cannot keep you here," he stated in a rumbling tenor. "I will not allow you to be trapped any longer. I will see you returned to Isla Perla, I swear it."

Evangeline scoffed softly. "She is a goddess, Erik. She does not concern herself over the desires of men any more than she does over mine."

Winters was unmoved. "I do not intend to ask."

THE *RIPTIDE* WAS JUST AS WE HAD LEFT HER, FLOATING MIGHTILY on the still-dark ocean waters. A shadow stood against the railing, a deep grey smear against a sky of lightening blue and purple. With the light behind it I could not make out a face, but it appeared to be staring in the direction from which we came, watching intently as we moved quickly out from between the cliffs. Jomo, Dunn, and Winters took turns manning the oars, rowing quickly and wordlessly. Little had been said since we'd left the black shores of Evangeline's cave, but more than once Dunn had stopped to scent the air, sniffing for something that only he seemed able to smell but never did he say what it was or how he might be able to identify it. Evangeline and I had barely spoken on the trip; when at first I had attempted to draw her into conversation she had held a finger to her lips and shook her head in the universal sign for quiet, motioning meaningfully at the water as if it might be listening. We had left the cave with little ceremony, lingering for a few minutes only so that Evangeline could rid herself of the golden gown and redress in the clothing the captain had brought along for her in the small bag. Had it not been for the unnatural gilded sheen that now laid upon her skin, she would have looked no different than the last time I had seen her as the scrupulous proprietress of Isla Perla, dressed simply in a linen shirt with smocked accents overhung with a simple, belted leather corset, and a striped, seersucker skirt. Her golden curls had been gathered and knit back into a simple braid. More than once the captain had hooked his fingers in the brass clasp of her belt and used it to pull her to him, staring at her as if he didn't quite believe her to be real. It was an oddly intimate gesture, but never once did his normal countenance break into anything other than what it always was. He remained hard and expressionless; the only hint to what may boil beneath the surface was the way he stared at her—as if she were the great treasure he had ever known—so that the look was even more desirous than it might otherwise have been.

When the lookout spotted our approach from the rail of the *Riptide,* the echo of his voice was loud enough to be heard across the water. "Haul anchor," he shouted, and I thought the voice might have belonged to O'Quinn, but it was hard to tell over the mermaid's song, which had started again, only this time it was devoid of its former sultry sound. Their cries were shrill and menacing and the noise of it stung my ears.

"The captain comes!" the lookout called again, more authoritative this time, and a loud, grinding sound followed next, and then the creaking of the capstan as it turned heavily, the men pushing the bars as quickly as they could to raise the anchor from where it rested on the seabed. Normally the job would have taken an hour or more, but the men moved with unique urgency so that the capstan squealed loudly as the wet rope coiled against itself around the barrel, and the heavy anchor groaned as it was carried along. A long, dark shadow moved underneath the water in the direction of the ship, causing a rippling wake that ran from near where our skiff floated to the ship's hull, stopping just under its keel. I hoped it was the anchor sliding upward, but I had never seen a rising anchor cause such a widespread stir. It moved with an unsettling speed and was too curved to be a simple length of straight rope. It lurked just below the water's surface and I refused to look at it again as the small boat bumped against the hull of the ship. Winters guided Evangeline to the ladder first, holding her hand as she scaled the few rungs and was pulled over in a flurry of skirts, and then the captain pulled me to my feet next, his hand wrapped securely around my shin as I found my footing on the ladder. Dunn and Jomo followed next, and we ascended quickly like a line of ants scaling the side of a great hill, leaving the small boat to bob uselessly in the water. Winters was last to leave the skiff, and as his boots stepped into the rungs of the ladder a shudder passed under the water like a note of terrible punctuation, rocking the ship so forcefully that had one of the men's hands not caught mine as I stepped over the railing of the deck I might have been pitched back into the sea.

The moment Winters' feet touched the deck he was barking orders and pushing men away from their toll at the capstan and toward other tasks, moving in the self-assured pace of the well-prepared. "O'Quinn, prepare the guns. You there, cut and run. Faster, damn you, or I'll leave you here and let the sea have her way with you!" He gave the order for the men to cut the lashings to the anchor's cables so that it fell lost into the water, and Domingo returned the wooden eye that he had been rolling nervously in his fingers to its socket, grabbed a knife, and set about to sawing the thick rope. Evangeline moved confidently about the ship, and I saw that she had added a belt with a half dozen knives and a short sword around her hips. The men acknowledged her as she moved among them, most giving small nods or even bows, but they did not linger with more formal introductions and she ignored them completely. Dunn was at her ear and speaking to her in the same rushed murmur that he often did the captain, and Jomo was sharpening a new edge to one of his many blades while his eyes stayed securely locked upon Evangeline. All around me the men prepared for a battle, moving in synchronized urgency in the same manner they had when we'd previously faced danger, and I freed my sword from my belt as another shudder rocked the ship.

A boom cracked the sky as the clear, dawning blue turned steely grey and the clouds covered the rising sun.

"The sea awakens!" Winters shouted, but his warning came too late. Before the last of his words had been spoken, a crimson-red cephalopod limb erupted violently from the water. It was overwhelmingly large, at least twice the width of the ship at its thickest point and bearing suckers that in some places were as large and round as I guessed the moon might be. It writhed above the water, flailing wildly in the air as another limb crashed upward, and then another, until all eight arms of a giant, red beast were twisting in the air above us.

I saw two things at once: first, a tremendous avarice overcame Jomo's eyes as he beheld the writing, red tentacles above him, eyeing it as one might behold a bounty of precious jewels, and then, the end of one of the arms swung forward and coiled itself tightly around Evangeline's waist, and before she had the chance to cry out, wrenched her roughly off the deck and beneath the waves.

"Evangeline," I screamed, reaching vainly for the air where she had stood half a second before as simultaneously I heard the roar of Winters' voice rise in an angry bellow above the noise. He yelled in a wordless thundering of fury as he thrashed his sword wildly at a tentacle that still hovered in the air above the deck, the remaining seven arms wrapping and tearing viciously at the ship's masts and railings. The edge of his blade caught the pointed end of one limb and sliced at it so that a sucker-tipped end fell squirming to the deck like the severed phalange of an undead hand, but he had already forgotten it, rushing to the rail of the ship and scaling it in two smooth leaps even as it cracked and broke beneath his feet from the weight of the monster's beating. With his sword raised in one hand, Winters grabbed hold of a length of rigging in the other and prepared to dive into the depths after Evangeline.

"Captain," Dunn called, arriving at his side. I could hear his voice even above the screams of the wind and the sirens as they buffeted around me. "Let me. I can make it."

The two men stared hard at each other, and then Winters nodded and Dunn flung himself overboard without another word.

"Wait," I screamed. For what I didn't know, but I was rushing toward them as fast as my feet would carry me, dodging men and falling debris as I made my way across the deck. But before I could reach them surprise gripped me as another slick red limb wound itself around my waist and lifted me into the air, holding me so tightly that I could not draw breath enough to scream. My sword dropped from my grip and clanged loudly against the deck as I was swung high over the ship, the figures of Winters and Jomo and the rest of them only small specks below.

The last thing I saw before the arm pulled me roughly underwater were the blood-red sails of the *Caleuche* slicing upward as a large spray of water lifted the Spanish galleon atop the ocean. Wraith-like grey men were stationed at the rails and at each gun port, and more hung over the edge of the ships to man the large canons that were pointed directly at what was left of the *Riptide*. I could see the waving eels of my father's hair and a hard, unfeeling expression transformed my father's face into that of a stranger's. Beside him the unmistakable form of Tom Birch stood still and brittle. I saw Erik Winters turn to meet them, a sneer on his mouth and his red hair whipping angrily in the wind as Jomo loomed at his back, and then I saw nothing but water.

XXII

WHEN MY EYES REOPENED I WAS BACK IN THE SEA COVE, lying in a heap on the hard, limestone floor, and the strange woman who inhabited the place was standing over me, her face still covered in its lacy mask though she was staring at me with the license of a goddess. I pushed myself up and got my bearings, feeling over my body to see what I had lost. My hat had managed to stay atop my head and I tugged at it reassuringly as I met the gaze of the woman. There was a smug look of victory on her face, but her smile was as sinister as before and just as unwelcoming. Evangeline was there in the cove as well, standing stiffly with her arms crossed over her chest and wearing a look of wrath and of fierce determination. Dunn was on his knees at her side, not in a posture of supplication but of defeat as if he had been forced there. His face, too, was twisted in rage.

For a moment, no one spoke, and when at last someone did I was surprised to find that it was me, and I heard a harshness in my own voice. "Let us go," I demanded, addressing the goddess familiarly, and unafraid. "Return us to our ship and leave us in peace, Mother."

Evangeline and Dunn darted startled eyes to me, as the sea goddess let loose one of her baleful laughs. "Oh, don't be cross, my darling. You are home now, and you will never have to leave our little island again." Her words were sweet, but her voice was cold and inhuman.

"We have no desire to stay on your 'little island'," I countered, without bothering to affirm it with the other two. This place may have once been home to Dunn, but judging by the expression on his face I believed that the sentiment had long since passed. I longed now to return to the open water, to Isla Perla, and Claudette.

"You, my dear Merrin, and your sister of course, are the daughters of the sea—of a goddess," she purred, motioning to herself in lazy, languid movements as she stalked away from me and moved closer to her vanity, utterly disregarding what I had said. The red silk of her dress was the same color as the beast thrashing above, and she looked terribly proud of her own reveal though I had guessed her identity long before. I did not know her name, or at least her real one, but it did not matter. I knew she was the sea witch who guarded this island, and had stolen Evangeline from Isla Perla, and that would be the destruction of us all if she were not stopped. It was her crimson limbs that were thrashing above, destroying our ship, and is was her minions that had attempted to lure the *Riptide* to crash on the cliffs of Bracile before making land. She was the *she* that my father had referenced, and though I knew that she was my mother, I had no great love for her in my heart. Only fear, and something like loathing.

"You are safe here, my darling girls," she explained, as if she were bestowing some great mercy, her masked face pivoting from mine to Evangeline's, who was as stony and contemptuous as it had been before. "I will not suffer you to endure the mortal world and its men."

"It is not your right to keep us here," I said. "To condemn us all to this curse."

"And what curse is that, dear? The curse of *Jones*?" she smirked over her shoulder. "Such a charming way to put it, isn't it? Davy Jones always had a flair for the dramatic, though of course he couldn't recognize that it was his own greed that damned him. You're so much like him in that way, Merrin." She made a tittering, scornful sound. "It's an unfortunate tragedy of your mortal coil, but it will pass over time as your heart returns to the sea where it belongs. In time, you will forget the curse of Davy Jones, just as easily as you will forget Isla Perla and all that you knew before you returned here, to me."

"Captain," I spat, angry despite my fear, of the implication of her words. "*Captain* Davy Jones. My father. The man you loved once, or have you forgotten who he was to you?"

"Forgotten?" She spun to face me, the red silk of her dress flying out around her like fiery fang tips of a red rockfish. "I forget *nothing.*" A deep, gurgling rumble echoed around her; it shook the cove and I had to anchor my hand against the length of a limestone column so that I didn't fall. There was venom on her tongue as she said the last, and her face whipped to Evangeline who rolled her eyes petulantly but said nothing. Dunn moved uncomfortably by her side and she touched one hand lightly on the roll of his shoulders to still him.

Our mother recoiled at this. "How can you touch him with such affection!" she seethed, her gaze landing angrily on Mister Dunn. "You, you miserable little monster. I know your face, even if it is old and cracked with age. It was you who ferried away my daughters, who stole them from *me* and took them across the ocean."

"Aye," he answered defiantly, rolling his eyes upward in a look of defiance. "That it were. I be followin' the orders of my captain then, and I be doin' it again if I could, witch."

I expected her to be furious, but she only smiled at him, and it was a smile that could freeze fire. "And tell me, dog, how has it felt all these long years to be trapped in one form?" She pulled something from behind her back. I thought at first it was the blanket that had covered me when I had visited this place in my dream, and indeed it was that, but I realized now that it was not simply a supple leather blanket of sealskin, but was sealskin itself. *His* skin, I realized, as I saw an expression of agony and desire brush past his face. If it had not been for Evangeline's guiding hand, he would have crumbled to the floor from the sheer pain of seeing it.

My mouth fell open. Mister Brandon Dunn, the wiry, white-haired quartermaster who had spent so much time longing for the sea and talking of its legends, was in fact not a man at all, but a thing of the sea itself. I had missed it before, but it was plain to see now. He was a selkie, a seal who could assume human form. Even my father had called him such; I had thought it was a just a pet name for the old sailor, but he had been trapped as much in this form every bit as much as Evangeline had been trapped on this island, and as I had been trapped in my own ignorance.

"What have you done?" I gasped in horror. I looked from my mother to Dunn and then to Evangeline, who shook her head at me in warning as my eyes caught hers, but it did nothing to stop the words that followed next. "You're not a goddess at all; you're a monster."

"A *monster*?" the woman repeated, dangling the sealskin just out of Dunn's reach as she advanced on me. Her lovely pearlescent hair and silken gown swirled angrily around her. "The distinction is a matter of perspective, dear girl. I am a *mother*," she insisted. "I *loved* that man once, that cursed Davy Jones. I loved him so much that I left the sea for him, and I bound myself to him so that he could sail the sea unharmed in immortality with me.

THE ISLE OF GOLD

But men are greedy, Merrin darling. Men are *weak*. And Davy Jones was no exception—no more than Erik Winters." Evangeline stirred angrily at this and narrowed her eyes into thin, blue slits. "They are *all* weak. I gave Davy Jones everything, *everything*, but he was more in love with his gold than he was with me, and so I gave him just what he deserved after he left me on that island to rot."

"He didn't abandon you," I argued. "He loved you."

Evangeline moved closer to me to take my hand in hers so that we stood united. She added to the story, "He set about to free you ... to free us all. And—"

"He *abandoned* me," she seethed. "And when he did he took the two of you in his hold, stealing you away so that I couldn't find you, couldn't bring you back to where you belonged." She waved her hands around the stark and inhospitable chamber. "And so I sank the ship he had you on and tried to bring you back to me, but you were lost—my two, precious daughters, along with the infant son of the captain who had tried to help him ..." She pointed now at what was unmistakably a human skull on her vanity. "Though he has already paid grievously for his error. Heavy is the price for stealing from the sea."

I looked at the skull with dread. Mother or not, the sea was cruel, and there was no empathy in her. "Name him," I demanded, though I already knew. "Name the man whose skull that is."

She sneered at me and waved her hand in a mock flourish. "Captain Amadeus Birch was his name, father of the boy Tom Birch, formerly of the *Riptide*. But don't worry, darling, I've kept him, too, on the *Caleuche*, and Erik Winters and his African prince will soon join him there. And perhaps you, as well," she said, her eyes spearing Dunn again at Evangeline's feet.

He didn't cower, but fear slid across his face and Evangeline stepped in front of him so that he was hidden entirely behind her skirt. "You will not harm him," she said flatly.

"Oh, I will not harm *him*," she seethed, and the corner of her lip curled upward as sharp and dangerously as a fishhook. "That would be too much of a mercy. I will do worse—I will destroy his hope. Whatever hope you had of shedding that miserable man flesh, it ends now." And with that she plucked a shell from her hair and stabbed it in into the fur, dragging it down so that it tore a hole into the supple folds of the sealskin leather. Dunn collapsed to the stone floor, crying out as if he, too, had been stabbed.

"And you, dear girl, my Mélusine" the sea witch addressed Evangeline now as she dropped the torn skin to the floor. "The queen of the thieves of Isla Perla. Have you not learned what I am capable of these past two years?" She raised milky white fingers to caress the side of Evangeline's golden cheek, and I saw my sister flinch and then regain her composure, staring boldly back at our mother. "You, poor girl, have the same unquenchable greed as your father—the same banal, myopic vision to control the waters. But if it is treasure you seek, then you will become it yourself, both in form and in legend. And because you have seen fit to bind yourself to your precious Erik Winters, he will enjoy the same sentence as your father. He will sail the world forever in search of you, but he will never claim you."

"You underestimate him," Evangeline said as she helped Dunn to his feet and held him protectively against her.

"No, my darling, you underestimate *me*," our mother taunted her, and she gathered up her skirts and pulled from their folds a piece of glistening white shell in one hand and the handheld mirror I had seen her wield before in the other. The stone was the same color and shape as the one I wore on my finger; identical to the one that Evangeline was touching now as she wrung her hands. The stone itself, I realized, as I remembered the ones that lay at the throats of Captains Winters and Jones, was somehow the link that bound those mortal men to the women of the sea. Our mother rolled it around in her long, pale fingers, and it sparked with life as she stared into the mirror with the sand dollar face that was the same as the one emblazoned on my journal and the gun ports of the ghost ship, *Caleuche*. I saw the ships in the mirror's reflection, the *Riptide* reduced to a smoking, burning mass as the *Caleuche* rained down cannon fire upon it. I saw Erik Winters, my friend and my captain, when he crossed blades with my father, eyes grey and unseeing as he fought back, advancing and indestructible against the man who would fight bravely until he could no more. I saw Jomo, cut and bleeding as he attempted to hold off the ghostly double of Tom Birch who bore down upon him.

Satisfaction shadowed my mother's face as her hatred consumed what little humanity was left in her. "My darling *Caleuche* will destroy what is left of your vessel," she said. "And you will watch as the men onboard are claimed by me, and then the *Caleuche* will own them, and will sail their souls to the other side of the world forever. It will be a fitting end for this *Curse of Jones*," she sneered. "Three souls for three men who dared so tame the sea—the one who began it will be forced to slay the one who tried to break it, and the last will meet them both at the bottom of the world."

I knew it would spell the end for me, but even this impending knowledge did not slow me as I sprung forward and grabbed both Dunn's skin from the floor and the mirror from my mother's hand. I sent the last shattering to the floor, destroying whatever power it may hold. "I will not allow you to do this," I said. "If it is only death that will slake your thirst, then I will destroy you myself before I allow you to do this."

"Don't be foolish, dear girl," she said. "Whoever controls the sea controls the *Caleuche*, and whoever controls her controls the fate of men who sail. And I control them both, and you are not strong enough to take it from me."

The answer was simple, but the task impossible. "I will. I will control the *Caleuche*, whatever it takes. I will bind it to me if I must, it and all the men, and I will save them."

My mother regarded me with a look of hostile disappointment as water began to flood the cove. She unwound the lace mask to reveal stunning white orbs, shaped of the same, iridescent stone that hummed atop my hand in place of where her eyes should have been. The red tendrils of her gown began to lengthen and take on life of their own, sucker pods erupting and winking evilly as they turned upward and the creature began to make its way out of the cove.

"Then you will perish with them," my mother said coldly as what was left of her mortal form dissipated into the crimson red body of the kraken.

XXIII

WHEN MY HEAD BROKE FREE OF THE WATER, EVANGELINE and Dunn were beside me in the sea, clinging to the edge of the small boat that had been left to float forgotten in the water. The air was filled with gun smoke and the sounds of men's voices as the crews of the *Riptide* and the *Caleuche* fought furiously to vanquish one another, the men distributed between the two ships that sailed side by side. The *Riptide*'s men fought valiantly—I could see the figures of O'Quinn, Gregory Nip, Domingo, and others as they brandished swords and guns like the fearsome pirate crew they were—but still the shimmering spectral men advanced on their mortal foe as they inevitably would. The men of the *Riptide* were powerless against an enemy that could not die, and the writhing arms of my mother's unforgiving, monstrous form rose up again from the waves to curl around the ship, squeezing and tightening as it bowed and then with a loud *snap* finally broke and sunk, taking anyone who remained onboard with it below the sea. The remains of the ship's once mighty frame was reduced to broken fragments of splintered wood that floated atop the thrashing water. On the deck of the *Caleuche* I could see the auburn red of Winters' hair and the grey of Jones', and beside their fighting forms I saw the ghost of Tom Birch rising over Jomo's as he bore down upon him with the point of his sword aimed at the man's chest. Gritting my teeth in determination, I swam for the ghost ship with all my might, leaving Evangeline and Dunn to follow behind me.

"Merrin, what have you done?" Evangeline cried, smoothing her curls away from her face as she swam alongside me away from the smoking mass that was the *Riptide* and toward the *Caleuche*. Her skirts billowed around her and she fought with them, pushing them down in great burping heaves. "You cannot win against her."

"I have to," I called back, fighting the waves that tried to push me under.

Water lapped against Dunn's face, and his hair was dark and sodden against his head as he, too, struggled in the waves. "We need to get to the ship," he said, as if he could read my thoughts and knew what it was I aimed to do. "None of it will matter if we don't reach them in time. She's already taken the *Riptide*. The *Caleuche* is our only hope."

The grey sky turned black above us as if it, too, knew my intent, and with her prey reduced to rubble the kraken's red arms loosened their hold on the remaining fragments of the ship and retreated back into the sea. I looked to see what was large and dark enough to obliterate the rising sun, and when I did my breath stuck in my throat. A rogue wave towered above us, taller and wider than the ship itself, like the ocean had gathered its body to stand upright so that it could swallow us whole and put an end to this madness, purging the ocean's surface of the evidence of the battle no man alive could have won. The wall of water was rushing toward us, growing larger as it inhaled the water in its path. When my hands reached the slippery rungs of the *Caleuche*'s side, I pulled myself upward and over the railing, ignoring the screams of the men as those that were still living jumped overboard, attempting to escape the blows of the *Caleuche*'s men, or the inevitable, drowning crack of the looming

THE ISLE OF GOLD

wave. I had to crawl over the dead to reach where Tom stood bearing down upon Jomo, and I rolled between them just as Tom's sword came down, stabbing deep inside the meat of my shoulder until it scraped across the wood of the deck beneath me.

I screamed in agony as the pain washed over me, and suddenly Winters had thrown off Jones and was there, forcing Tom back and away as Jomo wrenched the bloody sword from his grip and Dunn and Evangeline gathered me up, helping me to my feet. The pain was searing and intense; it blurred my vision as I held my wounded arm and tried to hold myself upright, willing myself not to lose consciousness. I staggered some, but when I had my footing I stumbled over to where Jomo held Tom with both arms pinned behind his back.

"Let him go," I ordered, and Jomo did so instantly though the expression on his face said plainly that he did not like it. Winters grunted his approval and positioned himself protectively in front of Evangeline. I knew, deep within my soul, that the cost of saving Tom was to bind him to me, the same as the sea had bound Jones and Evangeline had bound Winters. The sea was never-ending and immortal, and there was power within us that could be shared with those we loved. Our mother's heart was cruel and unforgiving, and she would not rest until the sickness within her had destroyed all that she might have once loved. Mine was pure. I would bind Tom to save him, and then I would give myself to the sea and save them all.

Tom advanced on me, and as he did he peered down with grey, alien eyes that did not know me. His skin was the pallor of death and there was no warmth in him, but as I held up my hand with the ring gleaming on my finger, he paused, his head bending sideways as if in curiosity.

"Stop," I yelled, not knowing if such a command would work, only that it must. Words that I had not planned rushed to my lips as the heat of the ring rolled over me, dulling even the pain in my shoulder. Davy Jones was coming again, his fingers white in the basket handle of his sword and his face still wore a blank, unseeing mask. Once again I used the power of my name, this time exercising the full weight of it as I staked my claim on the bridge of the ship. The *Caleuche* was a living thing that answered to the goddess of the sea, and I knew her legends. She had not always been a ship of the damned, but of the dead who had loved the ocean more than life and were content so sail forever. Perhaps its allegiance could be changed if I could summon enough power and free her of the sea witch's hold. "*Caleuche*," I cried, "hear me now. I am Merrin Jones, daughter of Davy Jones and of sea, and I would claim this ship as my own. You will be free to sail as you did before."

Immediately—unbelievably—the ship listened. Quiet fell around me as the crew of the *Caleuche* stopped and turned to stare, my father foremost among them. Then, gradually, things began to change. The *Caleuche*'s crew thickened and their bodies lost their brittle quality, strengthening into a more solid substance as color gradually began to return to their clothing first, and then their skin. My father pushed past whoever had been holding him back, stepping inside the inner circle that was Winters, Dunn, Evangeline, Jomo, and me. His eyes were hazel again and his hair was still grey, but his skin was tan and sinuous now, and no longer was he covered in fish scales and other debris of the deep ocean. He drew me into his arms and I could smell the sweet scent of the sea on him as he held me tightly against him while the wave yawned above the deck of the *Caleuche*, seconds away from crashing down and drowning us all. "I asked you before if you knew the power of your name," he whispered against my ear, his voice calm and reassuring even as I heard the cracking sounds of the water around us being sucked into the oncoming wave, and then the lift of the ship as she began to tip upward into the rush of water. "You had assumed I meant the power of the name Jones, but it was not that name. It is yours ... Merrin, the name of a savior. You, love, will save us all."

I stepped out of his embrace and looked at the circle of faces around me. An angry, hateful scream surged from below the water as the wave towered over us. It was coming, that much was certain, but for a moment I had everything. It was nothing like I would have ever imagined, but it was more and better than I could have ever dreamed when I left the harbor of Isla Perla searching for the answers to the questions of my past. I looked at my father, Davy Jones, and at my sister, Evangeline, whose fates had called me home to the sea. I saw Winters, my captain, and Dunn, my guardian, and Jomo, the warrior, these men who had become more than my crew, but my family and my friends, and who stood beside me now at the end of the world. At last I fixed my eyes on the man in front of me who looked so much like Tom Birch. His color was changing, but still his eyes were grey and unseeing.

"Merrin, don't," Evangeline cried, realizing at last what I meant to do as the first rains of the wave began to pelt violently down on top of us and the ship arched upward so that we all were forced to hold on to whatever was anchored down around us. "Someone must keep watch over the sea. If you do this you will seal that fate as your own, and you must face her alone."

I smiled at her, but I took Tom's hand in mine and wrapped

my ring into his palm, curling his fingers over it so that they encapsulated it in a weak fist.

"Forgive me, Mister Birch," I said. Then I pulled at his shirt until I brought him low enough that I could reach him, and standing on the tops of my toes I pressed my lips against his. I kissed him deeply, even as the sound of water rushed up and over us all. His lips were cold and lifeless beneath me, but I kissed even harder, tightening the coil of his fist, as I did ignoring the raging sea while it screamed around me. I kissed him until there was no air left in my lungs, and just when I thought it wasn't working, that I lacked the strength to bind my spirit to him, I felt his body relax and his arms loop around my waist, and then he was kissing me back. When at last we broke, I saw that life had returned to the boatswain's eyes and they were vibrant, saltwater green again.

"Oi, Rivers," he said as he leaned his forehead against mine.

"Not Rivers," I said, laughing sadly as I pressed my body against his, the last solid thing I would feel as the wave poured itself over the ship. "My name is Merrin Jones, and I will end the curse of Jones. I will save you all, that I swear."

EPILOGUE

WHAT HAPPENED BETWEEN MERRIN JONES AND THE DEPTHS of the sea is a story that has not yet been told. All that is known is what became in the moments afterward, when what was left of the crews of the *Riptide* and *Caleuche* awoke on the black-sanded banks of Bracile.

They woke in turns. First was Captain Erik Winters, though he stayed so still that only a slight change in the rhythm of his breathing proved him to be awake. The wounds he bore on his face and arms from battling the undead of the *Caleuche*'s crew had already begun to close over with crusted blood, and his red hair spilled out in careless tangles on the sands beneath him. The stone he wore around his neck was no longer a glowing white, but had deepened to the color of agate, darker at the edges and wound through with spirals the colors of a violet sky. Otherwise, he was unchanged and lay still with his faced turned profile to the heavens.

Shortly after the captain's awakening, the woman who lay clutched tightly in his arms opened eyes of brilliant chrysoprase blue and inhaled as deeply as if it were her first. The sea had washed away the golden plague that had covered her lovely skin, and her milky-white flesh was flawless under the light of a pale orange sun. Evangeline did not stir as she lifted her eyes to Winters'. The two spared a moment gazing at each other without encumbering the quiet with the weight of unnecessary words. At last Winters stood, and then drawing Evangeline up beside him they moved together in the direction of where rest of the crews' men lay scattered about on the sands.

Not far away, Jomo was the next to rise, pulling himself forth from the glittering black sands like a mountain rushing up from the dirt. He surveyed the beach around him with sharp, quick eyes, and then, deeming it safe—or safe enough for now—offered his hand to one of the men who had sat up near his feet. Around him, other men began to stir and mumble amongst themselves—Domingo and O'Quinn, the gunner, among them, along with others. He studied the faces around him, but then he saw the captain and Evangeline making their way toward him, and Jomo took his leave of his shipmates. When they were reunited, Evangeline swept between the two men, looping one of her slender pale arms in each of theirs. The trio stood silently, observing the blank expanse of tranquil ocean before them with calculating eyes. An endless expanse of jade green water laden with floating boulders of solid ice flowed between them and the other side of the world, and there was no sight of sails on the horizon that could ferry them home to Isla Perla, nor any trace of what had become of the *Riptide*, the *Caleuche*, or the two women who were somewhere beneath the water. For a moment, things looked hopeless, but at least they were alive. Not all of the men moving about the banks of the island had come from the *Riptide* and there were faces unaccounted for, but all here seemed alive and well.

Within a few minutes, the sound of impending footsteps signaled an approach from the craggy, granite cliffs looming behind where Winters, Evangeline, and Jomo stood watch. The three turned and saw that walking toward them, and at a quick and purposeful pace, was Captain Davy Jones. He strode confidently

THE ISLE OF GOLD

over the sand, and as he came closer it was apparent to all that he had been restored to his full and former glory. The evidence of the sea's curse had vanished from his form and he was a man again, full-colored and mortal with deep, ruddy skin and piercing hazel eyes. A look of resolve was stamped upon his face, and it was echoed in the countenance of Tom Birch who, reinstated as well, walked beside him. Both of the men now wore agate stones that matched Winters' around their necks.

Evangeline let loose Winters and Jomo and ran to her father, wrapping her arms tightly around his neck while he ushered her up in his arms. The two other men received Tom Birch; Winters offered his hand to the boatswain, and Tom accepted it with a nod, the exchange being of the sort that a prideful father might welcome a long-lost son. There were murmurs and greetings all around—the merest of which passed between the two captains, who still fostered a deep-seeded distrust between them—and the company looked anxiously around them for the one face still missing.

Brandon Dunn was not on the banks of the island, nor had any of the men of either of the shipwrecked crews laid eyes on him since before the great wave had swallowed the *Caleuche*. Very quickly the delight of finding themselves alive and well, even if stranded on a mystical island that threatened to collapse back into the sea, faded into mixed feelings of panic, fear, and loss.

Not soon after, twilight began to recolor the sky from vivid hues of orange and yellow to smears of purple and blue. The air ran cool. The assembly of nearly forty men, including the Captains Jones and Winters, Jomo, Tom Birch, and Evangeline, as well as Domingo Diaz, Elias O'Quinn, and Bim, Gregory Nip and the doctor, Horace Clarke, prepared to bed down for the night with rumbling stomachs and aching hearts. But just as they made ready to close their eyes a flash of ethereal green light flashed upon the sky, and moments afterword a burly man who had been assigned as lookout shouted, "Sails on the horizon!"

Then, their sounds rising, the voices of men joined in a steady chorus. "It's the *Caleuche*," they cried. "She sails still!"

And indeed it was the *Caleuche* in all her glory sailing toward them, her hull gleaming in the failing light and billowing sails of deep blood red rippling without wind. As the ship neared the edge of the beach one lone figure could be seen standing on the bow, curls of rich brown waving out from underneath a well-worn leather hat that was pulled so low over her eyes all that could be seen was a wide, grinning mouth. In her hand she gripped a thick wad of wasted red silk, and with this she gestured to Jomo, who shuffled his feet with desire. Beside her, rising no higher than her knee as it stood on all fours, was a big chested sea lion with tan skin wetted to the color of midnight black. Running in a ridge along the top of its sagittal crest was a distinctive shock of tall white fur.

From the ship a voice carried across the waves. "Aye," it came, and the voice was unmistakably that which belonged to Merrin Jones. "Fancy we leave this cursed island behind and sail for kinder shores?"

There was a cheer all around, and for the first time, Captains Winters and Jones met each other's eyes with a mutual look of anticipation. "What say you, Jones?" Winters, Evangeline's arm in his, asked in his usual, growling way, to which the older captain replied, "I think we best be sailing to the only place where we might be relieving my other daughter of that damned ship—to the very place it makes birth."

The pretty pink petals of Evangeline's lips curved into a cunning smile and she nodded in agreement, freeing a blade that she slid from hidden in her bodice.

"Oy," joined Tom Birch, who had said almost nothing the entire day, presumably lost in thought about the fate of the woman he loved. "I'll sail to the end of the world for Merrin, but tell me ... where exactly is that?"

"The end of the world be indeed where we sail," answered Winters, clasping his hand on the taller man's shoulder and looking approvingly to Captain Jones.

"Aye," Jones confirmed, eyes on the *Caleuche,* on Merrin, and on Dunn as he began to walk out into the gentle lapping waves of the dark night water. "To the end of the world it is."

ABOUT THE AUTHOR

Seven Jane is an author of dark fantasy and speculative fiction. She is a member of The Author's Guild and Women's Fiction Writing Association.

Seven is largely nocturnal, has an affinity for black and white photography, and exists almost exclusively on chai tea and avocados. She lives in New England.

www.SevenJane.com
Facebook https://www.facebook.com/sevenjanewrites
Instagram https://www.instagram.com/sevenjanewrites/
Twitter @sevenjanewrites

CPSIA information can be obtained
at www.ICGtesting.com
Printed in the USA
FFOW04n0501230518
46824259-49027FF